THE OTHER SIDE
SIDE
MIST, MIRRORS
& STRANGE TALES
E. Tayloe Wise

Fiesta Publishing
PO Box 44984
Phoenix, AZ 85064

www.fiestapublishing.com

Table of Contents

• *Italicized titles denote a poem.*

INTRODUCTION

In the following tales you will need to let your imagination **flow.** In my stories the protagonist usually has an otherworldly experience with ghosts, aliens, or other supernatural beings. There is, in these tales, a seemingly parallel universe existing alongside the present one in which we now live. I have always been fascinated by the possible existence of what I call "The Other World." Based on certain unexplainable phenomena I have experienced throughout life, I believe there is a strong possibility that some sort of parallel world—or dimension—might possibly exist here on Earth. I also cannot discount the fact that, in all likelihood, there are other worlds besides ours out there in the vast stretches of space. They are waiting for us to discover them, or they may have already discovered us, which I believe is a strong possibility.

In the following pages, you will also find that the majority of my short stories contain multiple references to combat events that happened during the Vietnam War. Advice that I was fortunate enough to receive over the past several decades from many people, generally revolved around one theme: write about what you know best or have personally experienced. Most of these tales are set in areas of the United States that I have visited many times or lived near for years, thus enabling me to use them as a background for the stories.

In 1968 I voluntarily joined the U.S. Army and, eventually, was sent to Vietnam as a combat rifleman. After three to four months, I ended up as a combat medic. If one did a good job in the jungle he was rewarded with a rear echelon job, and I was fortunate enough to get one. My combat tour in Vietnam is detailed in my first book, *Eleven Bravo: A Skytrooper's Memoir of War in Vietnam* (McFarland, 2004), which is still in print.

My second book, *Letters From Potsdam: Colonel John S. Wise's Impressions of the 1945 Berlin Conference* (Fiesta, 2022), took me over twenty years to complete. It details my father's experiences as an U.S. Army liaison officer at the Potsdam Conference held outside of Berlin where Truman, Churchill, Atlee, and Stalin divided up Europe after World War II—except Stalin was already in possession of Eastern Europe and wasn't about to divide or give back any of it to the Allies. The Cold War had begun.

I come from a family with a long military background—a great-great grandfather fought in the Civil War and my grandfather fought in the Spanish-American War—plus I experienced heavy combat fighting in a not so popular war. "War is," as R. F. Delderfield wrote in *A Horseman Riding By*, "a boring, bloody muddle, punctuated by moments of fear and disgust." What you see, what you do, what you experience in a war **_never_** leaves you. The dead and the dying haunt you day and night: they have never left me. The result is that I have suffered from post-traumatic stress disorder (PTSD) along with various physical crippling ailments for the last fifty-three-plus years. By finishing *Letters from Potsdam*, I realized I had a lot more to say about the Vietnam War and how it has affected me since 1969.

Some of this book's short stories were written between twenty-five and thirty years ago while others were written more recently. With the opportunity to publish them, I decided to use Vietnam as an underlying motif. I updated and expanded the Southeast Asian War details in my earlier stories and, in most cases, incorporated the war into the more recent tales. Many of the Vietnam incidents described herein actually occurred either to myself or others. I have altered combat events slightly and not used anyone's real name.

Despite the trauma of Vietnam and its lingering physical and mental aftereffects, I am still a patriot and do not regret my tour in that Asian country. I am proud to have served my country and agree with a quote by Senator John Kennedy (LA) in a 2022 speech, "I believe that Arlington National Cemetery contains four hundred thousand reasons why you should stand your ass up for the National Anthem."

I hope you will find these stories and the poetry, which I have written throughout my life, interesting, enlightening, and informative. If you are a Vietnam Veteran reading this, you will, most probably, recognize familiar scenes. I dedicate this book to you and to others I knew who did not return.

THE OTHER WORLD

Our God Is Dead -
Yet Satan Still Lives -
Because Our World Died -
Women Are the World
And, For Me, the World -
Is Now Dead!
I Discovered My World -
On the OTHER SIDE!

In That Other Dimension
Coexistent with Ours
Here on Earth -
Parallel with Us -
Where, Many Times
I Have Been -
There Are Doors
Leading to It
Here and There -
Invisible . . . Yet Shimmering -
Which Stand Ajar -
Admitting Only
A Select Few -
The Evil That Lurks
Within Us All -
Chases Us from Our World -
Into the Next -
Some - A Few - of Us
Are Fortunate Enough
To Escape Into -
The Other World

We Step Thru the Opening -
Into That Shadow World,
And Escape at Last -
The Grim Reality of Our World!
We Flee the Rantings -
Of Madmen -
Who Profess to Know
What Is Really Best
For All Mankind -
Yet - I Warn You -
To Escape to That
Next Dimension
Is Like Suicide -
Once You Step Over -
Or Pull the Trigger -
There Is No Return Journey -
Sometimes I Wonder
Which World
Would Suit Me Best?
Is Leaving Really
So Selfish Then?

For . . . By Departing
I Make Myself Happy -
Yet, Others Would View It
As a Selfish Act -
But, One's Inner Peace
Is Destiny!
And DESTINY
Must Be Paramount -
Else We Kowtow
To the Whims of Others!
So -
One Day - -
Soon - - -
I Intend to Take
That Step
Into That Other Dimension -
The Other World -
Ah, It Will Be an Adventure
Won't It?

BELIEVING

Scene I
Setting: War Zone

The stage is entirely dark. In the background is music from Barber's "Adagio For Strings" from the movie *Platoon* which slowly fades as a dim spotlight brightens and shines on a Soldier half kneeling on the ground.

He is dressed in camouflage and holding a walkie talkie. His shirt sleeves are rolled up. On his right arm is a bandage with dried blood stains. His face is smudged with dirt. An M16 lies on the ground next to him.

Offstage Voice #1

It is September 5, 1969, somewhere in the jungles of Tay Ninh Province, South Vietnam.

> Intermittent shots can be heard offstage.
> The soldier looks wildly around and then
> looks up. He keys his PRC-25 radio.

Soldier

Charley Charley, this is Bravo Foxtrot Tango, over.

Offstage Voice #2

Bravo Foxtrot Tango, this is Charley Charley, over.

Soldier

Charley Charley, we're running out of ammo, can you get one more resupply bird in to us?

Offstage Voice #2

Negative Bravo Foxtrot Tango. [static] ... past sundown [static]

... no resupply birds can [static] ... to you. Intel we've intercepted [static]

... you [static] ... probably [static] ... overrun tonight.

Take your weapons off Rock 'N' Roll [static]

... make every bullet count. We're returning [static]

... base. I expect you [static] ... hold the line. Out.

Helicopter sound fades into the background. More intermittent shots can be heard offstage. The Soldier looks around as if all hope is lost, spreads his arms in frustration, and drops his head.

Soldier

Damn! We're probably gonna be overrun tonight.

Not much chance we'll survive that human wave attack. Hey Sarge!

He turns and yells offstage.

Soldier

Radio the LZ. Tell them to lay down a ring of 105s around us and YOU make sure they drop the ordnance within 25 meters of our position.

Offstage Voice #3
(With deep Southern drawl offstage)

OK, lootenant. Roger that! Will do!!!

Soldier

Well, I guess I have to tell the guys. Geeze, there are only about twenty-five of us left.

He pauses and looks offstage. Then yells:

Men, we're in deep shit. We're probably gonna get overrun tonight.

If any of you survives—play dead

if necessary and then get away from here.

Check your compasses and take a 240 azimuth

until you get to the fork of two streams about half mile

from here and wait there to join up with

any other survivors. Stay there until help arrives.

     More shots are heard offstage.
     Soldier looks out into the audience and says,

Soldier

I gave up believing in God a long time ago.

I had so much religion crammed down my throat as a child.

Well, I guess I deserved this.

     He sighs.

Yet...

     He looks up, pauses for ten seconds,

I need some hope.

But there is no hope.

We're probably not gonna see tomorrow's sunrise.

     He pauses and looks into the distance.

Soldier

Shit, we'll all be dead.

     He drops his head.
     Lights dim. Incoming artillery sounds come from
     both wings of the stage sounding louder and
     louder as it comes closer to their position.
     The Soldier gets down on both knees and clasps
     his hands in front of him. He looks up.

Soldier

Well, God, here's the deal.

I know I can't bargain with you, but, if you let me and my men live tonight,

I promise, I'll never doubt your existence again.

I'll believe in you until my dying day. I guess I was weak for not believing in you.

You will be my comforter and strength. I'll hope you'll forgive me.

Lights fade into darkness.

SCENE II

When the lights come back on, the man is
asleep propped up against a log.
A stern and loud voice (Voice #3) (GOD) from overhead says,

Voice 3 (God)
Soldier, wake up!

The Soldier quickly sits up, looks around,
dazed and confused, then looks up.

Soldier
God?

God
Yes, My son?

Soldier
Is that really you?

God

Yes!

Soldier

I ... I prayed to you for the first time in years.

God

I heard you, my son.

Soldier

I've been lost, God. I left you. I'm sorry.

God

I know. But I never left you.

Soldier

I have no hope, God. I have nowhere else to turn. I've been weak. Please forgive me.

God

All members of mankind have to bear a burden at some point in their lives. That is why you will be able to understand that MY Grace is available to everyone, no matter what you have done ... or believed.

Soldier

Thanks God! I'm sorry for my lapse in not believing in you. No matter how much time I have left—even if it's only for tonight—I am truly transformed. I will NEVER doubt You again.

God

"I am the resurrection and the life. Whoever believes in me, though he die, yet shall he live, and every one who lives and believes in me shall

never die. Truly, truly, I say to you, if anyone keeps my word, he will never see death.'' [1,2]

Soldier stands and faces the unseen audience,
stretches his arms outward and says…

Soldier

I am truly blessed!! Thanks be to you, Almighty God!

The light fades into darkness.

Offstage Voice #1

"Therefore, if anyone is in Christ, he is a new creation.The old has passed away; behold, the new has come.'' [3]

Fifteen second pause as the light slowly comes back.

Offstage Voice #1

The enemy, badly mauled from artillery and numbering about five hundred soldiers,did not overrun their position that night.

---

[1] ESV Study Bible (English Standard Version). Wheaton [IL]: Crossway, 2008. John 11:25-26, 2045-2046.
[2] ESV Study Bible (English Standard Version). Wheaton [IL]: Crossway, 2008. John 8:51, 2041.
[3] ESV Study Bible (English Standard Version). Wheaton [IL]: Crossway, 2008. 2 Corinthians 5:17, 2230.

COME, PICK
THE FLOWERS

Come Quickly My Friends to the Fields
And Pick the Flowers at Their Ends
Gather Them - Sniff Them - Keep Them.

The Sun Shines Sweetly on Their Beauty
The Clouds Quietly Cover Their Upturned Faces
Which Droop - Wither - and Die.

The Rain Pounds Down upon Them
While Winds Forcefully Bend Their Backs
The Silent Cold Quickly Chokes Their Life.

They Drop - Decay - and Disappear
The Leaves of Autumn Fall Here
The Earth - Thus Naked - Lies Barren.

Pretty Spring in Beauty Now Approaches
Making Earth Lie Pregnant with Seed
We See the Flowers Born Again.

Come Quickly My Friends into the Fields
Pick Them - Pluck Them - Keep Them
Save Them - - For Beauty Fades Quickly.

THE CABIN, THE JOURNEY, AND THE VISION

Part I - The Cabin

My name is **Thomas West.** Shortly after I moved to Colorado, I lived in an isolated cabin on 139 acres of thickly forested land located on the west side of the Rockies. The nearest town, Gunnison, Colorado, is about thirty-one miles away. At an elevation of 7,703 feet, the town got its name from the first known European-American explorer of the area,

John W. Gunnison, who, in 1853, as a U.S. Army officer and surveyor, was trying to locate a route for the transcontinental railroad. He only spent three days in the area. In the late 1850s the town began to take shape from miners looking for gold.

During late spring and summer, I usually trundled down from my mountain lair to the town consisting of some 6,560 souls where I picked up my mail, plus stocked up on groceries and supplies. Although I had a three-hundred-gallon gas tank at my cabin, I always stopped at the local Sinclair station to top off my tank as an extra precaution to insure I'd always have an almost full tank of gas.

For most of my life I've been a loner … not exactly a sociable individual. Isolation from the rest of humanity was an asset, especially after THE WAR. I was perfectly content to live in my mountaintop hideaway. Little did I know how much my life would change, some fifteen months after I moved to Colorado. An unfathomable life altering event would completely alter my life in a new direction. I call it "The Miracle."

I'm a disabled veteran from the Vietnam War thanks to a North Vietnam Army Sharpshooter, or NVA for short, hiding in a tree in our patrol area near the Parrot's Beak area of Cambodia some thirty-five miles west of Saigon. My left arm was all but useless—not good for a lefty. Could hardly raise it without much effort, or feel much below my elbow, since there wasn't much left of my elbow area. As I was lying on the ground, the gook's second shot took off three toes on my left foot. My buddy, Jack "Gunner" Robertson, who carried our platoon's M60 machine gun, soon located the sniper and demolished the top of the tree. I watched the NVA's body fall headfirst from his twenty-foot perch to the ground followed by his SKS rifle. Tony, "Doc" Myers, worked on my wounds while our radioman, Bob Riley, called for a medevac.

"Well, Tom, you got two, one-million-dollar wounds!! You're going back to THE WORLD, man!" Doc grinned as he shot morphine into my arm and then my foot. I just grunted, gritted my teeth furiously, and prayed for the excruciating pain to go away, even though I knew it wouldn't totally disappear. But the morphine soon began to make me woozy and, imperceptibly, the agonizing pain dulled.

Medevac came in about twenty minutes later and whisked me off to the hospital in Pleiku, where they stabilized me and shipped me off to Biên Hòa airport outside of Saigon. I, along with about thirty-five other WIAs were then airlifted to Japan, where after five surgeries in eight days, the medicos told me I'd be shipped off to the states for further operations. Three more surgeries in Denver plus rehab took another two years of my life before they mustered me out just a year after the war had ended in April 1975. Now I had to incorporate either a cane or a walking staff into my daily agenda when ambling anywhere. And, in the beginning, walking consisted of moving at a snail's pace.

At first the VA only gave me 50 percent disability. I guess some government pencil pusher figured that since I still had one good arm and one good leg I only rated a 50 percent award. I hired a lawyer from the hotshot law firm Beasley and Graham in San Francisco, which specialized in VA disability cases. Finally, after a long hard slog of five years, the government bureaucracy caved and awarded me a full 100 percent disability. Because I had fought the VA's original 50 percent ruling and managed to ultimately win, I was entitled to back disability pay from the original award date until the full award of 100 percent. I took the tax-free money and banked it.

I gadded around the country for three or four years before I was accepted into a Texas grad school on the GI bill, where, in four years, I earned both a Master's and a Ph.D. in Asian history, taking one-

and-a-half times the regular course load every semester and during the summer. I wanted to know why the U.S. got into the Vietnam War. As expected, I didn't like what I found out. We had pissed away millions (probably billions) down the drain only to lose the war in Vietnam. We weren't the Greatest Generation by far. My Ph.D. orals turned out to be a breeze—hell, I knew more about the French and American participation in the Vietnam War than anyone else in the history department. Plus, a little personal experience didn't hurt.

After graduation, I was bored. I knew I didn't want to teach. I didn't like the stares and pitying looks people gave me because of my scars and disabling injuries. It probably didn't help that I had tattoos inked up and down both arms, especially on my left arm to hide the elbow scars. In the mid-70s tats weren't in vogue and often made people somewhat uneasy when they were around me. On my left arm I have the tat of a cobra wrapped around that limb from shoulder to wrist ending up with its mouth open and fangs exposed, as if to strike, on the back of my hand. So, perhaps, unconsciously, my use of tats was a purposeful means to keep people at a distance—a subliminal message … "DON'T F*CK WITH ME!"

Plus, were I to teach in a university, the college youngsters might latch onto my disability and try to make my life somewhat difficult. A few tried while I was in grad school until I had a personal one-on-one come-to-Jesus meeting, and they quickly learned never to cross me again. While I wasn't ashamed of my disability, it still made me feel incredibly self-conscious.

I decided to become a vagabond and roam across the U.S. I climbed into my truck and kicked off around the country desultorily traveling for twenty to twenty-two years, picking up stakes when I got bored and just moved on. What I received as a monthly disability from the VA—now $3,332.06—adjusted once a year for inflation, was more than enough to live on. Of course, the inflation figure used by the VA was minuscule; it never added up to the actual yearly cost increases of goods, services, and especially gasoline.

As I traveled up, down, and across the U.S., an invisible hand (or was it some type of benevolent force?) kept drawing me back to Colorado. I slowly began to realize I had been footloose for far too long. Plus, I was weary of KOAs, truck stops, Walmart parking lots, and trailer park camping spots for transients. I figured I needed to find a permanent place to live, somewhere remote where I wouldn't be bothered by next door neighbors throwing loud parties, Jehovah's Witnesses, or Mormons knocking on my door, or having to pay utility bills, etc.

In 2010, after hunting around Colorado for a year, I landed in Gunnison, which I decided to use as my area of operations (AO). There seemed, at least to me, to be some sort of invisible aura that guided me, albeit somewhat imperceptibly, to the town and its environs. Plus, this was mountain country and the locals tended not to ask you questions unless you offered information. It was my type of place.

Living in my 1995 Ford 150, I tried every realtor in the small town before finding Cyndy Continelli, an early fifty-ish auburn-haired woman with a cute smile and a nice twinkle in her eyes, who had a listing that both piqued my interest and intrigued me. On a bright Tuesday morning in early April, with hardly a cloud in the sky, we hopped into her two-year-old red four-wheel drive Jeep Cherokee, and she drove me up into the mountains. Cyndy first headed east out of Gunnison on Route 50, before turning south onto State Road 114, which we traveled along for almost twenty miles. At about the eighteen-to-nineteen-mile mark, she slowed for a couple of miles before finding and turning right onto an unpaved, and not well maintained, U.S. Forest Service Road.

We headed west and uphill on a dirt packed road covered with pine needles as it steadily rose in elevation toward the 10,514-foot-high Los Pinos Pass, which Cyndy informed me was closed six-to-seven months a year because of snowfall. It was basically a logging road timber companies used to cull trees from certain areas to help slow forest fires. After a few miles, she pulled over. We were there. A stream, which she identified as Cochetopa Creek, ran across a small meadow at the front of the property. It paralleled the Forest Service Road flowing down the mountainside from the Continental Divide. Thanks to the yearly snowmelt, I would definitely have a source of water. The property had another plus—it sat in an enclave with the Gunnison National Forest hemming it in on three sides, so there would be no neighbors to concern me.

Cyndy had two pairs of fisherman's waders, which we donned. As I carefully crossed the creek, which came up to my thighs, I was glad to have my solid walking staff. I prayed I wouldn't stumble, fall into the freezing ice-cold stream, and watch my walking stick, which I had become rather fond of, float off downstream. Cyndy arrived first on the opposite bank and extended her left hand to give me a boost up the short embankment. As I slowly climbed up the creek's side, I noticed she was not wearing a wedding band. On the other side of the creek, we unhurriedly tramped around a small meadow before ascending between sixty and seventy feet up a southward sloping hill, which was somewhat steep for me. Reaching a place where I could pause, I stopped, grabbed a tree limb for support, and swiveled around to look out through a break in the trees—the view was absolutely magnificent! The scenery revealed just how off-the-grid this Rocky Mountain property was. It suited me perfectly.

I purchased it immediately without haggling about the price. I really wanted a piece of Rocky Mountain Forest. Since I was paying cash, I was able to close in two weeks. The surveyors weren't happy because I wanted an actual plat of the property, which meant they had to do a lot of climbing and hacking brush to get straight shots with their transits to make their measurements and put their rebar rods at the corners. I was silently gleeful, as their two-foot-wide paths would make it easier for me with my infirmities to get around the property (at least for two-to-three years before the brush grew back).

My heavily forested land had a trapezoidal shape, steeply rising from the forest/logging road up a 200-foot hill that would have overlooked Cochetopa Creek had I been disposed to clear any trees for such a view. But I wanted privacy. So no massive destruction of trees. From the crest of the hilltop the land leveled off toward the back of my property, which abutted the National Forest land before steeply rising up the mountain. Yet, the back part of my lot was thickly forested with trees and brush. Instead, I found a secluded dell, some sixty feet lower down from the crest. It was a perfect spot for a small one room cabin. Plus, I wouldn't have to chop down too many trees. My ability to fell trees, much less hack away underbrush, as I soon learned, was a non-sequitur and a sobering reality check.

It was early May when I set up camp about a hundred feet south of the logging road in the small meadow area where trees overshadowed my campsite. Cochetopa Creek, about two-to-three feet deep, ran between my camp and the road. Its water was both cold to drink and exceedingly frigid to wade through. My newly purchased waders, looking like the bib overalls a farmer might use, enabled me to cross back and forth over the creek. Yet, I could still feel the coldness of the water through the thick plastic waders.

Vehicle access through or over the stream, due to its varying depth, was a minor problem which needed to be fixed.

Despite my disabilities, I slowly set out to clear an eight-foot-wide, eight-hundred-foot-long serpentine road up to the dell. After five or six days, however, I realized that just using an axe, or machete, was going to be far too much work and beyond my physical capacity, especially since my left arm made it almost impossible to chop down the numerous large trees. So, one day, while I was in Gunnison, I dropped by the small one room Farmer's and Merchants Bank (the only one in town) to check my account balance, which was rather large, due to my frugal use of money over the past twenty years and a nice monthly trust fund check from a long-ago deceased aunt. I asked the manager if she knew anyone with a bulldozer and she recommended a local guy, Dan Webley.

After withdrawing two thousand dollars in cash, I found Webley working on a backhoe in his shop located adjacent to his home. His dozer and a Bobcat were parked beside it. Webley was not only large—think the size of a former pro football lineman—but also topped out to at least six and a half feet. Despite his weight, he didn't appear to have one ounce of fat on him. We quickly discovered we were veterans, and immediately hit it off as we traded war stories and talked about hunting and weapons for a while. He'd been in Iraq—a totally different war from Vietnam. I discussed with him what I needed done. Reaching a tentative agreement on price, he said he would be able to start in a week or ten days, which was fine with me. Before I left, I gave him a thousand dollar down payment. I wanted to be able to park my truck in the glen and set up a camp, because winter was just four and a half months away.

In hindsight, living the life of a hermit in the middle of nowhere would have far more challenges than I ever could have anticipated. It didn't take long for me to realize I was a complete and inexperienced idiot when it came to wilderness living. I had no idea what surprises awaited me on the land. Yet, my pipedream was about to burst in the face of grim reality. To say I was naive would be a gross understatement.

Seven days later Dan showed up with his two high school aged sons as his helpers, and they set to clearing a road uphill to the dell area. After the teenagers stripped the bulldozed larger trees of limbs with their Echo chainsaws, Dan dragged the uprooted timber down to the meadow next to the Forest Service Road, where he stacked the various logs into a large pile. The young men also cleared the small brush and thin trees.

Dan's friend, a logger by the name of Joe Mudd came by early one morning a couple of days later. I wondered, as Dan introduced us, if he was a descendant of Dr. Samuel Mudd, the doctor who set John Wilkes Booth's broken leg after Lincoln's assassination. Joe set about to cut off the stumps with his extra-long bladed Stihl chainsaw, loaded the trees via a power hoist log grabber on the end of his logging trailer, and paid me an outrageous sum for the lumber. Then he poured gasoline on the remaining stumps and wood branches, lit it, and several hours later I had a large cinder patch on my land.

After four days, Dan and his sons had not only finished the serpentine road; they had also cleared the glen area. On the fifth day, he started clearing the creek bed, prepping it for the soon to be constructed bridge. Early the next day his friend, Bill Wellman, appeared with his dump truck containing a fifteen-ton load of ten-to-twelve-inch sized rock, which he dumped into the creek bed before returning twice more with further loads. Dan bulldozed the rock into position to ensure the soon-to-be bridge would have a solid rock foundation.

The next day, Joe Mudd arrived with four three-foot round by ten-foot long corrugated steel culvert pipes. Dan and Joe, using Joe's timber hoist, and Dan's Bobcat, installed the culverts side by side, which they welded together. Next, both men constructed a wooden concrete form on both ends of the future bridge and along the upstream and downstream sides of the steel pipes down to where each pipe touched. The next morning, they returned with numerous bags of Portland cement and a portable concrete mixer, and they poured the mud (what I called concrete) into the wooden form, carefully checking to confirm it had seeped down the sides to a point where the culverts joined from the previous welding sites. When they finished, I had a six-inch-thick concrete slab over the culverts. Next spring's snowmelt would be its first real test, and I hoped it would pass with flying colors.

Dan told me we would have to wait ten days for the concrete to cure before we could drive anything across the bridge. He said they would return to complete laying down the gravel road up to the glen.

Meanwhile, I used my free time to make numerous trips into Gunnison to stock up on supplies. While I was in Lee's General Store and Emporium, I ran into Cyndy, who was shopping. After a few minutes' conversation, I totally surprised myself by asking her if she'd like to get lunch. She said yes, so after putting her supplies in her Jeep, which was parked in front of the Emporium, we walked half a block west to Linda's Family Restaurant and Bar. At the time, I was just treating Cyndy to lunch. I was totally unaware of the fact that our luncheon get together would have further implications in a most surprising way.

A few days later, Dan arrived around seven in the morning. After offloading his dozer, Dan first tested the bridge with his heavily loaded Ford F-350 and then with the weight of his bulldozer. He pronounced it ready for use. Shortly thereafter Wellman arrived with the first of thirty-five truck loads of two-to-three-inch sized gravel for my road. I never ever imagined so much stone would be needed. It took Bill and his other driver over five days to deliver the rocks. When he made the last delivery of gravel, I paid him and gave him an extra special tip. As the stone was offloaded, Dan, starting at the dell and working downhill, used his dozer to flatten it out. His numerous trips back and forth both downhill and up helped to firmly pack the stone. In all, I ended up with a three-to-four-inch-deep graveled driveway, which, Dan assured me, would be more than enough considering what my usage would be.

After Dan finished, I drove up my road for the first time and parked my truck in the sixty-to-seventy-five-foot area of the now cleared dell. Using my walking stick, I traipsed down my new driveway to watch Dan load up his dozer. After he had secured it, he leaned against his trailer.

* * *

"Tom," he said, lighting his pipe after tamping down the tobacco, "you got a nice place to live now. But I gotta ask—are yew planning to live up here this winter with only a tent, or sleeping in yer truck bed?"

"That's what I planned on," I answered him wondering where this conversation was leading.

"Well," Dan nodded, "I need to tell yew some things about the wilderness, OK?"

"First off," he continued, "yer at about eight thousand feet in elevation here. The snows can get awfully deep up in this area. Eight, ten feet, or more. 'Specially with the wind blowin' in from the northwest up against these here mountains. They'll definitely snow you in and strand you up here for five-to-six months lessin' you got a snowmobile. There'll be six-to-eight-foot drifts piled right up against your cabin.

"You won't be able to drive out and with yer leg you'll never be able to walk out. You can get lost pretty easy out there in the snow—might even step on some thin ice with a stream under it and fall in. If'n that happens, yer an absolute goner. Count your life in hours—no minutes! With them war injuries, you won't be able to make it back to the cabin 'cause your body will be shuttin' down!" He emphasized before continuing. "An' even if yew had a cell phone, there ain't no coverage up this high so far back in the wilderness. Ain't nobody coming to rescue you."

I nodded, taking this all in, and began to realize my plan for living up here, until I built my cabin in the next year or so, might take a tad bit longer than I originally anticipated.

Taking a puff on his pipe, Dan continued, "Also, there's 'nother danger up here you might not have considered. Cougars. They hunt up this high in the winter lookin' fer deer or elk sheltrin' underneath trees. These cougars, they're extremely dangerous, 'specially, if they haven't eaten in a week or so. I know you tolt me you got a AR-15, but that ain't gonna do you a tinker's damn bit of good when you gotta take a call of nature. They'll be hiding out there in the brush," he pointed with his pipe to the edge of the woods, "maybe twenty-five feet away, where you might not see them as they'll be lying real low in the snow, frozen in place, so as not to catch your eye with any movement. Then, when yew turn away, wham! That cat'll explode and in three-to-four bounds, in 'bout five seconds or less, will be on your ass before you can even raise your rifle … that is if you remembered to take it while you're doing your stuff."

With every word he spoke, my plans seemed to shatter. Just like what might happen to a water glass during an opera aria when a soprano hits her highest notes. He was right. I knew he was right. I felt just a little more than uneasy. I realized how stupidly and naively idealistic I had been. My pipe dream was nothing more than a foolish hope.

Dan proceeded with his observations, "Lastly, yew got one more problem in the summer—black bears. While they're not as aggressive as their cousin, the grizz, which ain't nobody's seen in this area fer over a hundred years, them black bears can still do a numbah to you. When the snow melts, an' the weather turns warm, they'll be comin' outta their winter dens and start roaming throughout this area. And most likely, it'll be a momma bear, with two or three cubs. You DO NOT," he strongly emphasized while pointing his finger at me, "want to get between a momma bear and her cubs. You won't like the end result, which won't be nice."

"Now, as I see it," he continued, "you got two options. One, git a room in town for the winter, or two, git your cabin built before the first snows hit, into late August. And there ain't no way, with all due respect, Tom, with your disabilities, you're not gonna accomplish constructin' yer cabin all alone. Mother Nature," he took another puff, let it out slowly, and pointed to the sky "and minus 20 degrees cold will be on top of your ass before you even know it. I done heard freezing to death ain't for the faint-hearted. You go to sleep and never wake up, but yew sure do freeze yer ass off first!"

My heart dropped. I was f*cked, and I knew it as I listened to him. I thought of a phrase from Psalm 23:4 which we often repeated during our time out in the jungle with a slight variation to the Bible verse: "Yea, though I walk through the valley of the shadow of death, I will fear no evil." Then we added, "because I'm the meanest son of a bitch in the valley." After what Dan was telling me, I realized I certainly wasn't going to be the meanest son of a bitch in my wilderness neighborhood. There were two different carnivores out there that probably wanted to add me to their menu list. I could just imagine both beasts salivating at the thought of having me for lunch, dinner—or whatever. Plus, being mauled by a bear, as he added me to his dinner meal, wasn't something I would look forward to.

"Now Tom, you and me, we're vets. So, yew know I ain't gonna bullshit you." Dan sucked on his pipe before continuing, "Yew an' me, we knows 'bout hard times. We been there. Done that. But the enemy this time, fer you, is winter and cat critters. I ain't got no doubt you know when it's time to shit or get off the pot."

"But…," he paused, "I got a proposition fer you. I got some buddies down in town who need some work—carpenters, roofers, concrete guys, 'lectricians' [as he called them], and such. Oh yeah, you'll also definitely need a generator up here. As you know," he paused, "I also got a Bobcat, which we'll need. Now, iffin' you got between thirty and thirty-five thousand, I think we can get you a cabin built before early August. And that's only three months away now. If not, I got a small cabin back of my property down in town an' you could stay there 'til spring when we'd start back and finish it."

I was floored by his proposition. I sure as Hell didn't see that coming!

"Now, Joe Mudd, you know, the logger, he's got a small trailer with four-wheel drive an' can transport everything we need up here. He won't have no problem gittin' it up that there new gravel road of yours."

Dan and I started talking about logistics and costs and unforseen expenses. I gave him the go-ahead and asked him when he thought everyone could start, as I now knew we would be racing against the clock and good ol' Mother Nature.

"Let me go talk to the guys," he replied, "and iffin' if I can set everything up, maybe early next week. When you first see me and the crew, we'll be there to start. Meanwhile, don't forget what I said about them cougars!"

We shook hands; he left, and I hobbled up the slope as fast as I could. All the way, as I treaded slowly uphill, I kept imagining a silent killer was not only stalking but also eyeballing me, licking its chops, and creeping stealthily closer in the thick brush adjoining the road as it tensed ready to pounce. Fear is a great motivator, as I had learned all too well in Vietnam.

Once in the glen, I immediately strapped on a holster, containing my Ruger .357, which I had loaded with hollow point bullets. Next, I uncased my AR-15, cleaned it, and hung it on my shoulder. Now, I wasn't hunting Charley; I was after a noiseless stalker who wanted to eat me. I practiced holding the weapon in a firing position and limped around the clearing without my staff. While it was somewhat difficult and hurt a bunch, I managed it, so I took some practice shots and slowly fired off one 18-round clip. I had plenty of ammo—almost 2,500 rounds.

The next day, I drove to Gunnison and stopped at the bank. I had more than enough funds in my account. After withdrawing three thousand in fives, tens, and twenties, I also ordered some checks and asked the teller if she would print off twenty to twenty-five temporary ones until the real ones arrived. I'd need the temps to pay the cabin workers. She did.

I left the bank and headed across the street to Lee's General Store and Emporium, where I purchased several Igloo coolers, eight cases of beer, and six cases of soda pop for the work crew when they needed to take a break. I'd ask the crew to bring ice up every day, which I would reimburse them for. I also stocked up on about thirty days of food and purchased more ammo—after all, you can never have too much ammo. Just before I checked out, I accidently found a small guidebook on cougars and added it to my purchases. Might come in handy. As I didn't, on purpose, use credit cards, I paid cash for everything. Which probably made me even more off the grid. Plus, I didn't have a cell phone. Less easy to trace, which suited me just fine.

On my way out of town, I had a sudden and unexpected impulse to see Cyndy, so I dropped by her office. As I pulled into the parking lot in front of her office, I noticed her Jeep and knew she was in. As we chatted, I noticed her décolletage revealed she was wearing both a crucifix and a beaten-up Saint Christopher medal on two separate silver chains around her neck. The crucifix, about two inches long and one-inch wide with Christ nailed to the cross, was tarnished, and the Saint Christopher, also faded, with the words "Air-Land-Sea" around its outer edge hung from its chain via a tiny coiled-up wire instead of a regular clasp. I asked her about them, telling her I had worn similar medals in Nam and they had been my good luck charms—in that I had managed to come back alive, I chuckled, albeit not quite physically or mentally whole!

"Well, Tom," she sighed before replying rather sadly after a pause, "they belonged to my grandfather, Roy, who was killed in Vietnam during Tet of 1968. He was," she paused as her fingers fondled the medals, "a Marine officer who died at Hue."

I told her I was sorry to hear her obviously painful story and she didn't have to say anything more.

But, she continued, "No! No! It's OK." She answered, "I'd like you to hear the story. Unlike my Episcopalian Gramps, Granny Shelby was a staunch Catholic, so she gave Roy this crucifix," Cyndy said with some sadness as her fingers caressed each icon, "just before he left for Southeast Asia. Gramps' sister, Patricia, who, in turn, was not about to be outdone by her Catholic sister-in-law, gave him the Saint Christopher a day or two before he departed for the war zone."

"When Roy's body came home, we were told, due to his massive injuries that we could not expect to have an open coffin. So, sadly, the ceremony was conducted with a closed casket. We didn't really have a chance to view and tell him goodbye," she remarked before continuing. "The Marines sent his personal possessions along. Granny kept these two items and willed them to me after her death." She faltered as tears formed in her hazel eyes, so I stepped forward and put my arm around her shoulder, kind of hugging her as I reached into my jacket pocket and produced a small packet of Kleenex.

While she dried her tears, I commented, in hopes of comforting her in some small way, "Well, I'm pleased you still honor him because, as you know, we Vietnam Vets didn't get much of a fair deal when we returned from THE WAR."

She sniffled, but nodded, and we chatted a few more minutes. Then, I had to depart. *I really like Cyndy*, I thought after leaving her office and climbing up into my Ford. But my thoughts quickly brought me back to reality.

"What in the world am I doing?" I muttered aloud to myself, "I'm a frigging loner; she couldn't possibly want anything to do with a guy like me living so far up in the mountains."

But further unseen and unexpected developments would surprise me.

Three days later, while I was sitting on top of my picnic table, cleaning my .357, after firing two six shot rounds through it, I heard the rumble of trucks down below on the Forest Service Road and the subsequent slamming doors of men exiting their trucks. Holstering the Ruger, which I kept on the left side of my waist for a fast right-hand draw, I limped down my driveway until I could get a partial glimpse through the trees as to what was happening by my entrance bridge. Seeing Dan, as he looked uphill, I raised my arm to wave, and he returned my gesture. I watched him offload his Bobcat and start up my sinuous driveway. Joe Mudd started his heavily laden truck of building materials and followed Dan. The others followed on foot. I hoped all the noise would scare away any hungry mountain lions.

After introductions, the crew laid out the cabin site. Dan's guys quickly assembled a form for the concrete base. Using water from the creek, which Dan hauled up using four five-gallon orange Home Depot buckets hanging from his Bobcat's dozer blade, they mixed the cement. By the end of the day, the floor had been poured.

Meanwhile, using two-by-eight-inch boards as studs for the six-inch insulation, which would be inserted between them, and end up behind the Sheetrock, the two carpenters, having brought a small compressor, used their pneumatic nail guns to quickly assemble each section of the four walls. The cabin's front wall would be two feet higher than the back wall, so the snow, hopefully, would slide off the tin roof instead of accumulating and collapsing the cabin with its weight. At the top of the frame, they included several six-inch-by-two-foot slots for sliding glass windows, which would give me some outside light inside the cabin. The crew sorted out all the materials they would need by placing them in separate piles, all of which they covered with Visqueen, a thick plastic film to prevent rain from damaging stuff. By mid-afternoon they bid me goodbye telling me they would return in ten days when the concrete would be cured and ready for construction.

During that ten-day interval, I made several trips to town to purchase more ammo and enough supplies to last me the six months I would be holed up in my cabin during the long Rocky Mountain winter. While I was in Lee's General Store and Emporium, I asked the cashier where I might find a local arms dealer. She directed me to a side street a few blocks away, where I located Richard's Firearms and Ammo in a nondescript building with only a small two-by-two-foot rusty sign hanging over the front door. The faded rusty and paint-peeling sign depicted a lever-action .30-30 Winchester rifle, or "thirty-thirty" as it is most commonly known, which was first marketed in 1894. Richard turned out to be a Vietnam vet, so we easily established a rapport and traded some stories about the war. Like me, he had been wounded, but not as severely—just one AK-47 round through his ankle, which he showed to me. He had drilled a small hole through the bullet and wore it on a thin silver chain around his neck.

I told Richard I needed a weapon with a lot of firepower to put down a cougar—or bear. I told him I had an AR-15, but because of my disability, I wanted something less unwieldy but more powerful for in-close range than my rifle. From the wall behind his counter, Richard produced a Smith & Wesson M&P12—a dual-magazine pump-action shotgun, called a bullpup, with a capacity to load either thirteen three-inch magnum shells, or fifteen-inch shells, or twenty-three one-and-three-quarter-inch short shells. With its flexible sling, I could hang it on my shoulder with little difficulty. The bullpup carried an incredible amount of firepower for a compact 12-ga. shotgun. At twenty-seven-and-three-quarter inches in length and almost ten pounds fully loaded, plus using slugs, which were a solid lead, or copper, projectile, this potent weapon would be far easier to tote than my AR-15, and it would give me significant explosive power to stop a cougar or a bear—provided I had the time to do so! After a fifteen-minute ATF Bureau check and approval, I walked out of Richard's with my new purchase and hoped it would work when I needed it.[4]

On one of my visits to town, the invisible force again guided me to Cyndy's office. Entering, I said hello and we chatted a few minutes before I invited her to lunch. There was just something about her that I couldn't quite put my finger on. We relaxed over our midday lunch at Linda's and learned a little more about each other. Normally around women, I'm tongue-tied, but, curiously, she was able to get me to open up in a way that didn't appear to be prying. Actually, I think it was her pretty, mischievous smile. We finished lunch and parted outside.

"How come," I realized aloud with some shock, as I hopped into my truck to head back to my land, "I become such a motor mouth around her? What in the world is happening to me?"

On the tenth day, Dan and his crew returned. Over the next several weeks, they built my cabin from the concrete pad up. Dan, as we previously agreed, had purchased a small wood-burning iron stove. After being installed, its smokestack ran straight up through the roof. A wood stove chimney, if it was constructed with any sort of "L"—or 90 degree turn—in it, tended to cause wall fires because ashes accumulated at the "L" turn when the stack went through the outside wall and then made another "L" turn again as it rose above the roof line.

The roofers even used a green-colored tin to install on my roof, which would be great aerial camouflage. I really hoped the snow would easily slide off the slanted tin roof. I couldn't imagine being forced to scale a ladder, much less standing on a icy slick metal roof trying to remove snow. Plus, should a cougar appear, I'd be stranded on the roof and might end up freezing to death. Or, even worse, a

---

[4] Kelly Young, "Proof of Concept: S&W's M&P12 Bullpup," *American Rifleman*, February 2022, pp.44-49.

cougar might climb a nearby overhanging tree and jump onto the roof. *If that happened*, I thought, *I was a dead duck!*

My front door, as Dan pointed out one morning while installing it, was insulated solid metal with a locking six-inch deadbolt that would be seated into three two-by-four-inch, foot-long wood chocks nailed inside the wall next to the door frame. This, he told me, was to ensure it would be extremely difficult for any type of critter or person to get through. He also installed a screen door so I could get some air during warmer weather.

The "lectricians" wired me up and positioned the generator close to my front door. They also installed a starter switch inside to the left of the front door, just above the deadbolt, so I wouldn't have to wander outside in twenty below zero temperatures to start it. Yet, every third or fourth day, depending on how much gas I used, I would need to check its level to determine if the machine needed to be topped off. The guys not only constructed a small, enclosed room for the generator with ventilation screens at the top, but also installed a sloped roof over it and made the area large enough to store five two-gallon tanks of gas.

As part of the cabin's design, and at Dan's insistence, the bathroom, contained an eco, or composting, toilet (but no sink or shower for me!), which the guys attached to the outside back wall with an indoor entrance. I, thankfully, realized I wouldn't have to clumber through the snow to access the crapper or worry about critters. The carpenters also made a last-minute decision and installed a two-foot wide, strongly insulated metal door on one side of the toilet, which would provide an escape hatch if, for some reason, I was unable to use the front door. Without my noticing it, they also put a half moon on the door, which they had made and painted black. When I discovered it, I roared with laughter.

Again, I hoped the reason I hadn't seen either one of the predators was because of the noises generated by the cabin's construction. Then an ugly thought crossed my mind: *What would happen when there was no noise? Would they start casing the area—lining me up for their next meal? Hmmm, something to ponder.*

By the seventeenth day, the crew finished. I not only had a cabin, but they had also put together and installed a metal carport with sides for my truck. I personally thanked each of the men and shook their hands as I gave them their last paycheck—to which I added a 250-dollar bonus as appreciation for their efforts. Dan lingered behind.

"Hey, Tom! I got another proposition fer you."

Uh-oh, I thought, wondering what was going to come out of his mouth.

"I think you need a gas storage tank, sorta like those 275-gallon ones everybody uses for heating oil. We could place it over there," he pointed to a spot about twenty-five feet away from the cabin, "and yew wouldn't have to worry about running out of fuel."

"I can see getting a tank up the road, Dan," I replied, "but how's a loaded tanker truck going to get up my steep incline to fill it?"

"Easy peezee," he said. "This feller I know, Mark Tyler, he's got a small five-hundred-gallon tanker truck with a four-wheel drive. I know he can do it. I kin git him to come up here and give it a look-see, if you want to do it."

"Sure, fine with me! Let's do it," I said enthusiastically.

Around noon the following day, Dan appeared with a three-hundred-gallon gas tank in his truck bed, accompanied by Mark Tyler. After introductions, Tyler commented, "This here slope ain't gonna be no problem fer me, Tom. I can getcha filled up anytime you want, depending on yer usage, lessin' it ain't in tha middle of the winter!" He joked and we all had a laugh over his comment.

"Sounds good to me, Mark!" I replied with an eager smile on my face and giving him a thumbs up.

The two men slid the high-density polyethylene (HDPE) tank off the back of the truck and rolled it over to its permanent resting place. Mark and Dan then took some bricks off the truck bed and used them to chock the sides of the tank. Next, Mark pulled six four-foot pieces of steel rebar off the truck and, using his maul hammer, drove each one of the rebars into the ground on both sides of the tank as a precaution against a strong wind from rolling the tank down the driveway, or, even worse, into the woods.

The next day, Mark showed up with his tanker, installed a spigot for the tank, and filled it. I paid him, adding an extra hundred dollars as a gratuity, and thanked him profusely. He managed to turn his truck around at the crest of my driveway and waved as he left. I was set, or so I thought!

A few weeks later, I drove into Gunnison where I found a second-hand furniture store with an aging yellow sign proclaiming Nate's Used Furniture. I picked out some furniture—a full bed (with a new mattress!), four cushioned metal folding chairs, a cheap metal kitchen table with a blue-colored Formica top, which after long and heavy usage had faded, three-to-four small tables, and finally, a beat up foyer type of table. I had a piece of four-by-eight-foot by three-fourths of an inch marine plywood and two sawhorses, so I didn't need either a dining or a food prep table.

After making arrangements with Nate to deliver the furnishings in two days, I dropped by Cyndy's office. The invisible force kept drawing me back, because I wanted to be around her and talk with her. I hobbled in. My wounds were acting up and giving me some pain that day. She looked up then smiled when she saw it was me and we exchanged greetings.

"I hear," she said with a cute wink and a conspiratorial smile, as she stood and came around her mahogany stained desk, which looked like it was over a hundred years old and weighed a ton, "through the Gunnison coconut telegraph, that you've got a cabin!"

"Yup," I replied, "And, I would like to ask you to come up for a visit to view it and become my first 'official' visitor." I added, "I might even be able to rustle up some grub, but it won't be fancy."

"Why don't you let me bring a picnic lunch?" she offered before adding, "It will certainly beat canned food hands down! Plus," she laughed, "I'm not much into spam!"

We both laughed and, smiling, I nodded my head. We decided on meeting three days hence. I bade her goodbye and, after closing her office door, smiled—no, I grinned like a naughty boy who had done something he shouldn't—all the way back to my truck. As I pulled away, I shook my head in disbelief at my thoughts and feelings toward her. She must think I'm an absolute weirdo … or a doofus. On my way back to the cabin, I ruminated on our interactions together. *Was there anything there?* I wondered. And why now in my life? I had always thought I would be a confirmed bachelor. Yet, every time we were together, we just clicked. I felt a serene calm flow over me when we were together.

When I woke up at five, the morning of her visit, I took a quick sponge bath. I kept water, which I got from the creek, outside the front door in three five-gallon orange Home Depot buckets with lids. I made my bed and combed my hair. I looked forward to being with her. I was really eager—like a teenager on his first date. Lastly, I strapped on my holster with the .357 because I had a feeling if we took a hike I might need protection for both of us. I walked around the cabin wearing what I knew was a goofy smile while I cleaned and straightened up, but being the neat freak I am, there wasn't much to tidy up.

✳ ✳ ✳

A few hours later, I heard Cyndy's Jeep crunching up my driveway. I walked out and waved as she pulled in. She hopped out of her Jeep with more energy than I had ever seen in her. We greeted each other with cheek kisses and exchanged some pleasantries before I helped her remove a large covered picnic basket from the back seat. I started to lift the corner of the red and white checkered cloth.

"No peeking, Buster! It's a secret!" She laughed as she admonished me by pointing her index finger and shaking it in my direction. I knew my face was turning red. The basket weighed a ton!

"Wow!" I said. "It feels like you brought a feast for seven or eight people."

"Nope. It's just us." She grinned as she responded to my comment. Cyndy grabbed another paper bag from the back seat and followed me toward the cabin. On one of my trips to town, I'd purchased a cheap wooden picnic table with built-in benches on either side. I pointed to it, "Come lunchtime we'll eat on my outdoor picnic table," I started to chuckle, paused, then continued, "Professor Plum did it in the dining room with a rope dinner table!" She laughed then gave me a quizzical look and an enigmatic frown.

"What?" I looked at her with a surprised look, "You've never heard of the game Clue?"

"Of course, I have, silly," she answered as she took a swat at me. "I just wanted to see the expression on your face by my look of total befuddlement."

We both shared a good laugh.

I continued, "For now, we'll stick lunch inside to ensure no critters come out of the woods to sample the goodies before we're ready to eat." I opened the screen door, "But now, Madam," I intoned in a low formal voice, "Chez West awaits your grand tour." I followed her inside and set the picnic basket down on the beat up rickety table next to the front door—recently purchased at Nate's—which wobbled and creaked as if to protest the extra added burden.

Cyndy took a few steps, stopped, did a 360 degree turn, sweeping her eyes around the room and said, "Nice and comfy, Tom. I can tell you will be really happy here." Plus, she started to grin as she turned toward me, "I like the retro art deco look of your furniture!"

I burst out laughing, and she quickly joined me. We must have laughed at least half a minute or more as tears streamed down both of our faces. Well, when I was finally able to stop laughing, I thought, *That sure broke the ice!* There wasn't much to show Cyndy, so I hammered it up a bit by speaking in a posh British accent as I pointed to different parts of the room while intoning, "Now here's the scullery, but I'm in need of a wench to keep it clean. And over there," I pointed to the stove, "is the large *heating plant* and the four chairs in a half circle around it indicate the area is the living room and/or den, while," I pointed again, "the master bedroom is over there in the corner."

During our Chez West grand tour, Cyndy continued to hold the paper bag she had removed from her car. Finally, curiosity got the better of me as I wondered what was inside the bag. "Cyndy, would you like to set your bag down?" I asked her.

She nodded, set it down in a chair, and reached into the bag from which she removed a small hand-carved wooden box with a carved figure of an elk on its top. "Here's a housewarming gift for you!" Cyndy exclaimed with a big smile, as she took a quick bow and curtsy, and then, cradling it in both of her palms, she extended the box to me.

I lifted the box from her palms and raised the hinged wooden top. Inside was a plain hand-carved wooden cross. I looked at her, "Thank you so much, Cyndy. This means a lot to me. Wow!"

"There's a Native American Indian in town," she said, "by the name of John 'Two Bears' Warren. He's an artist who specializes in wood. He can carve anything you would like. He even carved the box."

I turned the cross over, on the back in the style of a grooved cow brand was engraved, "Best Wishes, Cyndy." There was even a small carved hollow for a nail. I thanked her again, gave her a long hug and patted her on the back.

"Now, let's find a place for it!" she enthusiastically exclaimed. Holding the cross, which she had lifted from my hand, Cyndy turned around the room before stopping and pointing to my sleeping area. Speaking in a French accent, she queried, "How about your boudoir, monsieur?"

"Sounds good to me!" I replied and nodded with enthusiasm as we moved toward the bed.

"I know you're bound to have a hammer and a nail," she stated. "Let's hang it on the wall over the back of the bed."

I went outside to my truck where I kept my tools and miscellaneous items of hardware—nails, screws, and the like in a large Husky tailgate cross box located in the truck bed just behind the passenger's seat. I soon found what I needed and returned to the cabin. Before I could put up a nail anywhere, Cyndy had me hold the cross up against the wall, asking me to move it back and forth and up and down until she nodded approval at the location. In a trice, I had the nail in and hung the cross. We both stepped back and agreed on its position.

"Thanks so much, Cyndy," I said for a second time to show my appreciation. "I really do like it." She just smiled.

Cyndy walked over to the chair, stuck her hand inside the bag and pulled out a magnum of Perrier Jouët champagne.

"Now," she commented, raising the bottle up in the air, "we can celebrate in style!" Cyndy insisted on our drinking the champagne. She strolled over to the picnic basket, and I couldn't help but think of it like a magician's bag of tricks, which always seemed endlessly full. Cyndy pulled out two champagne glasses—real glass, not plastic! We went outside, sat at the picnic table, and chatted about an hour as we demolished the champagne. Since I hadn't eaten breakfast, I was getting hungry, plus the champagne had made me feel a bit heady. After downing the last of the champagne, Cyndy got up, went back inside, and returned with her picnic basket.

"Now for some good food, Tom," she enthusiastically explained. Digging into her basket, she removed a plastic tablecloth with traditional red and white squares, which I helped her spread on the table. Next came some red Solo plastic plates and plastic silverware with red paper napkins, along with two red Solo cups, all of which she used to set the table.

Lastly, she dug into the basket, like a magician about to lift out hidden rabbits, and produced two wrapped salad plates. "I didn't know what kind of dressing you might like on your salad, so I brought Ranch, Bleu Cheese, Balsamic Vinaigrette, and Honey Mustard!" She grinned as she set the four bottles on the table.

"Well, that explains why," I said as I chuckled and smiled, "the basket had some weight to it!" I opted for the Vinaigrette.

"And now," dipping her hand inside the basket with a conspiratorial wink and smile, Cyndy produced two wrapped sandwiches, "the pièce de résistance! The main entree for your pleasure, Tom!" Cyndy unwrapped both sandwiches as she spoke, "I've got a roast beef and Swiss for you and a turkey for me!"

I thanked her as she set both sandwiches on our plastic plates. Next, she hefted out a 24-oz. container with iced tea, uncapped it, and filled our two Solo cups. After Cyndy sat down, we proceeded, between bites and conversation, to demolish the food. After lunch, I helped her clean up and put the items back in the basket.

Cyndy thanked me for helping her stow the items in the basket, and then inquired, "Tom, do you feel like taking a walk? Maybe let's walk up the forestry road?"

"I would love to," I replied, "but I don't know how far we'd get— my foot, you know?"

"Well, let's just take our time." Cyndy beamed energetically as she replied, "Even if we don't get far, it'll still be enjoyable! If, all else fails, I can always drag you back down the hill by the collar. After all," she continued, "it's a lot easier dragging a body downhill than uphill!"

We both laughed at her joke.

Before locking the cabin, as an extra precaution in addition to the Ruger I was already carrying, I slung the bullpup over my right shoulder. We set off down my driveway, crossed the bridge, and started up the pine covered forestry road, heading in the direction of Los Pinos Pass, though there was no way we would come close to approaching it. We walked silently and, although I had my staff, I managed to walk a lot farther than I thought. After fifteen to twenty minutes, maybe a half mile from the cabin, we emerged from the overhead tree cover to an overlook where we paused.

"That's quite a view," I observed. I could almost see Gunnison in the hazy distance.

Cyndy nodded then she turned toward me, put her arms around my neck, and kissed me. I felt like I'd been hit by a locomotive. I dropped my staff as I put my arms around her waist, and, drawing her closer, kissed her back. We stood entwined for several minutes, kissing, coming up for breath, smiling, and kissed some more. Not a word passed our lips during our intimate interlude.

When we parted, Cyndy bent down, picked up my staff and handed it to me. Then she grabbed my hand with sparkles in her eyes and nodded back down the road.

"Come on, Buster," she said. "Let's head back."

Afterward, as we lay in bed, we talked about our prior lives while we continued to caress each other before we both drifted off to sleep. It was growing dark when we woke. As I opened my eyes, Cyndy was staring at me. She smiled, then without a word, scooted over and gave me a long lingering kiss. An hour later we rose and dressed. It was late, eight o'clock or so, as we sat down on the chairs in front of the stove I had just filled with wood and lit.

"Tom," she said, "I really don't like driving in the dark. Is it okay if I stay over and leave early in the morning?"

"Sure!" I grinned.

"Well, I have one more surprise, a bottle of Pinot Grigio in the bottom of the picnic basket. Shall we drink it?"

I nodded. She rose and walked over to the basket sitting on the table next to the door and pulled out the wine. We sat, sipped, and talked until ten that evening before I mentioned I was tired and really needed some sleep. Plus, the wine had made me rather mellow. I stood, got some more wood, and filled the stove again before we retired.

I woke around five, having slept more soundly than I ever had during the past few years. A few minutes later, Cyndy opened her eyes. It was chilly inside the cabin because the stove's fuel had expended itself sometime during the early morning hours. We both got out of bed and Cyndy quickly rushed on tiptoes to the bathroom in her birthday suit while I waited my turn. The chill inside the cabin caused us to dress quickly. As I buttoned up my shirt, I realized Cyndy hadn't said a word about my scars, or especially my cobra tat. *Well, that's a good sign*, I thought.

"It takes almost an hour for me to get down to Gunnison," she pointed out, "and I'll need to hit home, take a shower, and be at work by nine."

"I'll walk you to the Jeep," I commented as I slid my holster on—after all, I had no idea when cougars ate—probably twenty-four hours a day.

At her car, she turned, gave me a quick kiss, and hopped in the Jeep. "Next weekend?" Cyndy asked as she nodded and gave me a big warm smile.

"I'll have to check my busy schedule, but I believe I can fit you in!" I replied with a silly British accent and a grin. She smiled, shook her index finger at me, and started her Jeep.

As she started down the driveway, she waved her arm out the window and I, in turn, waved back. *Wow!* I thought as I walked back into my cabin, *that sure was a surprise.* I never expected anything like this to happen. Yet, at the same time, I felt something indescribable changing inside, and I wasn't sure what exactly it was.

✳ ✳ ✳

Two days later, I got an even bigger surprise when I heard a large heavy truck with its engine screeching loudly at every gear change as it crawled uphill. It was Bill Wellman with his dump truck. I could see it was filled with cut logs piled above the top of the truck's plywood walls.

"Hey, Tom," Bill said as he stepped down on the gravel. "I got a reel surprise fer ya! Couple ah days ago, we had this reel big gust of wind blow through town an' this here tree fell acrost one of the streets. The city dun hired me to remove it. Normally, I'd chop it up and sell it to folks, but I dun run into Miss Continelli whilst I was cleaning up. An' Miss Cyndy, she dun tolt me that yew might need some split wood, an' could she pay me fer it if'n I would deliver it to yew. I tolt her you'd been real good to me with all the gravel hauling and that I'd get my wood splitter, chop it up, and deliver it to ya. So, here you are," he finished and swept his hand toward his truck.

"Bill, I don't know what to say. Are you sure I can't pay you for it?"

"Naw," he said, "just buy me a beer next time you're down my way."

"Okay," I paused and smiled. "But, how about, instead, I make that a couple of beers?"

"Dat'd be fine!" he said. "Deal." Bill extended his meaty hand and we shook on it. We then discussed where the best place might be for him to dump the wood and settled on the area next to the gas tank. After leaving me with enough wood to get through winter, he waved as he drove off down the hill.

I was just stunned at his generosity. Hard to imagine. My guardian angel must be looking over my shoulder. Over the next day or so, I carried a lot of the split logs into the cabin, and also stacked them into a four-foot-square pile outside my door.

✳ ✳ ✳

Cyndy showed up a few days later—early Friday afternoon. She'd purchased a lot of groceries, so I helped her tote the various cans and packages inside. We stuck them on my partially filled metal shelves in the kitchen area. She'd also brought in four or five different types of wines.

We had a compatible weekend. As she hopped into her car to leave Sunday afternoon, she turned and asked me if I'd like to come down the next weekend and stay at her home. I quickly agreed and off she went. Something went boing in my heart.

Part II
THE JOURNEY

My first summer in the mountains started my journey forward into an unexpected life. Little did I know, much less realize, what else would be in store for me.

Cyndy and I traded a couple of weekends back and forth. On my second weekend at her house, as we were washing some dishes after a well-cooked delicious dinner, she commented rather casually, "Tom, would you like to go to church? I occasionally attend this Bible church and would love for you to join me."

I immediately knew this was a biggie and intuitively realized I was perfectly okay with going to church with her despite my not having attended any church since childhood.

"Yes! Of course! Certainly I'll go, but I don't have any go-to-church type clothes," I mildly protested with a smile on my face as I spread my hands palms upward.

"Oh, Tom, not to worry," she said with a wave of her hand, "church nowadays is really casual. You can come in blue jeans, or bib overalls, with a tee shirt if you wanted—just not in your birthday suit!" She chuckled with that radiant smile of hers. And that was how we ended up at Gunnison Bible Church with a congregation of maybe fifty to sixty people. We sang a few hymns, and I was most particularly struck by, and remembered, a couple of lines from a song titled "Highlands":

"O how long have I chased rivers

From lowly seas to where they rise

Against the rush of grace descending

From the source of its supply."[5]

Those lines spoke to me. For most of my life I had drifted—chasing a will-o'-the wisp, looking for something intangible and never finding it. Perhaps now I had found the river's source and it had led me to Grace. Or, had Grace found me and then led me to Cyndy? I had a lot to think about. As I pondered this change, which seemed to be creeping over me, Cyndy drove us back to her place. As

---

[5] "Highlands (Song of Ascent)." Track 8 on *People*. Hillsong. Songwriters: Benjamin William Hastings/Joel Timothy Houston © Hillsong Music Publishing Australia. Capital CMG, 2019.

we drove, I recalled some verses from another song, or chorus, we'd sung that day:

"From the gravest of all valleys

Come the pastures we call grace..."[6]

I knew, in many ways, I had been in some incredibly deep and dark valleys during my life, especially following THE WAR as I dealt with my injuries. Although I believed in God, up until now I hadn't really thought about how He, or the Trinity, had affected my life. Yet, now from my mountaintop aerie, I could look down into the valley and experience Grace. Thus began a routine for me. Whenever I visited Cyndy for the weekend, we attended church and, haltingly, I began to feel a peace creeping into my mind. I felt I now belonged to something greater than myself.

After leaving Cyndy's early one gray Monday morning, I noticed the cloud cover looked somewhat ominous. It was mid-August. Then Mother Nature began her winter drill. By the time I returned to the cabin, two inches of snow had accumulated on the ground. Over the next several hours, the snow continued to deepen. Knowing I should prepare, I toted more wood into the cabin, stacked it next to the stove, and restocked the outside woodpile next to the front door. *Looks like Ole Man Winter is finally coming to visit and stay*, I thought to myself as I relaxed in front of the stove.

Several weeks earlier while I was in town running errands, I had discovered Susan's Used Books on a side street. I stopped, went in, and came out with twenty-four or twenty-five used paperbacks. I tended to read authors like Michael Connolly, Anne Cleeves, and Charles Martin, but I also purchased the first three books of Robert Jordan's *The Wheel of Time* series. As I stowed the books in my truck, I grinned and realized I now had lots of reading

---

[6] Ibid.

material for the coming winter when I would be confined to the four walls of cabin.

For the first couple of days of being snowed in, I worked at adjusting my body to the colder temperatures. Even though the cabin walls had six-inches of insulation and my stove spit out heat, it was still a bit chilly inside the cabin. I tried to use the generator sparingly but didn't need it for lighting the cabin. The two high up windows in the cabin's front wall and two Coleman lanterns to use when needed, provided light. I also went out once a day and shoveled to keep a path open to the wood pile Bill Wellman had so kindly dropped off.

About two weeks later at around ten in the morning, I heard the sound of snowmobiles coming up my driveway. Quickly donning my heavy Carhartt jacket and slinging the bullpup onto my right shoulder, I stepped out of the cabin. I should have known it would be someone I knew—both Dan and Cyndy. They shut off the engines, hopped off the machines, and started to walk to the cabin. I smiled and greeted them both. After Cyndy took off her snow goggles and pulled the scarf down from her mouth, I gave her a quick kiss then turned and shook Dan's hand and ushered them inside.

"Dan and I thought we'd give you a surprise visit!" Cyndy explained.

"It's great to see you both. I've just had," I paused and said in a fake British accent with the mock pretension of an innkeeper, "such a stream of visitors over the past few weeks." They both laughed at my joke.

I fired up the stove as Dan went back outside to his snowmobile and returned with a twelve pack of cold Coors beer. It didn't take long for the stove to start putting out some serious heat. We sat in front of it while they filled me up on the latest happenings.

At one point I asked them, "Did you park on 114 and come in from it?"

"Dan and I loaded our snowmobiles on his trailer," Cyndy replied. "After driving up here, we had to park at a turn around on 114 about a mile from the turnoff to the Forest Service Road. After unloading, it took us a little over half hour to get here as the snow is really deep in some places."

"Well, that sure is mighty nice of you both. I do appreciate it!" as I toasted each one of them with a Coors.

We spent a couple of hours chatting and sipping on the Coors, before Dan rose and said they needed to leave just in case a late afternoon snowstorm descended over the mountains. I walked them out to their snowmobiles, which they mounted. Dan waved and took off, while Cyndy lingered.

"Are you up for a visitor next weekend?" she asked.

"Of course!" I eagerly replied as I leaned over and gave her a nice long kiss which she returned with some enthusiasm. She started her machine, waved, and was off.

My first winter was, despite the cold, enjoyable. Cyndy would appear every ten to fifteen days or so, for a quick one- or two-day visit. Winter was her busiest season. The Gunnison airport brought in skiers from all over the country, who traveled the twenty-seven-mile snow cleared road up to the Crested Butte ski area, which had a plethora of single family lodges and condos, many of which were always on the market. Cyndy was on the road a lot because the winter season was when she made 90 percent of her annual income. The rich were always coming and going to Crested Butte selling, repurchasing, or buying property. They liked to throw their money around. Later on, she told me that, on average, she easily made between a hundred and fifty and two hundred thousand dollars during the winter months.

At Christmastime she appeared on her snowmobile early one morning and said, "Pack up your stuff and hop on, Buster [by now her nickname for me]. We're going to spend Christmas at my place." I readily agreed, as I not only really liked the woman, but I also knew I could take a nice long hot shower.

We traded visits whenever possible, which made my first winter pass quickly, more quickly than I anticipated. One cold morning in late March as the snow just began to melt, I stepped outside to shovel the windblown snow out of the two-foot-deep trench I had kept open all winter to the woodpile. At one time, during the coldest part of the winter, the trench had four feet of snow piled up on each of its sides. I walked about five feet when I immediately noticed large animal tracks.

I quickly pulled the bullpup off my shoulder and scanned the area. Nothing. Had to be a cougar. I backed up to the front door still scanning the area. It was just one set of lone tracks leading from the woods behind the cabin straight across the lot and down my driveway before veering off into the woods. I blew out a small sigh of relief. Because I needed to stack some more wood next to the door, I cautiously moved back and forth between Wellman's woodpile and the house making as much noise as I could in hopes of scaring the cougar away. As if any noise I might make would really keep a ravenous mountain lion away!

The tracks appeared for six straight days. Obviously, the nocturnal beast had decided to incorporate my cabin into his territory, which obviously, I had intruded into. I never saw my visitor, but I stayed alert to his probable appearance. I was somewhat uneasy. Was he stalking me? Lining me up for a quick and easy meal? And, then, one chilly morning something eerie occurred. A pair of his tracks stopped about 10 feet to the side of the woodpile path and simply vanished into thin air. I thoroughly scanned the area, but it was as if the cougar had either mysteriously taken flight or had been vaporized. It was most puzzling and unsettlingly eerie.

The next time Cyndy appeared, I told her about my silent visitor and the vanishing tracks. We both agreed that I had been presented with an unexplainable mystery.

"Tom," she proffered, "the next time you're down at my place, we'll go out and get a couple of bottles of Cayenne red pepper. You can lightly spread it on his tracks. It just might keep him away."

"Or," I said, "he'll lick it up and use it as a condiment while he gnaws away at my bones," I added, which gave her a good laugh.

Two weeks later I returned with five bottles of Cayenne pepper. I lightly spread it over his most used tracks. A few days later, I noticed the mountain lion's tracks were several feet away from his usual trail, so I applied the red pepper to the new tracks. After a week or so, the tracks disappeared. He didn't reappear. *Perhaps, I thought, he's waiting in abeyance until the snow finally melts and I can't discern his tracks.* He'd be lurking or skulking around and I wouldn't detect his presence so easily—until he pounced on me! While the cougar seemed to have disappeared, or moved on, it would not be my last encounter with him.

Spring came and the snowmelt flooded my little meadow and the Cochetopa rose. Its water rushed over and under my bridge with great speed, covering the bridge in two feet of water. I prayed and hoped that the bridge would hold and that the flooding stream wouldn't wash away my gravel road in the meadow. Over a period of a week, I was forced to put on my waders daily, walk down to the bridge, brave the icy cold water, and pull tree branches away from the upstream portion of the bridge. I knew if I left them they would pile up and form a dam that would eventually crack under the water pressure and destroy the bridge.

I always left my bullpup at the water's edge in case of any unexpected problem. I remembered that cats didn't like water, but that might not be bothersome to my mysteriously invisible feline visitor. I didn't want to take that kind of a chance. Especially because the frigidly cold water flowing against the waders numbed my mangled left foot making it difficult to walk. Once I exited the freezing current, my foot really hurt as I removed the waders and massaged it.

By early June, the flood waters had abated and the snow was gone. Cyndy and I were able to come and go with some ease. The summer blossomed, and so did our romance. Countless nights I prayed to God that I wouldn't somehow stumble and blow it. I knew I had fallen in love with Cyndy despite the fact I had never loved a woman prior to meeting her.

Part III
THE VISION

Beginning on July 7, I had two encounters that would radically alter my life. To succinctly sum it up, I experienced an unexplainable, incomprehensible, and indecipherable miracle. Like the Sphinx, it was truly an unsolvable enigma. Most people not only wouldn't believe me if I told them what happened, but also most certainly wouldn't hesitate in the least at writing me off as just another one of those kooky loners who must have been smoking way too much weed over the long winter in my mountain hideout. Afterward, I couldn't talk about it with anyone except

Cyndy. She was more than supportive because she immediately saw the physical change. Cyndy believed my story implicitly.

How does one comprehend, much less describe, an event that you logically know could never have possibly happened? Are we all trained from birth not to believe the unbelievable? That there has to be a logical explanation for everything? Yet, I know what actually occurred. I witnessed it. I saw it. I was an integral participant. It effectively changed my entire life and soul.

The morning of July 7 started out with a shock. I opened my front door, stepped out, and immediately froze in my tracks. The screen door was still propped open by the left side of my body. About twenty-five feet away in front of the woodpile, the cougar was sitting on his haunches. His bright yellow eyes, staring directly at me, seemed to bore a hole in my soul. No hair blowing in the breeze. No ear or nose twitches. Not an eye blinked. He looked like one of those lion statues at Karnak, frozen in place and guarding the entrance to the Luxor temple complex in Egypt. But I knew better.

I slowly moved the bullpup off my shoulder and assumed a firing stance. Now I was eye to eye with the beast. Yet, I really hoped that I wouldn't have to kill such a magnificent animal. After all, I was the intruder in his territorial domain—or so I thought at the time. Other men in my position might have immediately killed him, but not me. It was a standoff for five ... then ten minutes as I stood my ground and didn't move. I suppose I could have retreated and gone back inside, but what good would that do? The next time I opened the door, he might again be right there—waiting.

As we stared at each other, the mountain lion suddenly shifted and hunkered down, still keeping his mesmerizing yellow eyes totally concentrated on me. I felt as if he was trying to hypnotize me. Yet, at the same time, I had this unexplainable feeling that the creature was trying to communicate something to me. I knew I needed to act or do something, make some sort of loud noise, which might scare him into taking off. But nothing was close by that I could use as a noisemaker. Maybe a shot in the air? That might work.... But then I would need to bring the weapon back down quickly in case the barrel's explosion caused him to start coming at me for lunch instead of hightailing it.

Alas, I thought, *it's a Mexican standoff.* What to do? I continued to ponder. Perhaps, just perhaps, if I advanced two or three steps my approach would force him to either flee or go into attack mode. I prayed for the former to occur … not the latter. I took three quick steps toward him. He quickly rose on all fours and backed up a couple of feet, as his tail began to swing back and forth.

"GO! GIT!" I screamed, in hopes of scaring him off. I fired a shot into the air and quickly brought my weapon back down into firing position by my hip. And that's when it happened. *POOF!* He vanished into thin air!

No, I didn't see him run, or quickly slink off. He simply vaporized right before my eyes. Gone! I did a fast 360 degree look around but saw absolutely no movement anywhere. I knew cougars were incredibly fast, but not so fast that they could turn invisible right in front of me. I glanced into the tree he had partially been under. Nothing. This just couldn't have happened … not to me. I hadn't been smoking any weed or taking any psilocybin, much less any other drug—except for my pain meds. And yet the cat had, in less than a nanosecond, completely disappeared.

I more than just kinda freaked out. I shook my head back and forth scarcely believing what occurred. *Maybe*, I thought, *I had a brain fart. Perhaps I shouldn't be living alone in such a hostile and unforgiving environment. Had the forest turned on me? Naw, no way!*

Had I just imagined everything that just happened? Or, had I, suddenly, for some unknown reason, started to go bonkers?

I spent the rest of the day puttering around both inside and outside the cabin, making repairs and working at completing a general cleanup. While outside I was acutely aware of my surroundings and every three-to-four minutes scanned the entire area of the dell looking for any kind of movement. To say I was uneasy would be a gross understatement. The more I ruminated upon the morning's mysterious event, the more uneasy I became. What, just what, if what I had seen was really true? But my logical mind refused to acknowledge it. That night, I slept uneasily. But the cougar encounter was just the beginning of the miracle to come.

Two days later, as I sat outside at my picnic table, reading a novel, I heard someone walking up my driveway. Shouldering the bullpup, I sauntered over the sloped crest of the driveway, and saw the strangest sight ever to cross my eyes. *I am not hallucinating; I am not hallucinating; I am not hallucinating*; I silently repeated, like an Indian mantra, to myself several times.

Ascending my driveway was a deeply suntanned young man, about thirtyish, slowly walking uphill with a thick, wooden staff that shined liked a well-worn wooden banister. But that was not what startled me. The mountain lion was walking beside him! "No f*king way!" I muttered aloud. Every few paces, he patted, or scratched, the cougar's head. The man's long brownish hair fell to his shoulders, and he was wearing the weirdest clothing—a robe of sorts like one of those shepherds in a church nativity play, or maybe like Friar Tuck in the Robin Hood saga. A faded white rope was tied around his middle with two knotted ends hanging down to his knees. He wore some beaten up leather sandals. As he approached, I could see many lines indenting his furrowed brow. He had a tired look, as if, like the Greek god Atlas, he had hoisted and now held the weight of the world on his shoulders. Yet, as he drew closer climbing uphill toward me, he smiled, and I could have sworn a whitish aura, like a spotlight from Heaven, surrounded him. *Where, I wondered, had this guy come from?*

"Greetings, friend! Mr. Thomas West," he firmly stated. "I come in peace to talk with you a while." He had a strong resonate voice that seemed to echo and spread over the area. He turned, looked down at the cat, said something unintelligible, and it immediately dropped to the ground before starting, somewhat nonchalantly, licking its left paw.

He turned back toward me. His hazel eyes seemed to pierce a hole inside my heart, being, and soul. *What is happening to me? I wondered. Have I finally gone off the deep end? Is this real?* I tried not to look stupefied. *How? How the hell does this stranger know my name?* I asked myself as he extended his hand, and I shook it. He had a firm grip, but as he withdrew his hand, I noticed a round purplish mark in the center of his palm. *Strange place for a birthmark,* I thought.

"Mr. West, I know all people," he commented answering my silent, not so religious question. "My name," he commented, "is Hey-sus, I'm a wanderer looking for people to help."

Hey-sus. I thought. *Hmmm! Well, with a name like that and his coffee-colored face and hands, he must be of Spanish descent.* Yet, despite the eeriness of the situation, he seemed to radiate an aura of calm and peacefulness. I immediately felt both relaxed and at ease in his presence.

"Would you like some water?" I asked. Guess I needed to be hospitable. That's the least I could do. He looked thirsty.

As he nodded, I said, "Why don't you sit at my picnic table over there," I pointed with my left arm, which I could only raise so far. "I'll step inside and get us a glass." Which I did and hastily returned. He was sitting at the table, back to the woods looking down the driveway and watching his pet. His staff rested diagonally against the end of the table.

I sat down across from him, and bluntly asked, "Where have you been, and why have you traveled so far in this remote wilderness?" I blurted out before continuing, "and what are you doing with what appears to be a tame cougar?"

"Ah, Thomas," he leaned forward to reply. Looking directly into my eyes. "I am used to the wilderness, which I have lived in and out of these many years. The cat—how can I describe it?—is my guide. He finds and leads me to those I can help. He's my scout. As to where I've been," he paused and pointed to his heart, "here in your heart waiting to emerge at the right time and assist you."

"Huh? My heart?" I looked at him quizzically. I was thrown aback by his enigmatic and confusing answer.

"Yes," he continued, "I know you have been hurting for many years in mind, spirit, and body. I have decided to help you." He paused and took a sip of water before continuing, "The first action I took was to make sure your path found this wilderness where you would settle and build your cabin. After your many years of traveling and drifting through life," he paused, "I led you to this place. To find this property, I guided you into meeting Cyndy Continelli, who would then become an instrumental part of your life. She is," he paused, "a deeply spiritual woman and I believe you have found a great peace being with her. I knew you needed a helpmate."

I was stunned by what he was saying. Who is this guy? And yet, intuitively, I knew he was right. I knew my life had taken a turn. But, was I a part of some eternal plan?

"Thomas," he said, looking directly into my eyes, "I know you have suffered great physical pain. Would you let me help that pain go away?"

I nodded dumbly. *In for a dime in for a dollar*, I thought as I almost, but not quite, shrugged my shoulders.

He rose and walked—no he seemed to float—around the table. Standing to my left, he placed his hands on my disabled shoulder and arm. Wham! I felt like I had been struck by lightning! An overwhelming power surged throughout my body. He lifted his hands. I felt my arm. My entire limb, including the elbow, felt cured in some mysterious and unexplainable way. I could still feel the scars and withered limb, but something was different. Usually, when I ran my fingers up and down my arm, I always sensed the underlying pain, which, actually, had never really gone away. Now, nothing. No pain! It felt as if my injured limb had somehow been mysteriously rewired. I made a fist with my fingers and, tightening it, felt no pain running up my arm! Okay, now for the ultimate test. I started to raise my arm. Up and up I went with absolutely no pain or difficulty in raising it above a 90 degree angle.

I was astounded. I turned to him and asked, "Who are you? How did you heal my arm?"

"With faith, Thomas," he answered, "and I believe you probably have an idea as to who I am, even if you're not willing to accept it yet. And now, I have one last favor to ask."

"Fire away!" I replied.

"I would ask that you allow me to wash your feet. I believe I will be able to help your pain," he pointed to my left foot. "May I?"

After having had my disabled arm healed, I just nodded. I was too awe-stricken to give a verbal reply. I started to rise but he stopped me by laying his hand upon my shoulder.

"I know where it is. You stay here," he commanded as he rose and strove off to the cabin.

I sighed and removed my shoes and socks. A few minutes later he emerged from the cabin carrying my two-gallon Igloo water container along with a six-inch-deep pan I used for my hasty sponge baths. He laid the pan at my feet and filled it from the Igloo. Then he picked up my left leg and placed it in the pan. From his robe's pocket, he withdrew a small vial, and poured its contents into the pan. A smell of lilacs rose from the water. He slipped the now empty vial into his side pocket and produced a small blood red cloth with which he commenced to wash my mangled foot. I felt no pain as he touched me.

I had absolutely no idea what to expect as I was too astounded at this apparent miracle. He lifted the foot from the water and said, "This won't hurt as much as the arm." He cupped his hand over the area where my three toes had once been part of my now badly scarred and mangled foot.

I watched him in awe and wonderment. I tensed like I would do when getting a flu shot. Something, some power, surged through my foot and lower leg. It tingled—almost tickled—as it moved up to my knee and then vanished in a nanosecond.

"Stand," he commanded. "Put your foot firmly on the ground."

I stood. Placed a lot of weight on my left leg and foot. There was no pain. I looked down at my foot. The scars started to fade and then totally disappeared. I was shocked! I couldn't say a word, but just stared at my foot.

The miracle worker motioned with his hand for me to sit. He threw the dirty water onto the ground. I knew there wasn't going to be enough water left in the Igloo container to refill it.

"Should I..." I started to say and half rose.

"No," he replied in a kind voice as he waved his hand over the pan.

It magically filled with water! Right before my eyes, with a wave of his hand, he produced water from nowhere. And I knew it wasn't humid enough to make that happen. I was dumbfounded. I just knew I had to be dreaming. All this was just too unbelievable.

As he placed my right foot in the pan, he looked up and stared into my eyes, "Believe Thomas, believe!"

Again, all I could do was nod. Couldn't find any words because I was tongue tied. From his pocket, he produced the same vial and, miraculously, it had refilled itself. Pouring it into the water, this time a sweet gardenia aroma rose and reached my nostrils. I felt a deep abiding peace wash over and through me. He finished the other foot and stood, replacing the vial and folding the blood red cloth before returning both items to his pocket.

Laying his hands on my head, he started to talk, "Thomas West, you have been washed in my holy water and freed from sin. I have taken away all your pain and loneliness." Like a magician at a kid's birthday party, he produced a thin white wafer from out of thin air, which he proffered and pressed into my hand, "Take the wafer," he instructed. After I swallowed it, he took his finger and drew a cross on my forehead. "Believe, Thomas, and you will find heaven's rewards are yours to now enjoy. Go now and be at peace. It is time for me to leave."

He turned, picked up his staff that was leaning against the table, and started to walk toward the driveway. Stopping at the crest, he turned and said, "The night is dark, Thomas, but there is joy in morning, in the journey toward the light." He spread his arms wide and continued, "Many follow me and now you will also be one of my flock." He turned and started down the grade.

"Hey-sus, are you really who I think you are?" I asked him.

He paused, turned, and said over his shoulder as he smiled, "Thomas, some people call me Yeshua."

I watched as he and the cougar walked down my drive. Yet, it appeared to me, instead of walking, they floated, as if on an invisible water flume, down the gravel road. And suddenly, it seemed that just briefly, before reaching the first curve, they both rose off the ground and vanished into thin air.

I stood slack-jawed at the crest. I couldn't believe what had just happened. Was it a dream? Did I just go on some sort of psychedelic trip? Was I hallucinating? Or was it real? Yet, I could see that my wounds actually had been healed and now the scars around my elbow had begun to fade.

I stared down the driveway for several minutes after the man and his feline guardian and guide disappeared. I was just about to turn when I heard an automobile coming up my gravel road. It was Cyndy. *Wow!* I thought. *This certainly seems more than fortuitous. Did some unseen hand guide her to visit me today?* As she drew near, she beeped and waved. I waved back and stood aside as she turned around and parked at the crest of the driveway.

As she exited her Jeep, I walked toward her. We kissed briefly before she inquired, "Where's your staff?" Concern crossed her face, "You didn't look like you were in pain when you walked over to me. No slight wincing in your face."

"Cyndy," I asked, "did you pass anyone walking down my driveway or the Forest Service Road as you were coming up?" I wasn't about to mention the cougar! Not yet at least.

"Not a soul," she replied. "What's going on?"

"Let's go sit down, I have a tale to tell you, something I'm finding extremely hard to believe myself."

As we walked over to the picnic table, she slipped her arm in mine, patted it and smiled. "Okay, Buster, tell me whatcha got going."

We sat side-by-side at the table and I related the entire event to her. As I talked, Cyndy's eyes never left me, while she absent-mindedly stroked my left arm. I felt no pain and didn't even flinch once at her soft touch. Once or twice she stopped me to clarify a point. When I finished, I could see tears in her eyes. I proffered my handkerchief and she dabbed her face.

"Thomas, you've been given a gift. It's both an unexplainable mystery and a miracle. I truly believe that you've been touched by Him and have experienced the presence, power, and healing of Heaven flowing into and through you," she said. "Remember, now, there's not a mountain He can't move. I promise you, I will never tell a soul," she said and patted my arm. "Tom, this is our special secret."

The look on Cyndy's face was radiant as she leaned over and kissed me. "You've been in the mountains, Thomas. Now it's time to learn what the valleys contain. This is a sign. You have more important things that await you down in the valley below."

She gave me a conspiratorial wink as she hugged and kissed me.

A calmness settled over me like a wave gently lulling one to sleep. I thought that I saw some type of path, or trail, to take, but it was too nebulous to discern exactly what I should do.

I put my arm around her waist and turned toward her. As we rose, I swear a shaft of light came out of the heavens and encircled both of us. Yet, I couldn't feel anything, but I knew it was there as I spoke, "Cyndy Continelli, will you marry me?"

Tears sprang from her eyes, she nodded and said, "Yes! I will with all my heart, Thomas West." We kissed a long time—a really long time.

AFTERWARD

Cyndy spent the night with me on the mountain. A light breeze blew through the trees most of the evening as we sat outside at the picnic table and discussed the day's events and our future plans. Around ten, the moon shone down on us lighting up the area where we sat. *Was this another sign?* I wondered as we rose to retire for the evening. It seemed as if the beam followed us to the cabin.

We woke up early the next morning and headed out for Gunnison. Cyndy worked half a day and returned around noon. We drove to the courthouse, purchased a marriage license, and found a willing judge to say the words to splice us together. Returning to her home, we cleaned up, and I took her to John's Black Angus Steakhouse—Gunnison's fanciest (and priciest) restaurant. The bill, including two bottles of wine, was over two hundred dollars, but I didn't care. I was really happy for the first time in my life.

The next day, I returned to my cabin, cleaned and tidied up in less than an hour, and then locked it up tight. Cyndy and I decided during the summer—her slow season—we'd live in her town home during the week and at the cabin on weekends, unless she had business. In the winter, I'd lock up the mountain lair, and we'd live in Gunnison.

Three days after I'd temporarily closed the cabin, we flew out of Gunnison to Denver and on to Vienna, Budapest, and Prague for our three-week honeymoon. Upon our return, I applied to Western Colorado University (WCU) in Gunnison for an opening in the History Department and, since no one else had applied, I was hired to teach Asian history. Apparently, Gunnison just might have been too much of a backwater place for the radical, mass produced, leftist professors—who are now being taught in and graduating from some of the United States' most prestigious universities—to reside in and spread their rabid Socialist ideas. Westerners didn't like Socialists or Commies.

WCU also had a religion department leading to a Doctor of Divinity degree (D.Min). I felt a calling, so I applied and, between teaching classes and taking them, four years passed, and I had my degree. By that time the pastor at Gunnison's Bible Church, which Cyndy and I regularly attended, decided to retire. The church elders were happy to offer me, now considered "a local boy," the position. I agreed, but insisted on taking no salary. The elders demurred for about five minutes before we agreed, after rather quick and friendly negotiations, that I would be paid a dollar a year.

One day, while writing a sermon, I reflected on how much my life had changed and altered. I guess I had come full circle, from a bitter vet to a wanderer to a loner living in a cabin to marriage, teaching, and now to a minister. None of this, I intuitively knew, would have happened without my mysterious encounter with Him. Yeshua.

Then sings my soul, my Savior God to Thee:

How great Thou art! How great Thou art![7]

---

[7] "How Great Thou Art." Shane and Shane - Hymns, Vol. 1. Songwriter: Stuart K. Hine. Wellhouse Music. ℗ Wellhouse Records. 2018.

FOOTPRINTS IN THE SAND

A Thousand Footprints in the Sand
Are All Washed Away,
And No One Really Knows
Who Stood There Before
Watching the Sea Recede?
Only the Sand Knows -
For It Felt Their Step

And Then, with Water,
Washed Itself Flat Again.
Caesar, Maybe, Stood Here -
But He Is Gone,
And So Are His Footprints,
And the Footprints of All Other Men
Who Stood and Watched the Sea
Break upon the Shore.

Footprints in the Sand
Stay a While and Go -
Let the Roar of the Sea,
And the Crash of Waves
Wash the Sand Free Again -
Cover and Smooth It Out
For Some Other Man
To Make Footprints in the Sand.

THE CHURCH

The church was old. It had that used look and, sadly, neglect and decay had set in giving it a dowdy, dilapidated, and somewhat tarnished appearance. Its wooden siding had turned a light gray from age and paint on some exterior boards had started to peel. Strangely, none of its windows had been broken, which was a miracle giving that abandonment usually brought vandals and homeless people. Yet, there she stood, like a grande dame, apparently unmolested, in her majestic ancient grandeur, perched like, as John Winthrop said in his 1630 sermon to the occupants of the Mayflower, "a city upon a hill."[8]

---

[8] Barry, John M. *Roger Williams and the Creation of the American Soul - Church, State, and the Birth of Liberty*. New York: Viking, 2012, 2.

I passed it every day, sitting way back from the road in a weedy overgrown field, on my way to work in Gloucester Point on the south side of Virginia's York River. Its entrance road, consisting of gravel, was overgrown with weeds. No car had driven up it in a long while.

Oh, by the way, my name is John Dandridge. "My people," as one of my former wives was wont to say, have been in this part of Virginia for over three hundred years. I'm the chief cook and bottle washer of my own business, an outdoor outfit that I tritely named York River Outfitters, which basically caters to the camping, canoeing, and kayak crowd, mostly from nearby Williamsburg or Richmond, positioned further west. Now that the spring melt had disappeared and the nearby rivers had returned to their normal flow level, it was a slow time for us. But, by the end of May, things usually pick up, as that is when schools and universities break for the summer, leaving kids with no more homework and a lot of free time on their hands—including beer drinking. I made everyone who rented a canoe, kayak, or inflatable raft sign an airtight insurance waiver that the law firm I hired in Richmond, Wythe and Lee, had furnished to me. I made no bones about warning the college crowd that drinking and water did not go well. As if they paid any attention at all to an oldster like me.

One afternoon, in mid-April, I decided to take off early from work, leaving my assistant Mary Catherine Brice to handle the slow business and lock up. A lot of Southern women had two first names—Mary Anne, Mary Lou, or Anne Marie, etc. I lived in Hayes, a small town of maybe a thousand souls—if you included the outskirts for maybe two miles surrounding the rural village, which is located on the northern bank of the York River Peninsula. So, I crossed over the river twice on my daily twenty-mile round trip.

Every time I passed the church, I felt inexorably drawn to it as if some unseen magnetic force wanted to propel me to visit. Today,

I decided to stop and have an up-close look. I drove up the quarter mile driveway and parked in an unkept gravel lot just in front of the church. When I exited my 2015 fire engine red Chevy Silverado truck, I saw an old faded sign beside the front door. In faint black letters it proclaimed, "Washington's Church—All Are Welcome!" There was a slight breeze from the west, but the church seemed to exude a mysterious calmness and serenity. Oddly, I felt accepted by the old structure, which loomed in front of me.

I decided to walk around the church just to get a feel for the place and why I felt so drawn to it. Despite its shabby outside appearance, the abandoned old lady looked astonishingly well kept. I wondered about the history of the church and its approximate age. Little did I know, but I was about to find out the answer to my question in an unexpected way.

Having circumvented the church, I thought maybe I should just try the front door to see if it opened. As I strode up the front steps, and despite their apparent age, I heard no creaking or groaning from the wood underneath my feet. *Hmmm, that's really strange,* I thought. I tried the door's knob and surprisingly, it opened! I had a momentary hesitancy about entering the sanctuary, but a voice— was it in my head?—intoned, "Welcome, stranger." I looked around but saw no one. *My mind must be playing tricks on me,* I thought, as I stepped inside.

The sanctuary was immaculately clean. *How could this be,* I wondered? After all, from the outside this house of worship appears to have been abandoned for God knows how long. Yet there were pews that looked as if they had been oiled yesterday. I could even smell the oil—or whatever it was. Its aroma, some sort of flower, wafted toward me. I glanced down the middle aisle at the apse area and saw an old altar table with a plain, unadorned, three-foot-high cross set on top of it. I walked toward the altar and carefully mounted the two six-inch steps leading into the chancel area. I stood in awe as I turned around and looked back down the nave toward the front door. I wasn't quite sure what exactly was going on. This should have been a dusty, rat and pigeon infested, litter strewn church, but it wasn't. Instead, an eerie silence permeated the inside area as the fading afternoon light filtered through the sparklingly clean and clear windows.

Well, with my curiosity sated, I thought I'd better head home. Still, the unexplained cleanliness and peacefulness of the interior bothered me. Stepping down, I started to amble back down the nave, but an unknown voice came out of the air, "Stay awhile with us, John Dandridge! Go to a pew and pray." *Whoa!* Unnerved, I swiveled my head but saw nothing. I was the only person there. I decided to ignore the voice and picked up my pace as I headed down the nave toward the church's front door.

Suddenly, at about the halfway mark, an overwhelming desire crept over me, commanding me to sit in a pew. I felt as if an invisible hand was placed on the small of my back and was ushering me to the closest pew. So, I sat down almost semi-frozen. *What's going on?* I asked myself. *Am I hallucinating?* But, there I sat, contemplating whether or not to pray.

I hadn't been inside a church or attended a church service for over twenty-five years. Religion just wasn't my thing. After all, throughout my childhood, my high society, nose-in-the-air parents had crammed their Episcopalian beliefs down my throat by forcing me to attend church every long and excruciating Sunday.

Then, to my abject horror, they had bundled me off to the nearby Anglican Church School—originally a private boy's prep school—but now, in keeping with the "politically correct" times, coed and obviously affiliated with the Episcopal church. For four long excruciating years, I had more Protestant religion forced down my throat every day—chapel every morning and a history of either religion or the Bible during each semester of the interminable long and boring school year. In those days, I often wondered if the school's administration was hell bent on turning all of us into priests. Needless to say, when I graduated I was fairly sure I never wanted to experience any type of religion ever again.

Yet here I sat in what appeared to be an abandoned church. I reflected on my life. Yes, by all measures I ran a successful business now almost twenty years old. I lived modestly in a small two-bedroom house off the beaten track. Visitors never stopped in to say hello, and at Halloween and Christmas, I chained off my long driveway and shut off every light so I did not attract the little rug rats and their hoity-toity Generation XYZ526, or whatever. Yes, my reader, you guessed correctly that I don't have any kids. I don't like kids. I'd even been married a couple of times (well, three to be exact), but I'm basically a loner and my aloofness didn't inspire any wife to stay around that long or to want to bear my children, had I even been disposed for that radical interference in my life.

Plus, my biggest problem—the elephant in the room—as I continued to contemplate my past, was my family. I was a Dandridge, an FFV (First Families of Virginia for those of you who don't know!), going back to the 1650s. My great, great someone's ancestor's brother had been the brother of Martha Dandridge Custis, whose second husband just happened to be a fella named George Washington. Yeah, that George! So, over time I had gotten used to people asking me when I was introduced to them. Are you related to...? It was a mantle I didn't particularly care to wear. But I was stuck with it.

I guess I could have legally changed my name, but I was just too lazy to fill out the local government paperwork, much less pay the ridiculous fifty-dollar fee to do so. Besides, what good would it really have done? Plus, the FFV judges in Virginia—many with old revolutionary era last names, such as Byrd, Carter, Jefferson, or

Harrison—were deeply steeped in the importance of FFV family history. Not only would they frown upon my request, but they probably wouldn't even take the time to grant it. It wasn't a risk I wanted to take. My family, when—not if—they eventually learned about it, would be absolutely mortified. So, best for me not to embarrass "The Family."

Thus, I shunned most people and not only had little to do with my parents and their social snobbery, but also my two sisters (who had married "well" according to my progenitors as they looked down their noses at me wondering why I hadn't conformed). I also had an older brother, Randolph, who was an absolute prig. I didn't care for him, and he certainly despised me for some unknown crazy reason. Perhaps he was jealous that I refused to kowtow to my family's Virginia Brahmin caste system, or maybe he was incredibly frustrated because he didn't have the guts to do so. Being stuck and realizing you are surely doesn't help anyone.

Anyway, after Mama and Papa had departed this orb, I had no problem avoiding my siblings. One sister, Martha (guess who she was named after?), had fruitlessly tried to get me to attend family functions and the high-class society soirees she and her wealthy, old monied (and rich!) hubby, John Peter Jefferson (guess who he was related to?), seemed to throw every other weekend in Richmond, where they resided. I assiduously avoided their glitzy social shindigs, and especially her, like the bubonic plague. I knew she was hell bent on trying to fix me up with one of her "my shit doesn't stink" society girlfriends, or a newly minted divorcee. I was having nothing to do with it.

As I continued to sit in the pew, I felt as if I was stuck to my seat. Some force appeared to be holding me to the pew. I began to have this overwhelming feeling of drowsiness, which crept insidiously over me. I nodded off … or did I? I'll let you decide, dear reader.

I have no idea how long I slept, but I felt like Rip Van Winkle as I slowly regained consciousness. I sensed a presence hovering nearby. My eyes snapped open and was immediately startled and quickly scooted back against the pew bench. There was a minister of some sort standing not three feet away looking at me. I blinked my eyes several times.

The pastor was a rail of a person—thin, almost waif-like—he looked as if he hadn't eaten in ages. His face indicated he was in his fifties. Yet, he had a calm, reassuring look and wore an enigmatic smile. His deep red hair was mussed giving him a lost type of mien. Quickly, I intuited there was something not quite right with his body or clothes. He exuded an ethereal transparency. I thought I could see right through him, but not really. His appearance unnerved me.

"Ah, I apologize for falling asleep in your church, pastor," I commented looking up at him. "I had a strange compulsion to sit down, and I must have nodded off."

"That's alright, Mr. Dandridge. We were expecting you."

"Huh?" I asked myself, as I reared back in my seat at his use of my name. *What the heck was going on here*, I wondered, as my eyes quickly searched the inside of the sanctuary for other individuals. "Ah, Parson, who are you and what's happening?"

"Fear not, Mr. Dandridge, all will be revealed in good time. I am Minister Booker, and this is my church."

"But … but …" I stammered, "how did you even know my name?"

"Well, you have been a member of my church for thirteen years," he replied.

"Oh no, no Pastor!" I said vigorously shaking my head. "I don't attend church. Not since I graduated high school." I stood and stated firmly, "I think it's time for me to go. I don't want to keep you from your duties." I raised my arm in a sweeping gesture indicating the entire church area. Wanting to get the hell out of the church as fast as I could, I couldn't comprehend, much less believe, what was happening to me.

Booker just stared at me. "Mr. Dandridge," he started, "I'm sorry, but you will not be leaving for a while. Your expertise is desperately needed."

"What do you mean, sir?" I turned and walked toward the front door as Booker trailed behind.

"Open the door, and look out, but make no attempt to go down the stairs," he cautioned.

I opened the front door and froze. My Silverado had disappeared—as in gone and vanished! In its place was a horse and buggy. The outside environment surrounding the church had completely transformed itself. Where there had been woods on both sides of the driveway I used when approaching the church earlier there were now open fields with crops. I could see people harvesting in the distance. The topography even looked different. The car lot—I guess it was still a parking lot—was clean, no weeds. I looked down toward the main road I had driven on every day to work, but it had vanished. The building's siding had been newly painted. And the sign beside the church door had mysteriously changed! It now said, "Christ Emmanuel—Please Feel Free To Enter." How could this have happened while I slept? No way! I was totally flummoxed and beginning to feel rather uneasy.

I turned to speak to Booker, "What the h—," I cut myself off from using the word "hell" in front of him. Instead, I shook my head with puzzlement.

"Come back inside and I will try to explain, Mr. Dandridge," Booker answered before turning and walking back into the sanctuary.

I had this unfathomable and impulsive urge to walk down the steps and run as fast as I could toward the main highway, wherever the hell it was. I began to hyperventilate. My feet refused to move downward. I thought they were stuck in knee deep mud. *Calm down!* I said to myself. There must be some logical reason for what was happening to me. Only when I turned to reenter the church, did I feel unconstrained. A feeling of serenity swept over me, so I reluctantly followed Booker back inside.

The minister sat in the front row, where I joined him. Booker stroked his chin for a moment or two before turning toward me and speaking.

"Mr. Dandridge, you are familiar with Yorktown?"

"Yes, I have my business in Gloucester Point, which is close by the battlefield," I replied.

He just nodded, turned, and stared off at the altar. "And you have toured the battlefield?"

"Yes, many, many times. Usually, when an old acquaintance is driving through and gives me a call."

"Well, Mr. Dandridge," Booker commented as he again pivoted on the pew to face me. He paused a few seconds before continuing, "We know with your knowledge that you can help us with our plans."

"Er, what exactly do you mean, Padre?" I gave him a baffled and confused look. *What the hell was really going on here?* I kept wondering to myself.

"Mr. Dandridge, I am well informed as to your lineage," Booker said with some authority, "and…."

"Sorry to interrupt you, Reverend, but who is this 'We' you keep referring to?"

"I will explain, but first I need to give you some pertinent background information," he replied with an old age tiredness in his voice.

"Oh, alright. Okay," I grumbled while growing extremely frustrated by this unexpected change of events, especially since it seemed to involve me in some muddled way. I just wanted to get home, crack open a Blue Moon, and relax on my porch.

"Please, Mr. Dandridge, don't get upset at what I'm going to relate. Your ancestor, Bartholomew, leads a local group of men—patriots, if you will." Booker cleared his throat as I looked at him rather quizzically. I was dead sure I didn't have any living cousin by that name! "And he has taken ill. So," he paused, "he will be unable to thoroughly scout Yorktown for us."

Now I was really confused.

"I am part of Bartholomew's group," Booker continued. "With his illness, I am now the de facto leader of that band. And we need someone with an intimate knowledge of the area. Someone with prior knowledge who can point out where and how to bottle up Cornwallis."

This is getting weirder by the minute, I thought to myself. Booker continued, "I knew we needed someone intimately familiar with Yorktown and its environs. A person from the future who was also related to Bartholomew."

"But, what does this have to do with me?" I asked with some frustration creeping into my voice.

"Mr. Dandridge," Booker continued, "I have been gifted with the 'sight,' so I can travel into the future in my mind."

I really shook my head back and forth. *Is this guy nuts?* I pondered.

"For the last week or two, I have been observing you and I decided to tap into your expertise. I have brought you—no, transported you—to our time, now September 23, 1781."

I half rose from my seat and then sat back down, still not having a clue, or even an inkling, as to what had happed to me. It certainly didn't sound believable. No way this was happening! Not to me! Was Booker a nutso?

"As you know, General Washington is fast approaching us from the north with his army, which he has quickly marched south from Philipsburg, New York, over the past thirty to forty days. His Continental Army will be here within the next day or two. But, he has preceded them, is nearby, and needs your help. Our group also needs your expertise to locate certain strategic military positions."

From inside his frock, Booker withdrew a folded paper, which he opened. It crinkled as he unfolded it, and I immediately saw what was an ancient map of the Yorktown area. As I quickly scrutinized the map, I knew it had to be more than two hundred years old. Booker refolded it then handed it to me, "Keep this with you. You will need it when you discuss matters with The General." I took the map and kept it in my right hand.

"My men will start arriving within the hour," he firmly stated, "and they will be accompanied by General Washington. I would like you to use this crude map," he tapped it with one finger, "as best you can and point out to General Washington where his army will need to dig in, trench, and set up their cannons to take on and defeat the British."

All of this sounded rather too fantastic and far-fetched to me. But, I thought, *What the hay, anything for God and country, right?* I could feel sweat beads popping out on my face and trickling down my chest and armpits. I was extremely nervous. *Am I altering time?* I knew that wasn't possible. But … was it? I suddenly felt my fifty-plus years. *Okay, I'll go along with this, whatever "this" is*, I decided, though I was totally befuddled by the eerie set of events. *Is this real? Am I dreaming?*

I sat in the pew waiting. But what (or who) was I actually waiting for? Had something happened to me? Have I ended up in hell, or am I really going to meet George Washington? I could see the sunlight was beginning to dim outside the church. Quickly glancing at my Tag Heuer watch, I was astounded to see I had been here for five or six hours, maybe more, yet, it felt like only a few minutes had passed. While I sat and fidgeted, darkness began to descend outside then slowly it crept inside the church.

"Ah, Booker," I queried, "aren't we going to need some light?"

"Not until my people arrive with The General. Then I'll light some small tapers over in that niche in the apse to your left," he pointed before continuing, "We don't want any kind of unnecessary attention drawn to us. I have a thick black curtain I can draw so that not a lot of light escapes."

"Rather small area to use," I noted. "How are you going to get everyone in there?'

"Only you and I, The General, and his aide-de-camp will be there," he seemed to sigh as he answered. I guessed he was tensing up. He looked tired and sweat beads trickled down his face, which he wiped away with the sleeve of his frock.

"Yes, this has been a difficult time for us," he sighed as if reading my mind. "This war has uprooted and wearied us, leaving us so tired that I sometimes wonder how we can keep going. Now, though, that is moot. We are within weeks of the war's end, and your help will be most appreciated."

Wow! I thought. *What an incomprehensible experience—if it is real!*

About ten minutes later, or maybe more, I heard horses outside. I had lost all sense of time and I dared not look at my watch, no matter how tempted I was to do so. Time seemed distorted and out of whack to me. I sensed, almost intuitively, that the unseen riders had tied their mounts to the hitching rail located at the rear of the sanctuary, which I had noticed on my earlier circumnavigation of the ancient structure. When I noticed the rail, I figured that maybe during a prior time period local people had ridden to church and used the hitching rail before the sanctuary had been mysteriously abandoned. Yet now, I could hear the horsemen walking around the church heading for the front door. I also heard low murmuring and the crunch of men's boots as they surrounded the building on all sides.

Booker now rose, struck a flint and lit a small taper he had withdrawn from his pocket. He walked to the front door, and opened it. I heard him mumbling something like: "May God be with you," in a low voice as each man entered the church. Then Booker quietly said, "Follow me, gentlemen." His words echoed to where I was seated in the front pew.

I stood and turned to view the approaching entourage. In the lead, striding down the aisle was George Washington. Thomas Peale's 1780 portrait of him hardly did him justice. At six foot two, an aura seemed to surround him as he approached. For some unknown reason, I noticed his saber was hanging from his right side. Somewhere, in the back of my mind, I recalled reading that Washington was left-handed. Hence, he'd use his left arm to draw the sword. As he drew near me I noticed he definitely took command of the room. Yet he looked tired and dusty, having marched more than five hundred miles from Philipsburg, New York, during the last six to seven weeks with his combined five-to-six-thousand-man Continental Army. The army's number was increased by the accompaniment of Rochambeau's French troops. The French had marched even further—an extra two hundred miles from Newport, Rhode Island, to rendezvous with Washington at Philipsburg.

"General, this is John Dandridge," Booker intoned as he introduced us. "Due to his special expertise with Yorktown, he has offered to help us."

Washington stepped forward, extended his hand to shake mine, saying, "Mr. Dandridge, yours is a very familiar name to me," he pointed out as his piercing eyes swept over my shabby modern clothes.

I shook his hand. His grip was incredibly strong, and I tried not to wince. "Yes, sir," I respectfully replied, "your wife and I are members of the same family." He smiled and nodded knowingly.

"General, I've set up a black curtain over here," Booker said as he turned and pointed to the niche where faint candlelight emanated. *When did he accomplish that miracle?* I inwardly and surprisingly wondered. "I, as you can see sir, can easily add more tapers behind it. General, I've given a map to Mr. Dandridge, with which he will point out to you the best positions for your army to set up the siege."

Booker led the three of us behind the curtain. He lit a few more tapers, so the area was brightly illuminated for me to use the map, which I unfolded and placed on the floor. Taking out my Cross pen, I started discussing and marking the strategic points for Washington and his aide-de-camp, who had not uttered a word upon entering the church.

Washington interrupted me several times with pointed questions, which I answered with ease, as I was extremely knowledgeable about the battlefield. I wanted to tell him that his siege would end on October 19, but I didn't want to alter history. In three weeks, Washington, who had experienced so many setbacks and lost so many battles and men, would finally and decisively win the American Revolutionary War as a result of the blockade of the Chesapeake's mouth by French Admiral De Grasse's fleet and Cornwallis' capitulation after a twenty-two-day bombardment.

Completing my briefing, I stood with the map, refolded it, and handed it to Washington who quickly passed it to his aide. The alcove's increased candlelight illuminated the face of The General's aide, and I recognized him immediately as the twenty-three-year-old Major General, Marquis de Lafayette. I recalled from my numerous tours of the Yorktown Battlefield that Lafayette had arrived at Yorktown in mid-March 1781 and had engaged in several skirmishes with the British during the time leading up to the battle.

Turning to me, Washington almost smiled, "Thank you, Mr. Dandridge, for your insightful briefing. When this war is over, I won't forget your assistance," Washington commented as he stepped around the curtain before turning and looking directly at Booker. "Mr. Booker, we must depart. You and your patriots will know what to do with this vital information. Thank you for your help."

Booker just nodded as The General slid past him on his way back down the nave. "Well, Mr. Dandridge, you have certainly helped our revolution enormously, far more than you can possibly know," Booker spoke as he took my arm as we marched down the aisle to the front door. Washington had departed, Lafayette having quietly closed the door behind him. As we stopped at the door, Booker gave me a blessing and then, *Poof!* In less than a nanosecond, he vanished right before my eyes. Stunned, I turned and, looking around the church, I realized sunlight was pouring in through the windows.

I shook my head, not really believing what had taken place. Time was all mixed up in my mind. *Maybe I just took a long nap.* I opened the door and stared out in shock. My Chevy Silverado was where I had parked it. I twisted around to look at the sign on the wall behind me. It proclaimed, "Washington's Church—All Are Welcome!" I continued to stare at it for about half a minute.

"Well," I sighed as I turned around, "that was one hell of a dream I had." I glanced at my watch, it read four thirty-seven the same day I arrived to explore the ancient sanctuary. So maybe I had fallen asleep. I looked back inside the church. It was empty—no pews … nothing was inside the building. Time for me to leave.

When I returned home, instead of treating myself to a nice cold one, I poured a good two fingers of Benriach, a twelve-year-old single malt Scotch, into a whiskey glass and then sat on my porch to contemplate the afternoon's strange and unexplainable happenings. It was just all too unbelievable. I decided not to tell a soul about my mysterious adventure. After all, who in their right mind would ever believe me? Best to keep quiet and march on with life. But I broke that pledge to myself and wrote it all down in longhand then placed the story in my safe deposit box at the local Farmers and Merchants Bank.

I returned to my business, and over the next few months Mary Catherine and I were busy with canoe and boat rentals. Plus, our equipment sales soared that summer. Fall came, and, as usual, sales and rentals began to fall off, but not as badly as previous autumns.

One bright unclouded fall day—October 19—the day Cornwallis surrendered so long ago—Mary Catherine came in with the day's mail. "Hey, Johnny," she liked to tweak me by elongating my name. Seated at my desk, I looked up at her and scowled, which she knew was nothing more than a false front. "You've got a strange package here. Look at this wrapping. It almost looks like parchment or something! And someone has even tied an old string around it!" she exclaimed as she handed it to me before turning and exiting my office.

Yes, as I touched it, it almost did feel like parchment. I looked at it more closely and frowned. In the area of a return address was only one word, "Booker." The hairs on the back of my neck stood up, and I had a sudden queasy feeling in my stomach.

Uh oh! I thought as I turned the package over to see if anything was written on its back. How could anyone know about my "possible" church venture? The story was locked up tight in my safe deposit box. I shook my head, flipped the twine bound letter back over and looked at the stamps. There were eight twenty-cent stamps affixed in two rows of four each, with a picture of Gilbert Stuart's famous portrait of George Washington.

I now had an even more eerie inkling about what I would find when I opened the package. With some trepidation, I untied the string, which dropped onto my green felt desk mat. Taking my letter opener, I slit open the topside of the yellowish envelope and pulled out a folded piece of thick paper. Now I knew beyond a doubt what I would find when I unfolded it. As I started to open the fragile parchment, a small and faded ecru colored piece of folded paper fluttered onto my desktop landing on top of the string.

I opened it and my jaw fell to the floor as I read, "October 19, 1781. Thank you. Geo Washington." I was stunned—dumbfounded. I unfolded what turned out to be, as I suspected, the map I had marked for The General. *How can this be?* I wondered.

Now, I ask you, reader. Did this really happen?

THE CANYON

I Am Walking in a Canyon -
Deep . . . Deep . . . Down -
The Light Filters down Dimly
From the Overhanging Rim -
Large Sandstone Red-Colored Boulders -
Lie Scattered across My Path -
I Have to Wend My Way
Slowly around Each One -

NEVER Knowing What
Lies on the Other Side of Each -
As I Grope My Way Onward
In the Semi-Darkness
The Dark Is Fast -
Closing in on Me
It's Not Far Now -
From the Place
Where I'll Lie Down and Surrender
I'll Look Up to See the Fading Sun
As Night Approaches -
And the Stars Begin to Glisten -
I'll Finally Be at Peace -
No More Hurt -
No More . . . Nothing - -
No More Torture - - -
Of Living Each Day
Wondering How I Will
Make It to the Next -
I'll Close My Eyes One Last Time -
Take a Deep Breath -

And Pull the Trigger

To Oblivion!

Three Score and Ten Is More than Enough.

GHOSTS

had lived in Las Vegas for the past fifteen years teaching high school history. It was now early June and another school year had just drawn to a close. Tired of teaching, I asked for a year's sabbatical, so I could pick up some needed courses and further update my teacher's certificate. But, for the third year in a row, the powers that be, in their infinite wisdom, denied me that much needed scholastic break. I was burnt out and knew I needed a change.

So, with virtually no savings in the bank, I called it quits. Two days after graduation, I handed my resignation to Jeff Wolstone, the Scotch drinking and chain-smoking principal of North Las Vegas High, shook his hand, and walked out the door as if the weight of the world had finally been lifted from my shoulders. Next, I gave notice to Mrs. Delgado, my landlord of nine years, that I was leaving her small ten-unit apartment complex. I either sold or gave away most of my ratty furniture and threw tons of junk in the dumpster belonging to the 7-11 across the street. Finally, I neatly boxed up my books, placed them in a five-by-ten-foot U-Store-It warehouse, paid the rent for six months, and hit the road in my teal-colored seven-year-old Volvo that had 116,435 miles on the odometer when I passed the North Las Vegas city limit sign and headed north on Interstate 15 into southern Utah.

I had no particular destination in mind. Would I return to Las Vegas? I didn't know. If all else failed, I figured I could stop somewhere and teach part time to earn a little money. Life had not quite been the same since Mary Anne died. She and I had met in high school and had both gone on to graduate from Texas Christian University (TCU) in 1968. She earned a nursing degree while I gravitated toward teaching history.

At TCU, I studied under Boris Preston, an internationally known expert on Southwest American history who, in his younger days, had not only been a former All-American football player at the University of Tennessee, but also had played as an interior lineman with the Green Bay Packers. After his four-year pro football career, he entered Harvard and earned his Ph.D. in three years. In the classroom, the towering bald-headed Boris was a tyrant. He demanded the utmost attention from his students and gave them extremely difficult exams. Few survived his courses intact. We all knew he was incredibly knowledgeable in his field and expected the challenge. It didn't hurt that in the process we all learned a lot, especially when it came to writing properly. Boris taught us more about how to write a grammatically correct sentence than any English teacher we might have had in either high school or college.

Yet, despite his gruff exterior and demand for perfection, Boris' method of teaching inspired me. He was the main reason I had become a history teacher. I wanted to emulate him. I hoped to give my high school students the same kind of spark—or inner thirst for learning—Boris had infused inside me. It was sobering to realize that most of the teens really didn't give a rat's ass or a tinker's damn about history. They took the class because it was a graduation requirement. So much for learning, or history!

But Vietnam interrupted my idyllic seven-year courtship with Mary Anne. Drafted within four months of graduation, I was shipped out to Nam a bare six months later. I was so naive back then. I was a college graduate. I really thought the U.S. Army would give me a good job. I never, in my wildest imaginings, thought I would ever see combat, much less come anywhere close to it. Alas, I was dead wrong. In those days, the military war machine had an insatiable need for cannon fodder, especially after the U.S. losses suffered during Tet of 1968, so I was trained to be a combat infantryman—about the lowest job in the U.S. Army anyone could have—except being a cook. Such was the need for manpower in 1968. Even if you had crawled into the induction station with two broken legs and two broken arms, you would have been happily accepted into the service.

Two months after I arrived in Nam, I was on a medivac plane back to the states with major wounds in both my legs. We had walked into an L-shaped ambush near the edge of a rice paddy. The gooks, using captured U.S. claymore mines (which had seven hundred steel balls backed by two pounds of dynamite) caught our woefully undermanned nineteen-man platoon with its pants down. My legs had been shredded.

Most of my platoon didn't survive the initial onslaught—six of the men walking in front of me went down like dominoes and died. The rest of us were wounded in some form or another and, when

Charley opened up on us with AK-47s, four more young American teenagers died. We were pinned down and being picked off one by one. Had it not been for two Huey choppers and their machine gunners, plus a Cobra gunship returning from another nearby mission, we would have been dogmeat.

As it was, we had to call in air strikes practically on top of our position to keep Charley from overrunning us. We had also called in artillery from LZ Ike—a nearby fire support base—and they soon had encircled us with 105 and 155 rounds raining down. As the Cobra fired rockets and grenades into the wood line, the Huey gunships extracted those of us who were still alive. They had a slim cargo—only five of us made it out of the killing zone. We had to leave our dead—their stripped and rotting corpses would, I later learned, be recovered some five days later.

The army docs in Nam didn't expect me to keep either leg. Somehow, after three operations in Nam, four in Japan, and eleven back in the States, I managed to keep my limbs, but I needed a cane to walk with because my left knee was all but gone. A year after I had been Medevacked, I hobbled out of the McGuire VA hospital in Richmond, Virginia, with a Bronze Star for Bravery and a Purple Heart, along with an honorable discharge. The Army gave me 100 percent disability and discharged me barely eighteen months after I had been sent to Southeast Asia. Mary Anne and I married as soon as I mustered out of the service.

Mary Anne was my life. Originally, she had been born in Springfield, Missouri. Her father, an eye doctor, obtained a position with the University of Virginia hospital in my hometown, Charlottesville, Virginia, when she was seven. He moved his wife and three girls into a house just down the street from where I lived.

Mary Anne was a small, petite, black-haired beauty with a round face and the most enchanting smile I had ever seen. The first time I saw her, I fell in love with her. We started dating in high school and I never had eyes for anyone else. During our first twelve years together, Mary Anne and I lived in Charlottesville. I taught while she worked in the hospital.

But life is filled with terrible twists and turns. Mary Anne's asthma had worsened and desert air was said to be of help. So, we moved to Las Vegas in 1980. In actuality, we had both become bored with southern life. Charlottesville was a small town where everyone knew everyone else's business. It was time to escape. Finding a job in Vegas in those days was not hard. Five years later, she was dead. Not from the asthma, but from ovarian cancer. It nearly killed me watching her waste away and then die from this painful disease.

I continued to teach, but my heart really wasn't in it after Mary Anne departed. I was now, to use a 1983 title from the rock group, Yes, the "Owner of a Lonely Heart."[9] I merely went through the motions. Sticking to myself, I became somewhat of a recluse. Soon after Mary Anne's death, I sold our two-bedroom house and moved into a ground floor, one bedroom apartment owned by Mrs. Delgado, whose husband, I later found out, died in Vietnam. My legs had never really recovered from their injuries and alcohol lessened both my mental and physical pain. I saved little of my teaching salary—after all, I had my veteran's 100 percent disability check to fall back on if all else failed. Plus, for some perverse reason every time I went into a casino, I walked out with more money than I had when I entered. Finally, I quit going to the casinos. It was no fun anymore.

My car seemed to glide along the northbound interstate. I soon passed through what the locals called "the cuts" as I-15 angled across the northwestern corner of Arizona. "The cuts" involved passing through millions of years of geologic time. For some

---

9   "Owner of a Lonely Heart." Track 1 on *90125*. Yes. Songwriters: Chris Squire / Jon Anderson / Trevor Horn / Trevor Rabin. "Owner of a Lonely Heart" lyrics © BMG Rights Management, Carlin America Inc, Downtown Music Publishing, Musicnotes, Inc, Warner Chappell Music, Inc., 1983.

fifteen miles, the highway department had blasted its way through massive layers of sedimentary rock alongside the Virgin River Canyon. While this was, ostensibly, a magnificent engineering feat, I couldn't help but reflect how man had despoiled nature by tearing the heart out of these beautiful mountains. As I drove further into "the cuts" I was reminded of a verse from a Joni Mitchell song— "So, they paved Paradise and put up a parking lot."[10] It seemed rather apt for what man had done to this remote corner of the universe.

As I ascended up the gorge, I was overtaken by a vague feeling of unease, that perhaps some Indian spirits were looking down on me in silent disapproval, as I wound my way through this man-made desecration. I wondered what the various tribes that had inhabited this area over time thought of this defilement. Three hours after I had left Las Vegas, I topped out of "the cuts," and found myself approaching St. George, Utah. Seeing a sign for a Dairy Queen, I pulled off the interstate.

After winding my way through part of the town, I found the DQ on the left side of the road. It wasn't a regular sized DQ—more like one of those drive-through outlets. But I stopped and sauntered into the place to get a chocolate covered cone. A short beefy looking guy, wearing a red baseball cap backward, who looked like a former coal miner, served me. His badge said Jasper, Owner/Operator, so, since his business seemed to be slow, we chatted awhile. He told me he was in partnership with his brother David who operated a much larger DQ in Cedar City, which was just up the road a bit. He said I ought to stop there if I was planning on passing through Cedar.

I told him I had just quit teaching after fifteen years and was traveling around with no particular destination in mind. He suggested I stop and see the Kolob Canyon section of Zion National

---

[10] "Big Yellow Taxi." Track 10 on *Ladies of the Canyon*. Joni Mitchell. Songwriter: Joni Mitchell "Big Yellow Taxi" lyrics © Crazy Crow Music. Reprise Records, 1970.

Park on my way north. I finished my cone, thanked him, then headed back toward my car to leave. Even though I had left the windows down, the seats and steering wheel were blistering hot after sitting in the hot June sun. A mere wisp of a breeze lessened the intensity of the noonday heat.

St. George is a thoroughly Mormon town. I cruised slowly through the cool tree-lined streets passing the main square where there was a beautiful white spired Mormon temple. Just before I reentered the interstate, I stopped at a local outdoor camping and equipment store and picked up some trail food—the kind of stuff you mix with water to get an instant meal. At a health food store a couple of doors down, I also purchased some Gorp—nuts, raisins, and M&Ms mixed together—high energy food. I figured I might need something edible if I decided to camp out overnight.

I was soon back on the interstate heading north. I had no idea where I would end up on this journey—or if I ever wanted it to end in the first place. As I continued onward on my desultory peregrination nowhere, I thought a lot about Mary Anne and missed her. I remembered the first time we had made love in my two-bedroom apartment on 14th Street in Charlottesville. I had been home for about two months after my final discharge from McGuire. My parents wanted me to live with them, but I opted to be on my own. After making love that first time, I knew that I never wanted to be with another woman.

God, it really hurt now that she was gone! *Why*, I wondered, *was she the first to die, and not me?* With her gone, there was an ache and a terrible emptiness in my heart. After all, thanks to THE WAR, I'd already seen too much death in my life. I didn't need any more, but God had decreed otherwise. I hadn't slept with a woman since her death. No one could ever replace her, and I was just not sure I ever wanted to be with another woman again, much less love one. The hurt was still too raw. Mary Anne, a nurse, had understood the psychic scars from Nam that I carried with me every day of my life. Few, if any others, did—not even my parents. That's why after she died, the alcohol was much easier to use. It became my Lethe for the long and lonely, horrible nights I spent alone. I drank not to forget her, but to dull the numbness of the pain I felt at having lost her.

One evening, about five years after Mary Anne's death, Cecilia Rollings, another teacher at Las Vegas North High School, whom I knew on a nodding acquaintance, showed up, unexpectedly, and knocked on my apartment door. Cecilia was always impeccably dressed in the latest fashions—looking like she had just walked off the pages of Vogue magazine. I was mellowing out on my third (or was it my fourth?) Bacardi 151 proof rum and Coke of the evening when she tapped on the screen door.

I remembered that I had been surprised to see her. She walked right in and kissed me with that kind of directness that tells every man that he's about to get laid. Alas, I was a disaster. Although I tried to perform, I couldn't. She left in disgust and never spoke to me again except to nod in the hallway occasionally as we passed each other on our way to class.

I had often wondered if she ever mentioned to any of our fellow women teachers that I was a total failure in bed. Then again, maybe she hadn't told anyone because she had been married at the time she made a pass at me. I didn't really care. I just continued to stumble through life until finally coming to the realization that teaching just didn't cut it anymore, so I opted out on this journey of discovery—or was I really fleeing the ghosts of my past? And, there were too many ghosts.

My musings helped pass the time of day, and before too long I was approaching the Kolob Canyon exit, so I pulled off and drove up to the visitor center. After using the john, I wandered into the one room center where I purchased a plastic waterproof topographical map of Zion National Park. It showed the various hiking trails in the Park's Kolob Canyon section, which barely touched on the southern portion of Zion. Connecting the two sections was a grueling thirty-five-mile trail that led past Kolob Arch and down into the main portion of Zion, which 99 percent of the park's tourists visited.

The ranger on duty gave me an overnight camping permit and suggested I take the eight-mile trail down to see Kolob Arch—the longest stone arch in the world. He told me to be sure to lock my car, but that it would be alright to leave it at the trailhead parking area. Although it was still early June, he reminded me to take plenty of water, beware of flash flooding, and stay on the trail. It was to be a journey I would not soon forget.

Wandering out of the Visitor Center, I pulled two one-quart canteens out of my day pack and filled them at the water fountain just outside the Center's entrance door. Then I checked my pack's contents to be sure I had everything I might possibly need for an overnight stay in the park. For sleeping, I used an all-weather space blanket—"The Lightweight Super Insulator for Warmth & Protection!" proclaimed the attached outside advertisement. At the bottom of my pack was a two-and-a-half-pound lightweight nylon tent of indeterminate age and origin. In a small pouch I carried my survival cards (which began with the words "If Lost Relax"), a signaling mirror, matches in a waterproof container, and a compass. That was all I needed—plus, the food I purchased in St. George.

Leaving the Kolob Canyon Visitor's Center, I drove northeasterly up a long steady incline. Off to the west on the driver's side, a wide valley with golden fields of wheat stretched off toward far distant dark gray mountains. To my right, the beginnings of the canyon's red and pink sandstone walls towered upward. Rounding a right-hand curve, I entered the magical land of Kolob Canyon. In front of me, like a petrified waterfall, beautiful red sandstone cliffs rose upward toward the heavens. The brightness of the afternoon sun enhanced the rosy, pink beauty of these sandstone sentinels.

I soon passed a sign on the left indicating that Taylor's Creek Trail started in a quarter mile. The road, continuing upward, began to switch back and forth. I soon passed Lee's Pass, which the ranger had told me was the beginning of the trail to Kolob Arch. I decided to go to the end of the road and look over the magnificence of the Kolob Canyon area. To my left, off to the east, rose a sheer wall of reddish and pink mesas and buttes. Five miles from the visitor center, I finally arrived at the end of the road which had a large parking lot on top of a mountain. I parked in what was a picnic area overlooking a valley anchored by massive stone monolith mesas off to the east. No one else was there. A hot wind from the west blew past me, but due to the height of the mountain, there was still a faint coolness in the air.

Exiting my car, I grabbed my cane and limped over to a plaque set in stone that detailed the various mesas in front of me. The fresh air was invigorating. A slight breeze tugged at my shirt sleeve. Off to my right, I picked out Shuntavi Butte. Just below the top of the mesa was an impressive bright pink scar that was at least two hundred feet high and perhaps fifty feet wide where the rock face had recently spalled off the side of the butte. A jumble of freshly scattered rocks below the gash clearly indicated that a massive amount of rock had thundered down the butte's talus slope. Green pastures and scrub forest carpeted the top of each butte. Discerning sheep grazing on top of the distant buttes, I wondered how people got to the top without having to scale the rockface ramparts in front of me. The walk down to Kolob Arch looked intimidating. I wondered if I was fit to walk that far, or if my bad leg would hold up. Doubt began to nag at me, gnawing at my inner soul, while my inner voice said, in a most reproving manner, that I was making a big mistake.

Turning, I limped back toward my Volvo but, after taking a few steps, I jerked to an abrupt halt. A lone greyish cloud, drifting in the azure blue sky just to the west of mountain's crest, seemed to contain the vague outline of a buffalo. As I continued to watch, I realized that there was a white buffalo within the cloud and it appeared to be moving—walking about as if it was grazing. I blinked my eyes and shook my head, yet the nebulously palish white outline of the bison continued to materialize the more I watched it. The animal moved ever so slowly within the confines of the cloud.

I turned away momentarily, rubbed my eyes, but the massive and magnificent looking beast was still there when I looked back, except now it had been joined by another buffalo! Then another bison appeared as the cloud mysteriously and rapidly expanded from north to south. Was I hallucinating?

Suddenly, off to the left of the feeding bison, an Indian riding a horse and wearing a wolf's head materialized out of the mist. I really began to wonder if the alcohol had finally gotten to me. The rider seemed to be watching—or guarding?—the grazing bison. Behind the mounted Indian there appeared to be an vague outline of a woman following him. She was so ethereal that I could barely see her, yet something about her seemed oddly familiar.

The Indian turned directly toward me and raised his right arm in a salute. He seemed to fade in and out with the cloud's changing color and tone. I stared hard at the images in the sky before me. In an instant, the vision before me vanished as the sun filtered through the cloud, dissipating it within seconds. *My mind,* I thought, *must be playing tricks on me.*

What have I seen? I wondered. *Was this an omen? What was its meaning?* I decided to chalk it up to nothing more than my warped imagination. There had been no buffalo, no Indian, no woman. Besides, after all, logic told me that clouds don't just vanish within microseconds. I walked over to my car, climbed in and sat there speculating on what had happened to me. Just then another car, actually a small blue Toyota pickup truck, rounded the curve into the parking lot—a lone woman driving it. She parked several spaces away, got out, and wandered over in the direction of the plaque. Passing not ten feet away, she eyed me somewhat suspiciously on her journey to the plaque. I nodded in a silent greeting, but she just scowled.

Probably thinks I'm a pervert, I thought idly. Starting the Volvo, I backed up and turned the car to leave. As I began to pull away, I could see she was staring at me rather intensely. Her coal black eyes seemed to bore right through me. *Maybe she's memorizing my face and license plate,* I thought with sardonic grimness. She looked to be between thirty-five to forty-five, but seemed somewhat ageless. Her long black hair, tied in braids, ran down either side of her deeply tanned face. A thin, but distinct white scar, ran down her right forehead, crossed over her eye and continued across her high cheekbone to end just below her earlobe.

Thinking no more about this chance encounter, I quickly backed out of my space, turned, and drove down to Lee's Pass where I parked. It was time to fish or cut bait. If I walked in to see Kolob Arch, I was going to have to camp out somewhere along the way tonight. Digging into the cooler I kept on the passenger seat, I pulled out a Coke, opened it, and sat there drinking it trying to get up the courage to make the daunting eight-mile hike into Kolob Arch. I looked at my watch; it was a little after three in the afternoon. In my mind, I ran through every excuse in the book not to undertake such a foolhardy journey. But something deep within my inner being gnawed at me. My little voice egged me. It seemed to scream silently in my ear, *Go ahead and do it!*

Listening, I decided to hike down into the canyon for two-to-three hours, or as far as my gimpy leg would allow me. If I felt too bad, I could simply camp out and return in the morning. I put a couple of soda pops in the bottom of my day pack, rechecked its contents, making sure my two-pound nylon tent along with the Gorp and some trail meals were inside along with my two one-quart canteens. I pulled out my walking stick, locked the car, and started out at the trailhead.

The path leading down into the valley was between two and three feet wide and meandered along the top of a descending ridge line. There were many loose stones on the path, so I took my time negotiating the downward sloping trail, which after the first fifty or sixty yards, began to rapidly and steeply plunge into the valley. The ranger told me the walk to the stone arch normally took about four hours, but he hadn't reckoned on my lameness. What might be a sixteen-mile day hike for most people, would definitely be a two-day trip for me. My walking stick would be invaluable to me here. The farther I descended, the more determined I became to succeed in this quest. Some inner force seemed to give me extra strength. *After all*, I thought, *pain is only a state of mind*. Still, despite my self-talk, my leg began to ache after walking only a few hundred yards. Mind over matter doesn't always work.

God, climbing out of here is going to be sheer unmitigated hell. My thoughts were working against me. At that precise moment, having just negotiated a rather small gully across the pathway, I looked up. Something or someone seemed to move in the pathway some ten yards in front of me. I stopped dead in my tracks. I thought I saw the vague outline of an Indian, or was it merely a will-o'-the-wisp? Just then the wind picked up and blew the bushes on either side of the trail gently back and forth. Whatever I thought I saw vanished.

Yet, what appeared to be an eagle's feather now lay at my feet. It hadn't been there a few seconds ago. Had the wind deposited it there? I stooped and picked it up. A small red thread was attached to it. I wondered what all this meant. Why was I seeing Indians—or imagining them? I stuck the feather into a grommet hole in my pack strap and promptly forgot about it.

An hour and a half later, after carefully negotiating the steep path down the ridge line, I limped down onto the canyon floor. The trail wandered beside a dried-up stream bed. Hobbling along as best I could, I realized that my leg really ached. I paused and sat down on an old log beside the stream bed. Was I pushing myself too far? What happened if I couldn't climb out of this canyon? How long would it be before anyone started looking for me? I guessed that the rangers would find my car, check the license plate number against the one-day overnight permits issued and see that they had a problem if I hadn't shown up after a couple days. Well, I guessed I could survive that long—if I had enough water. I wondered if I had brought my water purification tablets.

Not good, Wilson, I told myself. *That's a defeatist attitude. We can't have that.* Whenever I started talking to myself, I always used my last name. Seldom did I ever think of my given name, Thomas, as no one I knew used it anymore. At school, I had simply been Mr. Wilson to both my students and colleagues. I hadn't encouraged familiarity, especially after Mary Anne died. Thus, I had been branded as somewhat aloof by my fellow teachers and, sadly, my students couldn't have cared less what my name was.

A camp jay, perched on a nearby bristlecone pine, mocked me from its lofty position. I took a small swig of water and watched as a small grey lizard darted up the arroyo chasing insects. As I sat there in the waning afternoon sun, I couldn't help but feel that someone was watching me, and the hairs on my neck started to bristle. I looked slowly around but saw nothing and heard no movement. I decided to find a campsite and settle in for the evening. It was just beginning to get a tad bit chilly already as the setting sun began to sink over the western horizon. Most of the canyon was in shadow, and I could feel the temperature dropping.

Looking around, I saw, off to my right, a small flat piece of land rising some fifteen feet above the canyon floor. Locals called this geologic feature a bench because it rose upward like one and it had a flat top. I struggled up a small slope and wandered over to the uplifted area. Finding a deer trail, I worked my way slowly up and over the edge of the bench as I gained the top. I quickly realized that, at some point in the past, someone else had had the same idea. There was a cleared spot and a circle of rocks for a campfire. Clearing the site of sticks and twigs, I placed them next to the firepit.

Next, I set up my green and blue colored North Face tent, gathered some more wood, and started a small fire. Taking a tin cup out of my day pack, I poured some water into it and placed it on a flat stone next to the flames. About a quarter of an hour later I had some lukewarm water. I poured it into one of my trail meal packages and shook up the contents. Using a spoon, I slurped up dinner and drank a 7UP.

I was extremely tired, and my leg still throbbed. As I sat on the ground next to the fire, I massaged my sore knee. It was numb. Tomorrow would be a long day if I decided to continue my journey to Kolob Arch. I wondered how far I had come. Probably no more than two miles at the most, so that meant I had at least six more miles and eight back. No way was I going to get out of here by tomorrow night. Maybe I had better turn back.

I continued to stare into the fire. I thought about my life and how wasted it had become during the past several years. Tears trickled down my face as I thought about Mary Anne. She had been the only woman for me. No other woman could ever replace her.

As I watched the wavering flames, the face of the same Indian I saw in the cloud, suddenly materialized out of the flames. I blinked and looked again. There he was! Who—or what—the hell was he? Suddenly the rest of his body appeared. He towered over me, staring directly at me, his onyx eyes, like x-rays, boring right through me. He raised his right arm in a salute with a flat palm and motioned with his arm as if to silently beckon me to follow him. But, just as quickly as he appeared, the Indian vanished.

What the hell is going on? *Is this my imagination or the beginning of DTs?* I wondered. I waited until the fire died down and then spread out the ashes. About three yards from the fireplace was a pile of loose dirt. I scattered some of it on top of the ashes to smother any remaining cinders. Now dark, it was rapidly getting chilly outside. The wind blew gently through the trees, and something rustled in the underbrush.

A bright full moon shone down upon my desolate campsite. The outline of Shuntavi Butte stood like a silent sentinel looming over my encampment. I stared at the alabaster moon a while, but then I thought I saw a wolf standing over it and howling into the night sky. He paused and looked at me. His yellow eyes seemed to suck out my troubled soul. Chills passed up and down my spine. I looked away and didn't look back. I wondered if a demon was pursuing me. It had been twenty-four hours since I had had a drink. *Maybe withdrawal from all the alcohol I'd been consuming was having this effect on me*, I thought grimly. Since it was past nine, I pulled my space blanket out, crawled into my tent, and, within minutes, fell asleep.

At some point during the night, I woke up. Even with the space blanket, it was chilly inside the tent. A dream about Mary Anne had awakened me. Staring into the darkness, I thought about her for several minutes. I missed her terribly. She had been my life, and nothing had gone right for me since she had died. Strangely, I felt as if she was physically present right there in the tent beside me. I could almost see her dim outline lying next to me—smiling at me the way she used to smile. Then, her apparition vanished. I drifted off into a restless sleep.

Birds chirping awakened me. It was a little past six in the morning so I crawled out of the tent and walked over to some nearby bushes to relieve myself. My leg felt better this morning, but it still ached. I fixed a small fire, heated some water, and ate a hasty meal, washing it down with a fruit punch I purchased in St. George. Finishing up, I took some water and poured it over the fire. Like a snake, the embers hissed at me as if to say, "How dare you extinguish us in this manner?" Smoke wafted up then disappeared in the bright morning sunshine while I doused the fire. As I had done the previous evening, I scooped up some loose dirt and proceeded to cover the now soaked ashes.

On my second trip to get more loose dirt, I pricked my hand on a sharp object. Looking down, I kneeled, brushed away some dirt and uncovered an Indian arrowhead. About two inches long, it was a beautiful piece of craftsmanship. I hefted it in my hand for a few moments as I further examined it. The main body was dark grey, but the point was blood red and still extremely sharp. Could this discovery be a coincidence or were the gods trying to tell me something? I slipped it in my shirt's pocket and promptly forgot about it. By 6:30 a.m. I was ready to start out on my quest to reach Kolob Arch. *What mysterious forces*, I wondered, *drew me onward?*

Having packed everything in my day pack, I checked out the firepit area one last time to ensure I had, indeed, thoroughly extinguished the fire. I then walked back down to the hiking trail. Within a few hundred yards, I crossed over a six-foot-wide shallow creek and began to climb what appeared to be a small ridge. The going would not be difficult for someone with healthy legs, but I found that I had to rest every two to three hundred feet or so. And this was a small ridge compared to the one I initially walked down to get into the canyon.

At one such rest stop, I found myself musing about why I had taken this trek. *How,* I wondered, *am I ever going to get back out of here? Why did I so foolishly decide to take this hike in the first place?* Then my inner voice reminded me that I had to make this journey to prove I still had something in me. *Yes,* I replied, *but I'm almost fifty, and I shouldn't have attempted such a physically exhausting feat.*

So, you want to quit? My inner voice asked. *No!* I silently replied. I have to do this. I didn't know what I was proving or what I had set out to do other than see that damn stone arch. But now, some mysterious force inexplicably drew me further onward. Maybe I would find some closure. *Maybe,* I thought, *I am making my last journey on earth and God is guiding me toward a finalization of sorts. Perhaps,* I mused, *I will experience my own personal Götterdämmerung.*

Finally, I reached the top of the ridge line. It had taken a good two hours of climbing. As I started to descend, I could see a small valley off to the east and the reflection of water. Glancing at my topo map, I discerned that the water was La Verkin Creek. I knew that I would follow it until I reached the Kolob Arch turnoff.

The thought of walking on flat land beside the creek gave me a great psychological boost. I could almost feel the adrenalin surge through my body. I hurried to reach La Verkin Creek but my throbbing left leg slowed my progress. It was another forty-five minutes before I finally descended into the small east-west valley that enclosed the creek. Sitting on a rock next to the rushing water, I dipped my fingers into the creek. Despite being early June, the stream's water was still bitterly cold, the result, obviously, of snowmelt in the towering buttes above me. Emptying my canteens of the chemically treated water I toted in, I refilled them with clean refreshing creek water. I munched on my Gorp for energy. Looking at my topo map, I reckoned I had about two miles to go before I reached the turnoff for Kolob Arch. I rested fifteen to twenty minutes before starting out again. It was, I noted, almost ten in the morning.

Walking on flat land is certainly a lot easier than either ascending or descending a rock strewn trail in rocky hills, especially when one has a gimpy leg. So, I made good progress alongside La Verkin Creek as it wound its way up the rosy-hued valley. As I tramped alongside the creek, I began to feel reënergized, especially as the warmth of the sun seeped inside of me, giving me the inner strength and willpower I needed to complete this trip.

It was a beautiful morning, not a cloud in the sky. Off to my left, the stony ramparts of Gregory Butte shone brightly in the morning sun. I paused to look at the butte's towering walls. For a brief couple of seconds, an Indian's face seemed to materialize out of one of the uplifted monoliths rising before me. I looked again, but my eyes must have deceived me because the image vanished. Finally, after a ninety-minute hike, I reached the side trail leading upward to Kolob Arch.

A small wooden sign, with an arrow pointing upward on its left side, declared that Kolob Arch was six-tenths of a mile up what appeared to be a densely vegetated draw. A small rivulet trickled downward beside and over the faint trail crisscrossing it several times. I paused and glanced at the path that wandered upward before disappearing around a curve as it wound its way uphill. Uphill—my eyes took it in.

This ascent would be a test for my leg, which was already aching from this morning's exertions. I rested another quarter hour before starting off up the draw. The trail's incline appeared to be gradual, but I still had to grab various tree branches with one hand while using my walking stick for balance as I scaled the small ravine. I hadn't gone more than fifty yards when I heard the eerily distinct sound of a flute. I froze. The first thought that came to me was that my ears had deceived me and that I had, in actuality, heard nothing more than the trickling of water in the tiny stream beside me. But the flute continued. It seemed to come from somewhere up ahead, yet I had not heard or seen anyone. The melodious sound enticed me onward. It always seemed to be coming from just around the next twist in the pathway ahead. As it drew me onward, I seemed to be marching to the tune of my own private Pied Piper. And then, after several minutes, the sound abruptly ceased.

After a fifteen-minute struggle up the trail, I heard branches cracking off to my left. A deathly ten-second silence followed before I heard another branch snap resonantly in the late morning air. Something large was moving through the bush. My heart pounded loudly in my chest—Thump! Thump! Thump! What sort of demon was about to spring out at me? Moving silently and cautiously, so as not to frighten whoever or whatever was moving through the undergrowth, I rounded a rather large boulder and stopped dead still with a start. Three large black cows stared at me, chewing their cud and intermittently pawing the ground. For a second my heart was in my mouth. I stared at them and they at me. I took note of the fact that one of them had a brand on its rump that looked like an arrow. Grasping my walking stick rather tightly, I banged it on the hard ground. The three dusty beasts turned and melted into the bush. I heard their rustling sounds for a few seconds, and then they were gone.

A slight breeze blew through the air. It moved an object on the ground where the cattle had been pawing in the dirt. I limped across the small clearing and looked down. It was another eagle's feather! Squatting, I picked it up. It, too, had a small red thread attached to it. What did all this signify? I stuck the feather in the same grommet hole that contained the first feather I found. Something, or some unknown being, told me to hold onto these feathers. For what purpose, I had no idea what all this meant. Limping back to the pathway, I sat down on a knee-high boulder and took a swig of water from my canteen. Sweat poured from my forehead and my armpits felt sticky. What the hell was going on here?

After a five-minute break, I decided to continue on my journey. Turning back to the path, I worked my way upward toward Kolob Arch. A mysterious force seemed to propel me onward. After a slow tedious half hour's climb, I finally reached the end of the trail where the stream broke off into two forks. My knee ached. High above me and off to my left, the huge span of Kolob Arch waited silently for my scrutiny and admiration. Except in pictures, I had never seen a stone arch. This one, although several hundred feet away in distance and height, looked beyond huge. I climbed up to a small clearing between the converging streams. A hawk circled lazily overhead. I watched it catch the updrafts and rise until it seemed to be at the same level as the top of the arch. Silence surrounded me. I vaguely wondered about the flute. Had I imagined it too?

I sat down, my back against a weathered three-foot-high tree stump. My leg throbbed, crying out in protest at what I had made it do this morning. In truth, the morning's climb had exhausted me. Looking at my watch, I saw that it was almost two in the afternoon, which gave me plenty of time to make a good start back to Lee's Pass. I knew I wouldn't make it back by tonight, but, checking my pack, I saw that I had enough food. There was plenty of fresh water within reach, so I wouldn't go thirsty. As I massaged my knee, I heard the high keen of the hawk. Looking up, I saw it dive at something in the rocks just below the arch.

The bird wasn't out of sight for more than several seconds before it rose again, but something about it was just not right. It wasn't the same bird. Instead, a bald eagle winged its way skyward from the point where the hawk had dove into the rocky bush covered talus slope just seconds ago. *What's going on here? What happened to the hawk?* I wondered. The eagle floated deliberately toward me and hovered where I rested. Strangely, I could feel its eyes boring into me. It was carrying something in its mouth, but not the hawk's remains. It looked like a red ribbon. The eagle swooped down in front of me. It's wide wingspread momentarily blotted out the afternoon sun. For a second, the bird seemed to take on the appearance of an Icarus-like Indian figure. I could feel the rush of its wings as it dropped the ribbon into my lap and flew off. I reached down and picked up the ribbon.

In a flash, the red ribbon turned into a small rattlesnake that rapidly entwined itself around my right hand and then struck me. As it injected venom into my body, I only felt a small pinprick of pain. In a panic, I grabbed the serpent behind its head, pulled it off of my hand and flung it to the ground about five feet away. When it landed, the viper immediately turned into a mature adult rattler coiled and ready to strike. I could now easily hear its distinctive hiss and its rattles. Looking at it with horror, I dared not move and willed my body to remain rigid and unmoving in case the damned snake decided to strike again.

After what seemed an eternity, the rattler slithered off and quickly disappeared into some nearby bushes. Looking down, I stared at the two fang marks on top of my hand. Drops of crimson red blood oozed out of the two puncture wounds. Oddly, I didn't feel any pain. Yet, a great feeling of lassitude crept over me. *Well,* I thought with some resignation, *this isn't such a bad place to die after all. What a beautiful place to rest one's eyes upon for the last time.*

Looking upward at Kolob Arch, I felt myself drifting off. But my eyes detected some sort of movement on top of the rock span. I rubbed my eyes trying to ward off a fuzziness in my vision. An Indian stood on top of Kolob Arch staring down at me. I wondered if I was hallucinating or if the venom was now working its way inside me, being pumped through my heart and then into every artery. Although he was several hundred feet away, I could still feel the power of his eyes delving into my innermost soul. I could see his jet-black hair blowing in the afternoon breeze. I tried to raise my snake-bitten arm, but it felt like a ton of rocks had pinned it to the ground.

And then I heard the flute music again. It was much closer this time, almost as if the musician was sitting next to me. I glanced to my left and there he was—sitting not five feet away resting his back against a nearby tree. He was there, yet … he wasn't there. I could see right through him. I realized he was a ghost! *The venom,* I thought, *must be making me hallucinate.* The flutist stopped, smiled, and nodded at me as if to say everything is going to be alright. I wondered if I had died. Reaching over, he dropped an eagle's feather in my lap. I looked down at it with some puzzlement. Then blackness descended.

The rhythmic beating of a stick on a hollow log brought me back to consciousness. It was nighttime. My back was now against a rock and my day pack lay next to me. About seven or eight paces in front of me the bright reddish-yellow flames of a fire wavered back and forth inside a yard wide circle of smooth well-rounded stones. The untended fire was surrounded by an open area of dirt approximately ten feet wide. Behind the fire a crescent shaped tangled growth of shoulder high bushes bracketed the open area.

My right hand felt somewhat constricted. Glancing down, I saw that it had been covered with some sort of grass and bound up with a leather patch. The leather binding had a white buffalo painted on it. My hand throbbed with little needle-like pricks of pain. Looking around farther, I quickly determined I was no longer in the clearing below Kolob Arch. In fact, it appeared that I was somewhere on top of a butte. How in the hell did I get here?

The rhythmic drum sound was soon joined by another sound— that of a gourd with rattles inside of it. Then the flutist joined in. I couldn't identify the origin of the music. Apparently, it came from out of thin air. Perhaps, I was only hallucinating it. But, suddenly before me appeared between ten and fifteen Indian dancers, both men and women, chanting and moving slowly around the firepit. I could see them, yet I couldn't see them. There was no substance to their bodies. I could see the outline of each person's body, but I could also see through it to the other side of the clearing. Even though they appeared to be ghostlike, I could still see their footprints in the dirt around the fire. *Ghosts don't make footprints,* I thought. *Am I in some kind of netherworld halfway between heaven and hell?*

A woman broke away from the dancing figures and slowly approached me. Kneeling before me, she proffered a bowl with a dark liquid in it. Pointing to my injured hand, she mutely nodded and held the bowl close to my mouth. "What the hell?" I said to myself. "I'm already dead, so I might as well drink it." *Perhaps,* I thought, *it's water from the River Lethe.* The river is one of five rivers found in Hades, the Greek underworld, that brought about forgetfulness to all who drank it. I hoped that imbibing it would put me to sleep until I awakened from this fantastical dream I found myself in.

She moved closer and supported my arm while I drank. I could feel her touch, yet ghosts didn't have substance—odd. The liquid burned, but it slid down my parched throat rather easily. It had a raw cactus type of flavor to it. *Whoa!* I suddenly wondered in amazement. *How do I know what cactus tasted like?* Had she infused me with peyote, a hallucinogenic drug containing mescaline? Yet, I drank it all, scrutinizing her as I did so. She seemed familiar to me. Where had I seen her before? I racked my memory. In the flickering fire light, I noticed a scar on the right side of her face. It was the woman in the parking lot! But how could this be? Who was she? Why is she here? Was I dead? Or was my mind playing another gigantic cruel trick on me?

"Where am ... uh, who are ...?" I tried to ask, but my tongue seemed to have an inordinate thickness to it. She shook her head, motioning with a finger against her lips for me to be silent. Reaching down, she lightly touched my injured arm, then reached over and detached one of the two eagle feathers I had jammed into my pack strap's grommet hole. She lightly caressed my injured hand and the arm below it with the eagle's feather. I could feel some sort of power flowing out of her through the feather and into my arm. It was as if she had infused me with her energy and life force, or maybe it was the cactus juice I had imbibed. She stood, dropped the feather into my lap, and silently returned to the dancing figures. Melting into them, she vanished. I picked up the feather to examine it. As I did so, I could feel the throbbing in my injured hand lessen ever so slightly.

For what seemed like hours, as I drifted in and out of consciousness, I watched the dancing figures as they wound their way around the fire never stopping or faltering. Their tramping feet raised small clouds of brown colored dust. Each time they circled the bonfire, the dancers' faces, and costumes changed. Some were young, occasionally I saw a woman or two, but mostly they were older men with sad eyes and multitudes of windblown wrinkles etched upon their faces. I saw hoop dancers, figures in traditional eagle feathers, and many more dressed as various kinds of birds or animals. Quite a few dressed as wolves or deer. I even saw a dancer with a beautifully ornamented butterfly headdress.

I idly wondered why the fire never seemed to diminish in intensity. It seemed as if an invisible hand replenished it every so often. There wasn't a cloud in the night's sky. A bright white full moon shone down upon this gathering. I couldn't feel the least wisp of a breeze. The night was neither cool nor warm. I felt as if I should sleep, but my mind was acutely aware of everything around me.

I couldn't understand why God had chosen this method for me to transition between life to death. What was His purpose? I reached for the thin silver chain around my neck and rubbed my fingers over the St. Christopher medal hoping for some kind of luck. The dancing figures seemed to never tire. My watch told me that it was fast approaching four in the morning. *Why am I not tired? I* wondered. *Why doesn't my hand ache from the snake bite?*

The moon had slid across the horizon and was about to dip behind a far distant butte. Without warning, the music abruptly stopped. The ghost dancers froze in place and slowly began to fade away. Within seconds they vanished. For several minutes, a deadly silence surrounded the dirt clearing before a figure began to slowly materialize on the other side of the fire. It was a woman, but she didn't appear to be dressed in Indian clothing. *Maybe Scarface has returned to get me, or maybe it's one of Charon's minions come to lead me across the river Styx,* I thought rather grimly. But, no, this figure wasn't Scarface, it was…. *Oh, my God!* my mind screamed. Mary Anne, my deceased wife was coming toward me. How could this be? She walked directly through the firepit and continued until she was standing about three steps away from where I lay.

"Mary Anne … I …" I couldn't think of what to say, so I reached for her.

"Thomas, you are not allowed to touch me," she said. "I can only be here for a brief time, then I must go, Love." She kneeled down in front of me.

"Am I dead, or what?" I asked.

"No, dear," she replied, "You're in a netherworld. Now listen closely to me. I'm fine. I'm at peace. No more horrible pain. But Thomas, you can't go on like you have been—drinking and continuing to mourn for me. You need to move on with your life and not be so sad that I'm gone. I'm a memory now. I am…."

"But Mary Anne," I interrupted her, "I still miss you so much. You were my whole life! I have never loved another woman as I did you! There is no one else who could be as good for me as you were." I could feel tears sliding down my face as the words rushed out of me.

"Thomas, it's time for you to find another woman. It's time."

"No!" I angrily retorted, "I don't want another woman! You were my life! I'd rather be with you, where you are now, rather than having to continue facing the life I've had to endure these past five years without you." I pleaded, "Take me back with you!"

"Thomas, listen to me," Mary Anne spoke sternly, "If you love me, if you truly love me, you will take another woman into your life. I am sending someone to you. Her name is Teks-Neh-Wah."

I just sat there shaking my head in mute disapproval. Tears continued to stream down my cheeks and dripped off of my jaw line.

"Listen to me, Thomas," she continued, "I have little time left. Teks-Neh-Wah will help you. She will love you just as much as I loved you. Promise me."

"But...."

"Promise me, Thomas," she scolded before raising her voice, "NOW!"

"OK," I nodded dumbly, "But who is Teks-Neh-Wah?"

"She's the woman dancer who gave you the cactus drink. She is not of our world," Mary Anne paused for a few seconds, "but of yours. Yet, she can enter ours when she wills—or when we need her. She is our link to your world. Love her, Thomas. Make love with her. She needs a child to continue the link, and you have been chosen," she continued.

"But why me?" I asked as tears continued to stream down my face because I realized that Mary Anne was beginning to fade.

"Because the Indian gods and our God have decreed it. You are a good man, Thomas. Do this for me. Promise me you will. I have to go now." She plucked up the remaining eagle feather from my pack strap, reached over and touched my injured hand, stroking it for a brief second. The pain receded even more.

"Will I ever see you again, Mary Anne?" I queried with anguish in my voice.

"Not in this life," she replied, as she shook her head and stood up.

"No! Mary Anne, please don't go. Please don't leave me again! I beg you! Please stay! I love you!"

I tried to reach for her, but my back seemed frozen to the rock I was resting against. She stepped back and moved quickly to stand in the middle of the fire. She turned to face me, then raised both her arms with palms upward. The firepit's flames leaped up above her head and within seconds she was gone. The flames quickly receded to a mere trickle. The clearing was empty and silent. An ominous silence permeated the clearing.

East of me I could see the first golden rays of the sun tinged with an orange reddish color that spread across the horizon. The music started again and suddenly the dancing figures reappeared around the fire. I could see the dust rise from where their feet stomped the ground. Teks-Neh-Wah detached herself from the dancers and walked deliberately over to where I sat propped up against the rock. Another bowl mysteriously appeared in her hand. Kneeling in front of me, she offered it to me. I reached up and grasped it. In the process of holding onto the bowl, I touched one of her fingers. It sure felt real to me. She smiled as I drank down the potion. It tasted of honey and flowers. Smiling back at her, I reached up and touched the scar on her face. She allowed me to trace it with my fingers. Then, she took my hand, kissed it, placed it on her abdomen, and smiled at me.

Everything seemed to spin around and around. Teks-Neh-Wah faded away, and I found myself spiraling downward into another black hole. What was in that drink?

When I awoke, the hot sun was shining down on me. It appeared to be noontime. I was still in the clearing. It was hot and extremely humid. I could feel the sweat in my armpits trickling down the sides of my rib cage. Glancing around, I realized that I was on top of Shuntavi Butte. Off to the northwest, I could just barely see my car parked in the lot at Lee's Pass. *How did I get here?* I wondered. When I looked back at the now bare clearing, Teks-Neh-Wah was standing in the middle of it. Behind her a small purplish cloud with a buffalo grazing in it drifted in the otherwise cloudless sky.

Without a word, she walked over to me. Reaching behind her, Teks-Neh-Wah pulled on a leather tie and her deerskin dress fell silently at her feet. The mist from the rising morning sun behind her caused Teks-Neh-Wah to appear as if she was an angel who had just descended from the heavens to alight on Earth. As she began to kneel, her long shiny black hair blew back and forth in the slight breeze. Its movement seemed to hypnotize me. Or was it the peyote? Leaning over, this incredibly beautiful and lightly tanned nude woman kissed me before she shifted and straddled me. I raised my good arm, touching her arm and face as she again leaned forward and kissed me. I could feel her removing my clothes but whatever was in the cactus drink prevented me from stopping her.

I felt as if I was floating on top of an invisible ocean wave— gently rocking back and forth. Tears began to stream down my cheeks as I thought about Mary Anne and the fact that I had not been with another woman since her death. Teks-Neh-Wah reached over and caressed my forehead before sliding her fingers down my cheeks and lightly brushed away the tears. Her touch somehow gave me great peace and banished my concerns.

I have little to no memory of how long we sat like this because my mind drifted off into an unknown eternity. Was I on Charon's boat crossing the River Styx into hell? At this point, I neither knew nor cared as I was surrounded by a serene feeling of peace. Neither one of us uttered a sound as Teks-Neh-Wah gently rocked up and down ever so slightly. Suddenly, she arched her back and thrust her hips into me. The explosion, coming so unexpectedly, drained me physically, mentally, and emotionally. Although I had filled her with my life force, I was completely spent.

In my almost unconscious state I felt totally exhausted, so much so that I was unable to lift my arms or move my legs. I wondered if Teks-Neh-Wah had put some type of magical potion in that last honey and flowered scented drink she had given me. She still had not said a word as she watched me intensely with coal black eyes that seemed to pierce deeply into my soul. She sat up, leaned over, and kissed me as she reached over and removed the bindings on my right hand. As I watched them fall to the ground, all the lights went out. I felt myself falling into a bottomless pitch black void.

Birds chirping woke me. I was lying on my back with my space blanket covering me. I realized I was inside my tent! But how could this be? I crawled out of the tent to find that it was set up in the same clearing where I had camped the first night on the trail to Kolob Arch. *What is going on here?* I wondered. Looking down at my hand, I saw the two small round scars from a healed puncture wound. At least I didn't dream that! Checking my campsite, I realized all my possessions were intact. The fireplace was still covered with the reddish-brown dirt I had sprinkled over the ashes of that first night's fire. I drank some water and decided to head back to Lee's Pass. Within minutes, I had everything rolled up and packed tightly into my pack.

As I walked down toward the trail, something shimmered off to my left. As I watched, a figure materialized at the next bend. It was Teks-Neh-Wah. She was wearing the same clothes I had seen her wearing in the parking lot. She smiled as I approached her.

"I see you rested well, Thomas," she said as she smiled and took my hand.

I looked at her. Around her neck was a red ribbon holding an arrowhead. It was dark grey in body with a blood red tip. I felt my shirt pocket, but the arrowhead I had found was no longer there. She was wearing my arrowhead! I looked at her in amazement.

It took us several hours to make the climb up the ridge line to Lee's Pass as my leg needed a lot of support from my cane and I often had to rest. As we wound our way toward the trailhead, we talked about everything. By the time we reached my Volvo, we knew all there was to know about each other. She was, I learned, a Navajo who worked part time for the Park Service. Teks-Neh-Wah told me she was hired because she had an instinct when it came to locating lost campers.

"So, when I didn't show up after my one-day hiking permit expired, they hired you to find me?" I inquired.

"No," she replied, looking at me rather enigmatically. "You only left yesterday."

"No," I shook my head before continuing, "I left more than two days ago." I looked at my watch. I knew that I had departed on Wednesday. If I spent one day hiking into Kolob Arch and one day on top of Shuntavi Butte, then, according to my memory, it should now be Saturday morning. My watch, however, indicated that it was Thursday. I stood staring at it for over a minute as Teks-Neh-Wah held my arm and gazed off into the distance to Shuntavi Butte with a distant yet dreamy look in her eyes.

I decided there and then not to ask her about the Indian dancers or what had happened between us on top of Shuntavi Butte. Maybe all of this was a dream. Or, maybe, remembering a verse from a hymn I knew, "That's When Death Was Arrested and My Life Began."[11]

We drove together to Cedar City that afternoon, got a marriage license, found a small Episcopal church located in a private home on a side street, and were married. Nine months later, less two days, Teks, as I had come to call her, delivered a healthy baby girl. When Teks suggested we name her Shuntavi, I readily agreed.

---

[11] "Death Was Arrested." Track 2 on *Nothing Ordinary*. Songwriters: Adam Kersh/Brandon Coker/Paul Taylor Smith/Ryan Heath Balltzglier "Death Was Arrested" lyrics © Capitol CMG Publishing. 2017.

THE ROAD

I Am Walking down a Road
Which Stretches Miles before Me -
In the Far Distance I Can See
A Dark Cloud Slowly Advancing
Towards Me -
It's Going to Sweep over Me Soon
So I Keep Heading for It -
The Road's Surface Changes

From Asphalt -
To Gravel - -
Then Dirt - - -
Still, I Trudge Onward -
As the Darkness Looms Over Me -
Soon It Will Envelop Me -
And I Will Finally Be at Peace
Having Left All the Agony of Life Behind -
When I Finally Emerge from the Dark -
I Won't Be Here in Our World Any More -
It's Been a Good Trip -
But I'm Anxious
To Forge My Way Home -
Wherever That Is?
Because No One Really Knows -
What's on The Other Side -
So, I'm Weary and Tired -
It's My Time to Go -
I'm Ready for the Whirlwind -
To Take Me!
Guess I'll Close My Eyes, Now
For the Last Time.

THE KOOL-AID KID

first noticed Tyler Westbrook when we scrambled off the Greyhound bus that brought us to basic infantry training school at Fort Benning, Georgia. We were jumping down the bus steps and running for our lives because drill sergeants on every side of us were screaming bloody murder in our faces as we desperately tried to assemble into some sort of a straight line, which we had no idea how to form. The Negro drill sergeant in front of us was having an apoplectic fit due to our ineptitude as we ran hither and yon around like idiots who have just escaped from the funny farm, while being screamed at with every expletive in his repertoire and then some.

Tyler got into the front line with me, extended his right arm to touch my shoulder, and whispered loudly, "Mark off your position every arm length and pass on to the next guy." The guys behind us caught on quickly and we formed up in four ragged lines.

The Negro sergeant walked over in front of Westbrook and screamed, "Mr. Pussy, who taught you how to form a line?"

"Sir, I had some training in civilian life, sir!" Tyler replied. What he didn't mention, but later told me on the Q.T., was that he had graduated from Fork Union Military Academy in Fork Union, Virginia, and the Virginia Military Institute (VMI) in Lexington, Virginia. But, upon graduating from VMI, he refused to accept a commission as a Second Lieutenant. I, in turn, told him I'd graduated from Texas Christian University in Fort Worth, Texas, with a Geography degree.

"Well, Mr. Pussy, I'm making you an acting platoon sergeant. You better not f*ck up! You hear me recruit?"

"Sir, yes, sir!"

For whatever reason, Tyler became the go-to guy in our platoon whom we looked to for guidance, advice, and help whenever we screwed up. He seemed to have his shit together while most of us were a herd of cows chewing our cud looking for a leader. He was always there to offer a helping hand from showing us how to properly clean our M16s to using a toothbrush to clean toilets. During the interminably long marches, he walked beside our column and continually encouraged laggards to keep up and not despair. Invariably, he always gave them a thumbs up and a big smile as encouragement. In all, he and our drill sergeant were responsible for molding our platoon into a lean mean fighting machine that bested the other three platoons in our basic infantry training company in almost every endeavor from drill marching to M16 competition firing on the range.

As we underwent infantry training, Tyler constantly repeated over and over, "Get this right guys; we're going to war. There are NO SECOND chances!"

Our drill sergeant, a man named Vinson, who was from Mississippi, let Westbrook take command on the marches. But Tyler always deferred to him, asking permission for this or that, and clarifying what Vinson wanted us to do if his orders were confusing or ambiguous. It seemed to me that they were in cahoots with one another. Except, Tyler kept the sergeant's heat off most of our backs until someone really faltered or f*cked up.

After eight weeks of unmitigated hell, everyone in our platoon graduated—thanks to Tyler. If you really did well in basic training, you received a promotion from Private E-1 to Private E-2 and both of us had no problem obtaining that raise. After graduation, the battalion brass approached Westbrook and asked him if he wanted to go to Officer Training School (OTS), but he declined telling them, "I volunteered, and all I want is to get my two years in and get out."

So, ten days later, Tyler and I found ourselves on a Trailways bus heading to Fort Polk, Louisiana, where we would undergo the rigorous Advanced Infantry Training (AIT). Fort Polk lay just outside of Leesville, Louisiana. We soon learned from others on the post that if the world needed an enema injected into it, Leesville is where it would be applied. Polk was in the southern swamp lands of Louisiana and Leesville, which we were allowed to visit on weekends, and was a horrid place of strip joints, prostitutes, and lowdown crooked used car salesmen. Everyone in that shit hole of a town wanted a piece of your hard-earned paltry military pay, which at the time for us was a few dollars short of a hundred dollars a month.

AIT was a grueling training period. You knew at the end you'd be shipped off to Vietnam as an 11B10, or just 11 Bravo—

the Military Occupation Specialty (MOS), or in plain words, the description for a combat rifleman. Tyler and I hung together and bunked next to each other. He always had a genuine and encouraging smile and never hesitated to assist someone, whether the trainee started limping along during the numerous excruciating marches the drill instructors (DIs)—all Vietnam combat vets—put us through or helping the less educated among us assemble or disassemble the M16 rifles we were issued.

I say less educated to be kind. Many of the draftees, and even some of those who had voluntarily enlisted in the Army, were from the South and had little or no education beyond seventh or eighth grade—or a lot less. Most couldn't read much less write. I'm sure there were a lot of "X's" on the enrollment papers we had to sign after passing our entry physicals.

Those educational deficiencies, however, didn't bother the mighty U.S. Army. After all, the year before, in 1968, Tet, the celebration of the Vietnamese New Year, had taken place. Tet caught the inept generals sitting in their plush Saigon headquarters by total surprise. Not to worry. Now, the ruthless military machine needed bodies—lots of them. We were going to show those "Viets."

The military brass couldn't have cared less whether or not anyone was educated. The training machine just continued to grind you up and spit you out as a rifleman as long as you knew how to fire the M16. Nothing else mattered, not even failing the shooting range tests. If you knew how to load, point, and pull the trigger of an M16 or M60 machine gun, you were deemed not only proficient in weapons, but also physically fit for the rigors that lay ahead for you in the fetid jungles of Southeast Asia.

On graduation, if the drill sergeants had done their job, you were now ready to be chewed up in the meat grinder of the damp and insanely humid jungles of South Vietnam. After all, a plethora of GIs were needed as sacrifices to the North Vietnamese Army (NVA), so both our "superior" infantry numbers and artillery fire could overwhelm them. That, it turned out, wasn't as easy as the Pentagon brass envisioned. Had they but read Bernard Fall's several books on Vietnam, their thinking might have enabled them to understand the Vietnamese people and adapt accordingly. But, we were the U.S. We could NEVER fail! BULLSHIT!!!

On the day of our AIT graduation, Tyler and I, not surprisingly, got orders for our Asian sojourn along with a thirty-day leave so we could go home and spend some time with our family, wives, or girlfriends, since a lot of us would be returning home in a wooden box. I wondered, *How do you say goodbye to loved ones who may never see you alive again?*

My name is Ed Wire, and I'm from Cave Spring, Georgia, a small town located northwest of Atlanta and lying almost next to the Alabama border. The town is home to twelve hundred souls and the Georgia School for the Deaf, where my father, who was deaf, worked as a teacher. After flying from New Orleans to Atlanta, where my folks met me, it took about ninety minutes to drive home.

The thirty days passed quickly, and before I knew it, I was off to Fort Dix, New Jersey, via a flight from Atlanta to Philadelphia. Then I crossed over to New Jersey by bus, where an airplane waited to fly me and two hundred others to our destiny. At Dix, we were issued our lightweight jungle fatigues and packed our civilian clothes away in our Army issued duffle bags. Fortunately, Tyler was on the same plane. When he saw me coming down the aisle, he gave me his thumbs up and his big smile. So we sat together on our plane trip to hell.

The first stop after Dix was Anchorage, Alaska, where the powers that be made everyone exit the aircraft while it took on fuel. Needless to say, despite it being late April, it was f*cking cold in

Alaska. We were forced to stand around on the tarmac for about twenty minutes freezing our asses off before we were allowed into the terminal to briefly warm up and use the facilities.

The next leg of our journey took us to Yokota AFB in Japan, which adjoined Tokyo. Just before landing, we passed by the 12,388-foot Mount Fiji, which the Japanese considered both sacred and a pilgrimage site. Later on in life, when I was studying for a Ph.D. in geography in graduate school at Arizona State University in Phoenix, I learned the mountain was also the subject for numerous pieces of art by the famous Japanese painters—Hokusai and Hiroshige. After refueling, our journey continued until we landed at Tan Son Nhut Air Base outside of Saigon, where Army buses awaited to take us to the 90th Replacement Battalion at Long Binh, which was located just north of Saigon.

After our in-country processing at Long Binh, we were issued our military gear. The one item that would turn out to be incredibly uncomfortable was our rucksack, with its exposed aluminum frame that dug mercilessly into our lower backs. Several more days of in-country training passed. The 90th was basically like a cattle holding pen where we, as cannon fodder, waited to be allocated out to whatever recently decimated unit needed fresh bodies the most. At the end of our third and final day of in-country training, both Tyler and I were assigned to Company B 2/8 First Air Cavalry Division—a helicopter outfit—which had its headquarters at Quan Loi, some fifty-to-sixty miles north of Saigon. Now assigned to the First Cav, we quickly learned we were now called Skytroopers.

It was in Quan Loi that I discovered Tyler hated the taste of the potable water issued to us. Yes, it was nasty and tasted god-awful, but we had no other options.

"Ed," he said, turning to me, "All my life I've always hated the taste of water, but this water tastes no better than shit and makes me want to immediately regurgitate it. Eeech! It really makes me want to puke! If anything kills me in Vietnam, it'll be this f*cking indigestible water!"

So Tyler spent an entire day while we were in Quan Loi writing to everyone he knew begging them to send him Kool-Aid.

Two days later, we were flown by helicopter out to Fire Support Base (FSB) Caroline, also known as LZ (Landing Zone) Caroline. Caroline had been partially overrun the previous night. As we approached, we could see hundreds of dead NVA bodies not only surrounding but also inside the LZ's perimeter. Our dead had already been removed but we saw that a bulldozer had dug a huge hole outside of the perimeter's fighting berm and our troops were tossing bodies into it like lumpy and amorphous sandbags. Hopping off the chopper, we were directed to Company B's position where an E-7 Sergeant named Gibbons, who was from North Carolina, instructed us to join Blackfoot, one of B Company's three platoons. We were warmly greeted by the twenty something members of Blackfoot and were immediately put to work filling sandbags.

After three days on Caroline, First Cav choppers arrived and whisked us off to some unknown spot in the jungle located close to the Cambodian border. Our job was to patrol the area looking for Charley—what we called the enemy. After several hot, humid, sticky days, all we found were a few bunkers but no NVA. The 115 plus degree heat was excruciating, which caused us all to sweat profusely and tempted us to chug our foul tasting Army issued water. Our squad sergeants had to continuously warn us to drink judiciously, space it out, because we wouldn't get water resupply for another day or so.

Of course, there was a lot of inviting water in the numerous bomb craters we encountered. Yet, to drink that water was hazardous—if not downright dangerous. After all, the NVA could have pissed or taken a dump in it. Also, water lying in the bomb craters usually contained chemicals from Agent Orange, which was used for defoliation. Agent Orange was sprayed on the trees and was subsequently washed off by the rainwater. Eventually, it seeped into the craters. Not long after, the sprayed area looked like a devastated wasteland of ghost trees with no foliage. Plus, the craters also contained various types of minuscule bugs and germs, which had a horrible effect on our intestinal systems. Dysentery was not something you wanted to have while in the jungle. A person would become incredibly dehydrated in just a few hours as the bugs quickly ravished his body. Yet, time and again, I saw guys scooping up the bomb crater water and gulping it down. Were they looking for a quick way out of the jungle? I didn't know or care. It was their problem, not mine.

On our fifth day in the boonies—our term for the jungle—we were due for resupply. We tramped through the jungle, with its numerous thick bamboo thickets and vines waiting to entangle or trip us. After two hours, we arrived at a large open field and waited in the late afternoon for the supply choppers. We could hear the birds before we actually saw them. A string of four helicopters soon appeared about a half mile up in the azure sky. We popped yellow smoke, which they acknowledged. They dropped rather precipitously down to the field and hovered about three-to-four feet off the ground. We rushed out and hurriedly pulled both the supplies and the water containers off the hovering birds and hightailed it back into the tree line. As each chopper's supplies were pushed out into our waiting arms, the machine lifted off heading upward as fast as it could rise.

As the last supplies were tugged off the fourth bird, gunfire broke out across the clearing. The bird's two machine gunners returned fire and the chopper quickly ascended to get out of enemy fire range. Meanwhile, we were involved in our first firefight. Lying prone, we returned fire across the hundred-yard-wide clearing, but after five minutes the enemy went silent. Our captain decided to employ a pincher movement. He sent Aztec platoon around the left side and Cheyenne platoon around the right side of the field. We, in Bravo, acted as a support for the encircling platoons. It took the better part of two hours for both platoons to hook up and report back that they had found nothing but a well-used trotter, or trail. Our captain ordered us to cross the clearing and hook up with the other two platoons, which we hastily did at a slow run, not willing to risk any prolonged exposure as targets to the enemy.

Once across we were ordered to set up for the night. Resupply had brought us mail. Many of us didn't receive anything, but Tyler really scored. He received eleven letters—all containing two-to-four packets of Kool-Aid. He was in seventh heaven and immediately poured two packets into one of his canteens and chugged almost all of it down.

"Hey, Tallboy," he said with a contented smile, "I think I'm gonna live!"

In Vietnam, out in the jungle, most of us had nicknames for each other rather than use our given names. By not using our real name, it was a way we were able to isolate ourselves so that no one ever got that close to us. It was our way of making ourselves impersonal—non-existent. Joe, for example, became "Alabama" because he was from that state. So, if Alabama, who was walking in front of you got blown away, it was Alabama who died, not Joe.

My nickname was "Tallboy" because, at six foot five, I towered over everyone in our platoon. I knew my height would make me an easy target for Charley, so I tended to hunch over anytime we were on the move. Tyler quickly acquired the nickname of "The Kool-Aid Kid," or just "The Kid." He was always generous with his Kool-Aid, passing out packets left and right to anyone who asked him for one and always giving them not only a thumbs up but also a large wide smile. One day several months later, he told me that he usually had no less than fifty packets in his rucksack. His correspondents, he told me, kept him steadily supplied as each letter always contained three or four Kool-Aid packets.

"No way," he told me one day as we were stumbling through the 110 degree fire pit of jungle, "do I ever want to get myself in a position where I have to drink that foul piss water!"

A few weeks later, we were involved in a heavy firefight. Even though we called in both artillery and Cobra gun ship support, the three medics assigned to our infantry company had their work cut out for them. Our seventy-five-man company had four Killed in Action (KIA) and seventeen Wounded in Action (WIA). So, the brass pulled us out of the area, flew us back to the nearest firebase, LZ Ike, and over the next three days, pumped us up with fifteen more raw recruits, or FNGs—F*cking New Guys. We usually called the FNGs, Cherries, a derogative name because they hadn't yet been under fire, so we compared them to girls back home in the world who hadn't done it the first time. All of us tended to be wary of the Cherries until they had been under fire a few times because Cherries died at a higher rate than us old-timers. With the numerous firefights we'd already endured, the Cherries would soon be bait for the jungle's meat grinder.

Then, just as we thought we might get a break for a few more free days on LZ Ike, the Cav flew us back out to the same area. Within an hour, we stepped in the shit again. Resistance to our intrusion was massive, almost overpowering. We had to call in artillery almost on top of our positions. Two medics, while assisting the wounded, were killed and the third, badly wounded.

It was then that I saw Tyler stand, crouch, and run over to one of the dead medics. He grabbed the guy's first aid equipment and, dragging it, started crawling around to assist the wounded and dying all the while as our artillery pounded the area surrounding our position. Shrapnel flew everywhere.

"Hey Kid," I yelled as I crawled to him, "I'll cover you! Watch out for the f*cking shrapnel!" I joked.

The Kool-Aid Kid turned his head, gave me a quick smile and then a thumbs up behind his back as he moved over to the next wounded Skytrooper. I put my M16 on semi-automatic so I didn't expend my ammo. Whenever I saw any movement or muzzle flashes in the jungle, I targeted that area and sent three bullets into the brush.

Our artillery, which seemingly took forever to rain down in front of our position, forced the NVA to retreat farther back into the jungle until they cut off contact with us. The butcher's bill that day was grim. In addition to the two medics, seven others lost their lives. Three of those were some of the Cherries we had just acquired on LZ Ike. We had fifteen wounded. With the third medic being airlifted out due to his wounds, our company now had no Army trained medics.

Lieutenant Knoll, our platoon's leader, who had seen what Tyler did during the firefight, called him over and said, "Westbrook, you're now Blackfoot's platoon medic." The Kid just nodded, smiled, gave Knoll a thumbs up, and returned to his hastily dug foxhole. The other two platoon lieutenants also appointed non-Army trained medics. So, on four hours first aid training in Basic, Tyler became our medic. A medic's mantra was, "Apply pressure and elevate." And that was about all any medic could do until the injured were whisked up and out by Medevac.

The Kid had once told me that he only weighed 110 pounds, which was now somewhat worrisome to me. In addition to his regular fifty-five pounds of necessary gear, including two bandoliers

of M60 machine gun bullets, which we all had to carry, he now had
to tote an additional thirty pounds of medical equipment. The fifty-
five he still carried on his back, but the thirty he now carried on his
chest. It would take two of us to pull him up off the ground when
we needed to move out. As medic, The Kid got to choose where he
would position himself as we moved through the jungle in search
of the ever elusive NVA. Usually, he chose the seventh or eighth
position in the advancing column.

"Because," he told me, "when we hit the shit, I'll be close to the
guys up front and can quickly come to their assistance."

It seemed to me that becoming our medic really changed him.
He was more daring and willing to take risks. After all, in firefights,
when everyone else was lying flat on the ground returning enemy
fire, The Kid had to stand and run to the wounded or dying, thus
making himself an easy target for the NVA to take out. Somehow
The Kool-Aid Kid survived unscathed. Of course, every so often
he got nicked in the leg or arm by shrapnel. Nothing serious. In
firefights, I always kept as near to him as I could. In sum, I was sort
of acting like his bodyguard, firing whenever I saw an NVA muzzle
burst. I guess I was his guardian angel.

At the end of every firefight, The Kid was responsible for
tallying up the KIAs and WIAs and giving the list to Lieutenant
Knoll, who passed the information along to the higher ups, so that
the proper Purple Heart medals could be awarded. Although The
Kid had taken minor hits from shrapnel several times, he never
put himself in for a Purple Heart. He just bandaged up the cuts or
pulled out the small embedded shrapnel pieces, usually from enemy
Chi Com grenades, and went about his work.

When I asked him why, he replied, "I'm not here to win medals.
I'm here to help you, or the Skytrooper next to me, make it back

to THE WORLD in one piece." Yet, after all he had done so far, the Army awarded him three Bronze Star medals for heroism.

In August, we really hit the shit. We had twenty-three straight days of combat. Somehow, The Kid and I survived. By the end of fighting on the twenty-third day, I hardly recognized anyone in Blackfoot because almost the entire platoon had been replaced by FNGs. Knoll had been wounded and replaced by a new officer right out of Shake and Bake OCS. His name was Greene, and he was right out of the cracker South, with a big Southern drawl. Realizing we were the only old timers left, he quickly discovered that he needed our knowledge not only to stay alive but also to keep Blackfoot as a lean mean fighting machine. The Kid got Greene on his side from the git-go by offering him some Kool-Aid packets. The packets, in some ways, served as bribes, even though The Kid never used that name. Still, when he needed a favor from someone, he usually got it.

After our twenty-three days of combat, the brass pulled us out of the field and gave us a three-day R&R (rest and relaxation) in Tay Ninh. We needed the rest, and the guys who chose to get some boom boom in the local Vietnamese massage parlor would soon need a certain type of medicine from The Kid until we returned to an LZ where a long-needled penicillin shot in the ass awaited them. On our third day, we were airlifted to LZ Becky, where we pulled what we called "castle duty."

Life on the LZs was always a pain in the ass. We all hated it. If we weren't filling innumerable sandbags or burning shit, we were on guard duty, sometimes for twenty-four, even thirty-six hours straight, depending on incoming NVA mortar fire to probes as they tried to locate our weak spots. When we did get to sleep on the LZs, we had to contend with the numerous rats that infested every LZ and climbed over our exhausted sleeping bodies. Even though we kept a candle burning in our bunker's sleeping quarters to scare away the nasty rodents, they still ventured out to harass us. One night a rat perched on my chest and commenced to chew on my shirt's button. Awakening, I swatted him, and with an irritated and high-pitched squeak, he scurried off into another part of the bunker. No wonder we all yearned for a return to the jungle where each night we could not only get some peace and quiet but also four or five hours of sleep.

The only good thing about being on any LZ was that we could openly smoke weed. After all, we sure weren't smoking out in the jungle where it would give away our position. Here on the LZs the Gooks knew where we were. Plus, officers gave us some slack and didn't object, mainly, I think, because none of them wanted to get a bullet in the back or be fragged.

After a week on Becky, we were airlifted to a part of the jungle adjoining the Cambodian border. We figured things would get hot. And they did. More days of combat. Somehow The Kid and I survived.

The last day I saw The Kid, we were wandering down a trotter, which twisted back and forth around large clumps of bamboo. The Kid was walking backward handing the guy behind him a packet of Kool-Aid. I was following about ten feet back. The Kid, about to turn, glanced up, saw me, gave me thumbs up and one of his big smiles just as a sniper's bullet entered his brain.

I guess he finally got the Purple Heart, which he had so assiduously avoided.

HEROES

The Only People
Who Are Heroes
Are the Dead,
Because We, Who Lived
Are Now in Hell.
There Is No Heaven -
No Peace of Mind
For Us Who Survived

For We Have Indelible
Reprints of the Hell
That We Have Seen.
And Each Day
We Arise To Die
A Little More Within.
The Hopelessness
Of Our Situation
Dulls Our Minds -
Numbs Our Bodies -
Until Nothing Is Left -
And We Flow Onward
Like Wraiths in the Night
Searching for That Happiness
That We Will NEVER Find
Because We're Not Dead Heroes.

THOUGHTS

What Was

Can NEVER Be -

What Should Have Been

Will NEVER Pass - -

What Should Be

Will NEVER Be - -

Because Time

Cannot Be Relived

To Alter

What Cannot Be Altered

Is to Dream

The Impossible Dream - -

And To Dream - -

Is To Die

A Little Bit Every Day

Life Without Her

Will NEVER Be - -

Can NEVER Be Again

And So I Die

A Little

Each Day.

THE RETURN OF THE GHOST MIRROR

At first, I thought I was quite mad. Then I thought maybe I had only imagined it. It certainly was too vivid to have been a dream. But what was it? Did it really happen? Or had I merely imagined it all? Hallucinated it, maybe? I will, dear reader, let you decide whether or not what occurred to me on that day (or was it a month or a year?) in 2013 actually took place. But first, a little about me and what happened leading up to that fateful day in May.

My name is Andrew Jackson Ward. Jack for short. Yes, I am a direct descendant of that famous Confederate general, but I never openly admitted to it. Also, I'm a loner. Always have been. Can't take direction from most people. My wretched childhood apparently caused my aloofness as my father mentally abused me, leaving me with a lifelong feeling of worthlessness. A third son—I was born in a middle-class southern family somewhere in central Virginia. My two older brothers were out of the house and gone before I hardly knew them, so I grew up alone. Which gave me time to become somewhat introspective.

At age fifteen, my parents trundled me off to prison. Well, it wasn't exactly a real prison, but it might as well have been one. Instead, it was a boys prep school—one of those exclusively snobby boys prep schools in northern Virginia called St. Anselm's of Canterbury. I hated those upper class muckety-muck eastern coast Brahmins, especially since the school operated on an archaic rat system (similar to that of West Point) where older boys taunted younger ones unmercifully.

During my three years in that religious affiliated prep school, I rebelled and flunked out each year. I did it on purpose. But, my parents were adamant. So, each summer I was forced to make up my yearly failures by being privately tutored. Except, one summer I got a break and attended a local public high school for a class. Thus, with no summer break for each of those three excruciatingly long and wearisome years, I suffered along and took the make-up exams that shuffled me into the next grade. Why didn't I deliberately flunk those reexams? I don't know. The thought, for some reason, never crossed my mind. Finally, at the end of my junior year, the snotty St. Anselm's told my parents that, due to my continuously poor scholastic performance, they would not permit me to return.

My parents told me they were going to look at other boys' schools. I totally rebelled, telling them if they sent me to another prep school I guaranteed I'd be thrown out in twenty-four hours.

They caved and sent me to the local county high school instead. Needless to say, I was ecstatic.

So I graduated, but much to my parent's displeasure I was not accepted by any university. Both of them were horrified that none of the exclusive East Coast universities would accept me. Meanwhile, I'm pretty sure it was my subpar high school grades. So what did the old man expect? Yet, miracles do happen. Two weeks before fall semester started, a mid-sized college in North Central Texas, Grapevine Christian, accepted me. I was relieved, as I wasn't looking forward to living with my parents. Who knew what they might come up with next?

Amazingly, I bloomed in Texas. Living far away from Virginia and my parents was good. *Not too bad,* I thought of my academic progress. I didn't flunk out. And, miraculously, I made it through college with a 3.2 GPA. Finally, graduation arrived in May of 1968— the height of the Vietnam War.

Three weeks after graduation the U.S. Army opened its arms wide and accepted me. I enlisted. I was not drafted. And I was sent to Nam. If any single experience has defined my entire life, it is what happened to me in Vietnam between 1969 and 1970. Not a day goes by that I don't think of that war and my participation in it. I saw so much combat that it seared and rewired my entire thought processes, especially since I was a combat medic.

Having survived the firefights and the war, I guess I could survive anything. Including what happened to me when I bought the mirror—but I am getting ahead of myself. The airplane flight home, which we GIs called the Freedom Bird because we were leaving Nam, dropped me off in Oakland, California.

I never returned to Virginia. Never called my family. Never saw any of them again. What did they care? They had all but written me off anyway, so what use was it to return and take their continued abuse? In 1970, all Vietnam vets were deemed to be crazy unstable pot smokers. Upon returning to the world, what we called home, we were spit upon and called all sorts of names like baby-killer and the like.

It just didn't make sense for me to return to Virginia. I had nothing to look forward to back there—except more grief. Besides, after Nam I felt more alone than ever. I felt cut off from the "real" world. So, after mustering out in Oakland, I started drifting. I worked odd jobs here and there but hated taking orders. I lost more than a few jobs after telling the boss to "stick it up his mother f*ckin' ass." One supervisor got so incensed when I told him what he could do that he took a swing at me in front of seven or eight witnesses. Big mistake. What I did to him wasn't pretty. He'll live the rest of his life with the scar I left on his face from the beer bottle I used to calm him down. I left town rather quickly.

So, what to do? Nam had definitely turned me into a loner. I hated taking orders and decided I wouldn't. My money began to run out while I was in Santa Fe. One day, I spotted some Indian paintings that looked damn good. I talked the artist, Joseph Rainwater, into my being his agent with a 25/75 split for anything under a thousand dollars and 35/65 for anything over. He thought I was just another crazy white man. I took seventeen of his paintings and lit out for Albuquerque where I caught a plane to New York. I was down to my last hundred dollars.

One of my college roommates had connections in the city. I averaged fifteen hundred dollars for each of Joseph's paintings. In one trip I had made over eight grand. So, I returned to Santa Fe, signed an exclusive agreement with Joseph, put down some money on an old building just west of town and opened an art gallery just off an exit ramp about a half a mile west of I-25. I lived in the back room, which was once a storeroom. It was about six feet wide and ran the entire thirty-foot width of the building. At the far end, in addition to the wash basin, was one of those old pull-chain toilets with the tank of water hanging five feet above the throne. There was no wall or curtain.

By the 1980s, Joseph's paintings were going for ten thousand and up, depending on size. Plus, he was also doing private commissions at twenty-five thousand a pop. I spotted two or three other Indian artists and started moving their works too. One day, a drunk Navajo staggered into my gallery. I sobered him up and gave him a job sweeping floors. It didn't take long for me to find out he was a Vietnam combat vet like me. He said his name was Raymond and that he was a Navajo. I agreed to pay him in cash. The years seemed to fly by as my modest arts and antique business struggled along. Still, I was able to set something aside and keep the bills paid.

One day, sometime in the summer of 1997, Joseph came in with two paintings that he had done for a rich disc surgeon in Cincinnati, Ohio, and a sleazy timber baron in who lived in Eufaula, a southern Alabama town with loads of Antebellum homes along its main street. He and Ray, who was polishing the floor at the time, started to chat. I didn't listen to their conversation as I was too deeply engrossed on the telephone with an art dealer in Cleveland who wanted to take some of my paintings on consignment. I was trying to tell him politely that I didn't operate on consignment, but he wouldn't listen, so I hung up on him.

"Hey Jack!" Joseph yelled, "Ray here seems to know something about antique art."

"Whattaya mean?" I asked.

"He spotted my antique ring and told me all about its craftsmanship and what tribe probably manufactured it."

I should have listened to my little voice right then and there and not continued the conversation. Had I done so, what happened to me with the mirror might not have come to pass. But I didn't.

"So, Ray," I queried, "where did you learn about antique art?"

"Well..." Ray faltered, somewhat unsure of himself, "before my mother died, she made turquoise bracelets, rings, and such."

Without thinking, I dug into my pocket, pulled out a wad of bills, and peeled off a thousand dollars.

"OK, Ray, here's a thousand bucks. Go out and buy up some antique stuff. What you find, we'll sell here in the shop. I'll give you the same split, minus the upfront costs, I give Joseph."

Both men looked at me as if I was nuts. Joseph knew Ray's history. He and I both wondered if Ray would take the money and drink it up.

A week passed without any sighting or call from Ray. I thought for sure I would never see him again, or if I did, I wondered how sober he would be. When Ray returned, he didn't say a thing—he simply laid on the counter seven of the most exquisite pieces of Indian jewelry I had ever seen. We made close to five thousand on those pieces. I never asked Ray where he found the stuff, but after a year, I had pocketed close to twenty-five grand from his sales. It was time to expand.

In 2004, I bought both my building and the premises next door. Then I set up a separate limited liability company (LLC) partnership and opened an antiques business with Ray as the manager and junior partner. He handled the acquisitions and sales. Soon, besides Indian jewelry, lots of antique whatnots started to flow into the shop. It wasn't run of the mill stuff either. Much of it was high class stuff. Pieces families had hoarded for decades but now wanted to unload. We gave good prices and made more money. And then it happened.

I was working in the art gallery one morning in late January 2013 when the girl appeared. I didn't see or hear her enter the premises. I was too engrossed in reading an art catalogue from a gallery on the Outer Banks of North Carolina to notice. They were exclusive agents for a Florida artist who specialized in brown ink etchings with East Coast seascapes and various water birds. I liked his work and was thinking about trying to sell it.

Some sort of movement caught my eye. I looked up and she was standing there, eyeing me somewhat nervously. She was young— thin as a rail, almost waif like. Maybe twenty-two or twenty-three. Her shiny raven black hair, streaked with a henna color and parted in the middle, hung straight down the sides of her pale white face coming to rest near the small protuberances that were her breasts. She had no makeup on that I could discern. I had never seen someone with skin so white. *Is she an albino?* I wondered. A long grey-blue dress hung from her shoulders ending at her ankles, a row of pearl white buttons located every two inches and running up the front of the garment held it in place on her body.

"Mr. Ward?" She tentatively asked.

"Yes, how may I help you?" Instantly alert, I wondered why I hadn't heard the jingle jangle of the bell over the front door. It always rang whenever someone entered the shop. Plus, the burglar alarm also beeped twice every time the door opened. I hadn't heard either one of them. *How could I have missed those two sounds? Was I really concentrating so hard on the Outer Banks catalog that my ears had stopped working?* I wondered.

"I have this mirror I want to sell," she replied. "I tried next door, but it's closed and the sign in the window said to try here."

"Oh, yes, my manager is out today looking for some Hopi and Zuni jewelry."

"I have the mirror in my truck if you would care to look at it," she commented.

"Sure thing! Let's go."

I put my green corduroy jacket on and stuffed my Stetson on my head. After all, it was chilly in Santa Fe during the winter. I didn't want to catch a cold. *Why*, I wondered, *doesn't she have a coat?* Her faded and washed-out dress looked awfully thin—almost translucent and extremely ancient. She looked somewhat ethereal, as if one could see right through her. The bell over the door jingled as we went out, and I could easily hear the two beeps of the burglar alarm when the door opened. What's going on here?

She was driving an old Ford pickup. It looked ancient—60s to 70s-ish? Maybe? Tires almost bald. Holes rotting through the fenders. The color was so faded that it looked like dull red mud. The glass behind the driver's seat was cracked. The mirror rested on the truck bed. It was about eighteen inches wide and five feet high surrounded by a gold frame. There were a couple black spots, almost like brush strokes on the surface of the mirror. As I gazed at it, I saw a flash from the surface. Must be the reflection of the sun. I glanced at the mirror one more time and couldn't believe my eyes! In the mirror, I saw some horses tied to a hitching rail. Or at least, for a microsecond, I thought I did then the image was gone. *I must be imagining things!*

"Well, young lady, this mirror looks to be more than a hundred years old. It's not in the greatest of shape." I offered her $250 dollars for it. If I was lucky, I might be able to get $300, maybe $350, for it. She just nodded. I pulled out some bills and handed her two $100 bills and a $50. She carefully folded them twice and deposited them in a small pocket on the right-hand side of her dress that I hadn't noticed before. Turning, she walked to the driver's side, opened the door, which should have creaked or groaned with old age since, I was sure, hadn't been oiled in forever. Instead, not a squeak permeated the air as she got into her truck.

"Mr. Ward," she said looking at me somewhat enigmatically, "that's a special piece. Take care of it, and don't let just any old customer buy it. It's," she hesitated, "kind of special. You'll know when the right person wants to buy it."

"OK. I'll take good care of it." *What did she mean?* I asked myself. She smiled enigmatically then turned to start the engine.

I lifted the mirror out of the immaculately clean truck bed. It was heavy. WOW! It must have weighed sixty to seventy pounds. I could almost feel the sweat beads beginning to pop out on my forehead. I carried it toward the shop, paused at the front door, and turned to wave goodbye. She and the truck were gone. I could have sworn I hadn't heard her depart because I didn't hear any tires crunching on the gravel in my parking lot. The street in front of my shop ran straight for over a half mile in either direction, and there were no side streets down either stretch. I didn't see the truck. It had vanished. I wondered if my hearing was suddenly going south. After all, I had lost a lot of high frequency hearing after a vicious North Vietnamese Army attack on LZ Becky in Tay Ninh Province on August 13, 1969.

Pushing open the front door, I heaved the mirror inside and set it down next to a counter. *I'll get Ray to take it over tomorrow,* I thought. I leaned it up against my catalog counter and stepped back to contemplate it. There was something eerie about this mirror that seemed to both baffle and draw me toward it. I could almost see a mist rising up and swirling within it.

The next day Ray came over from his shop around ten in the morning. "Hey! Jack, what's the story on this old mirror?" he asked. I told him about the mysterious woman who had dropped it off.

"We'll need to hang it somewhere in your shop. I doubt anyone will pay a lot for it, but why don't we ask three hundred for it?" I asked him.

"Sounds good to me, Jack. Let's carry this thing over, hell, I bet it's heavy. I can't imagine you carrying it in here!"

So, we toted it over to Ray's premises. The thing seemed to get heavier and heavier with each step. We got it into his place, and, after moving a few antiques around, found a wall to display it on. After we hung it, I went back to my gallery.

About ten minutes later Ray came rushing back in. "Jack, quick ... you gotta see this mirror!" he said breathlessly.

We entered his shop and walked back to the wall where the mirror was hanging. As we stood in front of it, it began to mysteriously mist up. We both took an involuntary step backward and started to shiver just a small bit. We both felt as if some type of electric charge had passed through our bodies.

"That young woman you purchased this from ... she had to be a Spirit Woman," Ray said.

As we stood looking, the mist cleared, and we saw a desert scene with saguaros in it. A coyote suddenly appeared on the right, turned, and looked directly at us through the mirror before nonchalantly trotting off to the left. Then, unbelievably, the woman I'd purchased the mirror from, suddenly appeared. She stared through the mirror looking at both of us before a grey cloud obscured her and the mirror turned blank.

"That's the woman who sold me the mirror," I told Ray with some amazement in my voice.

"Jack, you got a Ghost Mirror!" Ray exclaimed with some fervent awe in his voice. "You can't sell this!" he continued. "I don't know why the Spirits chose you, but you gotta keep it in your office out of sight from the customers. Maybe even put a cover over it. Plus, I'm going to have to find a shaman and learn what we need to do about this. It's sacred. We really can't do anything to it, like sell it, because we might defile it. And the spirits would not be happy with us!"

So, we took the mirror down, hauled it back over to my premises, and hung it in my office. No sooner had we hung it and stepped back to take a look at it than the mirror fogged up and a nebulous greyish cloud spread across its entire surface. A sudden flash startled us, so we quickly shuffled farther backward. The mirror cleared and we saw a different scene consisting of red rock stretching to the distant horizon. Stark high mesas and smaller buttes stood out with multiple rock columns, or hoodoos, soaring next to the red monuments, which dominated the scene before us. Off in the distance we saw a horse with a rider behind what appeared to be shimmering heat waves. They appeared to be floating within and behind the waves.

"What the hell have I done and gotten myself into?" I wondered aloud. "This has to be the absolute weirdest thing I've ever encountered." We remained in front of the Ghost Mirror in awe at what was occurring right before our eyes.

Suddenly the rider and horse turned toward us. The rider was an Indian. He dismounted slowly and looked directly at us. His face was furrowed with a thousand age lines. After tying the reins to a Palo Verde tree branch, he uncapped what appeared to be a deerskin water bag, took a long swig, wiped his mouth with his forearm, and turned to stare at us. We stood mesmerized as the Indian's eyes bored right into and through us. Then, the surface was obscured by what appeared to be a dust storm.

"Jack," Ray observed, "the ancients are letting us see them. We need to be extremely careful."

"Is this for real, Ray?" I queried. "Have you ever seen anything like this?"

"No, I sure haven't," Ray replied shaking his head. "But while growing up I heard a tale from my elders about it. I need to find a shaman who can explain this Ghost Mirror! Back in an hour or so," he said as he rushed out, leaving me to contemplate what exactly was happening.

I found a black curtain and covered the mirror. Then sat at my desk and started trolling the net, hoping to find anything on Ghost Mirrors. My search turned out to be fruitless. There was nothing on the web, which made me uneasy. It was as if the entire web had been wiped clean of Indian mirror items.

About two hours later, while I was rehanging some paintings, Ray entered the shop with an elderly man (perhaps in his early-to-mid 70s) who wore faded blue jeans, a nice white shirt with a large Indian pendant displaying a mountain with stars streaking past it. His almost white hair was plaited and hung down both sides of his face. Lastly, he wore a dusty sweat-stained cowboy hat with a couple of long brown feathers stuck into the left side.

"Jack," Ray said, "This is Two-Feathers-Man-Who-Rides-A-White Buffalo. He's...."

"Excuse me for interrupting, Ray, but you and Mr. Ward can just call me Two Feathers. I'm an Apache shaman and Ray told me about your mysterious mirror. Would you mind if I take a look at it?"

"Well, Two Feathers, you can call me Jack and, no, I would be happy for you to do so. Perhaps you can solve this enigmatic mystery."

I led him to my office while Ray followed. I removed the covering and the mirror immediately clouded up and then, as before, the same Indian appeared in the desert landscape. He had collected some rocks, placed them in a circle, and had a fire of small twigs burning. He looked directly at us as if he knew we were watching him behind the mirror.

"Oh, Jack," Two Fingers sighed, "You not only have a mirror … you have The Ghost Mirror," he emphasized "the." "This is most troubling."

"What is The Ghost Mirror?" I asked him.

"Our legends speak about this mirror. It is a sad tale. Many moons ago, when the White Man was moving west in search of land, there was a wagon train traveling west across our land. Not many wagons, maybe four or five." He paused, then continued, "Our ancestral Apache warriors attacked this train, and thinking they had killed everyone, started looting the wagons. Suddenly, from inside one of the wagons, a white woman appeared, perhaps materialized would be a more accurate description. She was dressed all in black and bleeding badly from her head and fingers. Blood streamed in rivulets down her face and copiously dripped from her fingers. Our people were stunned by her sudden and mysterious appearance. They sat on their horses staring at her. She lifted this large mirror from the wagon and flashed it in the faces of each of the mounted warriors in the war party. Each warrior felt as if something had been pulled, or jerked, out of him."

"I curse you all!" the black dressed woman screamed. "You will never go home to your Spirits when you die," she staggered against the frame, as bright red blood continued to drip down her fingers onto its shiny surface. "I've captured each of your faces in my mirror and when you die you will be trapped in here forever," she pointed at and tapped the mirror's surface. "You will never be able to escape!" she screamed. "You will burn in hell forever!" she screeched as she pointed to each of the warriors, who shifted uneasily in their saddles. The war party, startled by both her appearance and curse, shied back at this last statement. As they looked at her, the red blood streams on the mirror's surface seemed to split, divide, and reform as an image of the black clad woman. The warriors became unsettled at this development. They now realized she was an evil spirit.

"And then, according to the myth," Two Feathers continued, "she pushed the mirror back into the wagon, fell to the ground, and died. One of the warriors dismounted and started to walk toward her body when suddenly there was a tremendous flash and sound, as if both a lightning bolt had struck and a thunderclap had boomed in the heavens above. Each person in the war party felt a shock going through their bodies from head to toe. Again, their horses neighed and screamed as they shied and started to back away. And…" he paused, "as the warriors looked on, her body spontaneously ignited then blazed up in flames that disappeared in seconds, leaving only a trace of blackened ashes."

As he paused a few seconds, I asked, "What happened to them? Did they continue to loot the wagon train? Or just leave?"

Two Feathers replied, "Each warrior thought he had experienced some bad medicine. Their leader, a man called Two Wolves, told them they needed to take such a suspicious object and hide it in a dark cave where no one would ever find it and where it could rot away. To destroy it, Two Wolves told them, might bring instant evil upon them all. No one must ever reveal the location, he told them. Then he made each one of them cut their thumb and swear a blood oath as their blood dripped down into the sand. If the mirror was ever found again, Two Wolves told them, the Spirits might destroy their entire tribe. Being extremely superstitious, the warriors found a dark and long crevice nearby, where they hid the mirror. Two Wolves also told them not to scalp anyone on the wagon train or remove any possessions because they had encountered bad luck with the curse of the evil black-haired woman.

"So, what do we do with it?" I asked Two Feathers.

"See that warrior in the mirror?" Two Feathers pointed with his wizened arthritic hand. "That is Two Wolves. He is trapped as the legend tells us. Forever bound within the mirror. Forever to roam outside heaven."

"Is there any way he could step through it to where we're standing?" Ray asked.

"I think so," Two Feathers replied, "but I would pray to my gods and hope such a thing would never occur."

"Two Feathers," I said looking directly into his eyes, "then who was that woman who brought it to me?"

"She is a Spirit Woman. I have no doubt about it. I think she must have found the mirror and accidentally touched it. It made her a ghost woman who can now live in both worlds—ours or the past, perhaps around the time of the strange happenings during the wagon train massacre. Or maybe she was living in this day and time and found it, and it turned her into a ghost. She could also be a direct descendant of the ancestor who saw the original warriors hiding it. That ancestor may have passed down the location within her family, who had been sworn to secrecy."

"But she definitely looked Navajo to me, Two Feathers," I stated. I had become somewhat uneasy over the shaman's tale. Plus, I felt a momentary tingle spread throughout my body, almost like static electricity.

"Yes, that is possible," Two Feathers answered. "The wagon train could have been in Navajo territory when the Apache warriors, who may have been on a raid for loot and wives, encountered it."

"So, what is your thinking about who she might be?" I asked the old man.

Two Feathers leaned over, touched the mirror's faded golden frame, stroked it, being careful not to touch the surface before turning toward me and answering, "I think she may have been out looking for plants and seeds. Perhaps she was a medicine woman."

"Are you saying she witnessed the massacre?" I queried.

"I think so," Two Feathers nodded as he continued, "she may have seen the slaughter and hid herself. Perhaps, she may have seen what happened with the black-clad woman who cursed and put a spell on each of the warriors."

"Do you think she might have followed them to the site where they cached the mirror?" Ray asked.

"My medicine training tells me that such an occurrence is possible. I feel some sort of connection to this woman, but I don't know how or why," he answered. "It's just speculation on my part, but I sense she may have been a medicine woman too. And since I am a medicine man, perhaps that could be the tenuous connection between us, even though we both may be members of two different tribes."

He paused and we three continued to stare at the mirror. The Indian within, sitting cross legged, had caught a rabbit, and was slowly roasting it over the fire. Suddenly, a huge rattlesnake slithered into the campsite and headed directly toward the seated

Indian. It must have had at least ten rattles. The Indian eyed it with some resignation. The snake coiled in front of him. We could see that the tail was rattling so fast that it was a blur. Without pausing, the snake struck the warrior at lightning speed on his right thigh then recoiled itself. The Indian appeared not to have felt the strike as he made no move to flinch at the poisonous bite. Instead, he raised his head and stared directly at us standing behind the mirror, which turned cloudy and the scene before us vanished. All that was left was the surface of the mirror reflecting the images of all three of us.

"This is not a good omen," Two Feathers sighed and continued. "Jack, I think you better cover it up again. We all will have to think about our next steps. I have another much older friend who is also a shaman. I will need to discuss this situation with him and see what he recommends we do with this mirror. Meanwhile," he turned and faced both Ray and me, "this has to be kept a secret. This Ghost Mirror has a sacred purpose for our people. Plus, we will need to find the Spirit Woman. Without her help, we may see something horrible brought down upon all living Apache. You both must swear a sacred oath to me not to mention this mirror to anyone. Bad things might happen to all of us, especially if news of this discovery leaks out."

Nodding in unison, both Ray and I quickly swore an oath of silence agreeing to the secrecy surrounding this object. I now felt somewhat uneasy about the mirror being on my premises, much less hanging shrouded in my office. Ray and I both bid goodbye to Two Feathers, who promised to return in two days.

"Jack, I'm going back to my shop," Ray remarked. "Do you feel okay about sleeping in the back with The Ghost Mirror in your office?"

"Well," I reluctantly admitted, "I'm just a little worried, but what can I do? It's there and I just have to live with it and hope someone on the other side doesn't decide to come through it uninvited—especially that rattler!" Ray nodded, turned, and left for his store.

That night my sleep was uneasy. I kept thinking about the story—or legend—Two Feathers related to us. The Indian and the rattlesnake in the desert scene bothered me. Was it some kind of a subliminal warning to all of us? Was some sort of poison going to surreptitiously seep into our bodies?

I was happy to be a loner. I was in my mid-60s now. I had never married. Oh, along the way, there had been a woman here or there, mostly those I had picked up at a bar. We had one-night stands, but nothing serious ever developed. Some were married and needed the release, or thrill, of doing something so intimate outside of what had to have been their lonely marriages. No family—I guessed they all must be dead by now, so no reunions would be possible, not that I wanted any kind of a meeting with any remaining members of my family. Although, I grimly realized the internet, where you can find almost anyone in seconds, might lead to a family member tracking me down and showing up unexpectedly one day.

I mused that this Ghost Mirror episode might be the highlight of my life. Who knew? But I still had a hard time wrapping my brain around this entire strange saga, which was unfolding before my eyes. I wondered if I was trapped inside a dream, that wouldn't stop or let me waken.

Not surprisingly, my sleep was somewhat fitful that night. Finally, after an uneasy night of off and on waking up going back to sleep, I arose early, around five. After some bathroom ablutions, I fixed some coffee—black, no sugar or cream. Taking a steaming cup of joe into my office, I stood before the shrouded mirror. The shroud seemed to move a bit. *Is there some sort of air current in this old building that I don't know about?* I wondered. I did a quick 360, but I still felt uneasy, as if some unspeakably evil presence lurked in the room with me. The sensation lasted only a few seconds or so and then faded away, but it still made me shiver. What if this really was the legendary Ghost Mirror? Did it actually have the potential to destroy the entire Apache nation? That certainly seemed a bit far-fetched to me. But I wasn't about to discount the mirror's supernatural force.

I worked on paperwork for several hours but continued to feel a looming ghostlike and ominous aura surrounding me while I worked. Ray came by shortly after he closed shop and we chatted a while in my office. He too said he could feel some sort of presence, but to him it felt magnetic.

"I feel, sitting in this chair," he said somewhat uneasily, "that I'm being pulled toward the mirror."

"Well," I commented, "it'll be interesting to see what Two Feathers has to say tomorrow."

Ray rose to leave and told me that he'd be in early tomorrow. I nodded, followed him out, and locked up shop for the night.

The next day, I was awake at dawn. I'd had another uneasy night trying to sleep. Ray came in around eight, and we talked shop until he left to open his store at nine. The day just seemed to drag so slowly. I had a few customers and sold some minor pieces of art and recommended they look at Ray's antiques next door. Two o'clock came and Two Feathers had not returned. I found his absence rather worrisome. I was antsy and started fidgeting, walking around the shop, adjusting picture frames and getting more and more anxious by the minute.

Around five, Two Feathers walked into my shop. He was accompanied by an even older man, who looked so ancient that I figured he had to be at least ninety-five or even a hundred years of age. His face was lined with more furrows than Two Feathers' face had, but this elderly man was singularly small, wiry, and sinewy—perhaps five foot high and not a pound over a hundred and twenty-five.

Two Feathers introduced him. "Jack, this is Matthew Red Horse. He taught me many years ago how to become a shaman."

I reached forward and shook Red Horse's hand. His grip was incredibly strong for such an ancient individual. "Thank you, Mr. Red Horse, for coming. I'm pleased to meet you." Just then the jingle jangle of the front doorbell sounded followed by the alarm system's two beeps. In walked Ray, so introductions were made again, and I told Red Horse he could call me Jack. I left the office and hurried out on the main floor, locked the front door, and brought a padded folding aluminum chair into the office for Red Horse. Then we all sat down.

Two Feathers began, "I told Matthew everything and he would like to see this mirror," he nodded in the direction of the covered mirror. I stood, walked over to the side wall and uncovered it. Immediately the mirror began to cloud over. Red Horse stood and walked over to the mirror.

After standing in front of it for about thirty seconds, he spoke, "Yes, Jack, I am almost sure that this is the missing mirror." As he talked, the gray clouds vanished in a trice, and we stared at the scene before us. Two Wolves was still there looking toward us. The rattler coiled silently beside him and he had rested his hand on top of it. The serpent's tongue flicked in and out. Then it appeared to yawn and we could see that its fangs were curved and long.

"Oh, this is not good," Red Horse observed. "That man is definitely Two Wolves and the snake is the symbol of evil that follows him wherever he rides. Ah, let me see something. I will try something to confirm my suspicions." He placed his right hand on the mirror's surface and stood there. We looked in awe at him as smoke seemed to sizzle around Red Horse's hand and we heard a crackling, as if his fingers were being fried in oil. He turned to look at all of us and said, "Don't be worried at what happens next." Red Horse pushed his hand and it disappeared into the mirror.

We all gasped then stood up with our mouths gaping, looking both aghast at him and mesmerized by what we could not believe even though we were actually seeing it with our eyes. Red Horse slowly withdrew his hand from the mirror, and as he did we sensed, or smelled, a hot desert air blowing through the mirror, swirling around us and flowing out the office door. I was so shocked that I took a quick glance through my office wall window because from it I could see the front door. I wondered if I had really locked the front the door. *Maybe it somehow opened without the bell or beeps,* I thought. *That would explain the hot desert breeze.* But the door was shut tight. The hair on my neck tingled.

"I knew there was one test I had to do to confirm that this is The Ghost Mirror," Red Horse continued. "And, yes, it definitely has a magnetic pull to it. Fortunately," he paused, "not quite strong enough to pull my arm and the rest of me into the abyss on the other side. Jack," he turned toward me and spoke, "this Ghost Mirror must be returned to its original hiding place and then sealed up forever, or the evil spirits behind it might somehow escape and wreak havoc upon all Apache, perhaps," he paused, "eradicating the entire tribe."

"Why do you think the Spirit Woman found it and brought it to me?" I related her last words to me and continued, "If so, how can we find out where it was hidden in the first place?"

Red Horse turned back toward the mirror and looked intently at the scene within. The Indian had stood next to his firepit and appeared to be most agitated. The rattler had slithered toward us and now appeared to be striking the backside of The Ghost Mirror. Its mouth looked huge.

That's not a good sign, I thought, vigorously shaking my head.

Red Horse replied, "Jack, I think the Spirit Woman rests uneasily in this world. She probably saw the massacre and also where Two Wolves and his band of warriors hid it. Maybe, after they departed, she waited several hours, or a day or so, before getting up the nerve to enter the cave. I think she may have touched its surface and been drawn into it, then spit out again because she was not Apache. But she had changed somehow. I think, since that time, she has continued to live and is still caught between her ancient Navajo spirit world and the spirit world of the present."

"Is she looking for peace? Or, do you think she wants to return to her world of some 150 years ago?" I asked him. Red Horse walked over to his chair and sat down. The rest of us seated ourselves and listened intently to his every word.

"Well, as you have suspected, the mirror has some type of magnetism. It draws people in. Who knows what or who this Spirit Woman really is, or how she arrived on your doorstep. BUT," he strongly emphasized and pointed at us, "you, and perhaps Ray were chosen. We probably will never know the true answer, or why. Now," he continued, "I believe that she is nearby, waiting for us to do something."

Ray spoke, "What?"

"I think," Red Horse replied with some sadness in his voice, "we have to return the mirror to its hiding place."

"But, how?" both Ray and I asked at the same time.

"I must think on this tonight and confer with Two Feathers alone. We will both decide what comes next," Red Horse answered. Both shamans stood. Ray and I escorted them to the front door, which I unlocked. We stood outside. It was after nine p.m.—the sky had begun to darken, and an eerie purple color spread over it.

An owl hooted somewhere nearby.

"Well," Red Horse observed, "That is certainly a good omen. The owl is considered sacred to us; his wisdom will show us the way. We all must keep our eyes open for an owl. I think he is watching over us." He and Two Feathers then turned to leave.

Ray and I bid them goodbye. Afterward, Ray looked at me, shrugged his shoulders, and silently departed. I returned to my showroom to make sure—I tested it twice—that I had locked the front door. I was sure I was in for another restless night of sleep.

I tossed and turned that night, thinking about all that had happened and what had been said. I felt all this was some sort of dream or enigmatic riddle that needed to be broken down, taken apart, and solved. But I knew I wasn't the one who could find the answer. With Two Feathers and Red Horse, it looked as if we were going to search somewhere for the convoluted answer. *Maybe,* I thought, *we're facing something enigmatic like the riddle of the Sphinx: What goes on four feet in the morning, two feet at noon, and three feet in the evening?*[12] Well, I guess, we would find out.

I rose again at five, fixed some coffee, zapped two cinnamon buns, and ate quickly. Next, I puttered around the office doing the continual paperwork that comes with owning your own business. I

---

[12] https://quatr.us/greeks/riddle sphinx oedipus.htm.
The Answer is Man. A man is a baby in the morning of his life and he crawls on four feet.
A man is an adult in the noon—the middle part—of his life and he walks on two feet.
But when a man is old, in the evening of his life, he walks with a cane, on three feet.

tried to keep my mind off the mirror, but even shrouded it loomed ominously above me. *I'll be damn glad to rid myself of this irritating problem*, I thought. My mind conjured up the old Shakespearean quote from Macbeth, *"Out, out damned spot."*[13]

I pondered when both men would show up and what conclusion they may have decided upon. I decided not to worry as I was on Indian time now. Yet, I was mildly surprised when both shamans walked through my showroom's door around eight that morning. Ray followed behind the two medicine men. *Well, this looks auspicious*, I thought as I greeted everyone. As they entered, I saw Ray flip the deadbolt and turn the Open/Closed sign to Closed. We all assembled in my office again. A silence permeated the room for a minute or so as the two shamans settled into their chairs.

Matthew Red Horse spoke first. "Jack, both Two Feathers and I concur that the mirror has to be returned to its original hiding place then sealed up in such a way that no one will ever be able to stumble upon it again."

"Ah," I queried, "just how do we do that?"

"Ray told Two Feathers a while back that you have used dynamite in the past?" he asked.

"Ahhhh," I sighed, "Yes, but that was in the war some forty years ago. And how in the world are we going to acquire some TNT? I sure as heck don't have any stashed away; that's for sure!"

Two Feathers spoke up, "I have some 'connections' so to speak, and they will give me as much as I need."

"Well, I don't know how much we'll need, but I think not less than twenty sticks, plus twenty-five or more blasting caps to be on the safe side," I observed.

---

[13] Hudson, Rev. H. N., A.M. *The Works of Shakespeare - Vol. 5.* Cambridge [Great Britain]: John Wilson and Son, 1881, 328.

"Good," Red Horse spoke as he stood before continuing, "We will use your truck. Be ready to leave early tomorrow morning."

"But … but," I mildly protested, "how do we know where we're going?"

Red Horse replied, "Either a guide or a sign will come," he said somewhat cryptically.

We stepped outside. As we stood there taking in the bright and beautiful day, we heard a high-pitched whistling up in the sky. All four of us looked up to the azure blue sky. A bald eagle soared about fifty feet over our heads, circling over us as if to line us up like a target to swoop down upon.

"Oh, that is extremely strong medicine for us," Red Horse intoned. "That eagle is my spirit eagle, and he will be our guide tomorrow. We must keep our eyes peeled for it."

How? I wondered to myself, *how will he or any of us know for certain that it's the same eagle?*

I decided to not worry about it but just accept on faith that Red Horse certainly wouldn't be taking us on a wild goose chase. I glanced up at the eagle again. It circled lower, and then, without any warning, it swooped down and landed on Red Horse's left shoulder. We were stunned. The bird had blood red eyes and surveyed each one of us individually—its eyes seared into each of our souls. Red Horse lifted his right arm and hand and gently stroked the bird's back. Being no more than three feet away from Red Horse, I looked at the eagle's yellow talons, which were long and extraordinarily sharp. Yet Red Horse didn't appear to mind that they were holding onto his shoulder rather tightly. It was then that I noticed an inch wide blue band around one of the talons.

"Red Horse," I questioned, "why the blue band?"

"Because," Red Horse replied, "he is my Spirit Eagle. He will only come to me and has been with me when I first became a medicine man in my early twenties."

"Ah," I looked somewhat incredulously at him and asked, "since your twenties?"

"Yes, I put that band on him eighty years ago,"

My mouth dropped, "You are over a hundred years old?" I questioned.

He just nodded, stroked the eagle two more times, then spoke to it in a language I didn't understand. The eagle lifted off his shoulder and almost effortlessly soared so high, so quickly, that we all lost sight of it within half a minute. It vanished before our eyes. *I sure wish I knew what was going on*, I silently said to myself. We parted. The shamans walked away and both Ray and I returned to our shops. *So, tomorrow is the day*, I thought, as I entered my showroom. *Tomorrow maybe, just maybe, this nightmare, or dream, or whatever the hell it is, will finally be over*. But I continued to wonder if it would really be over?

I rose early—at six—and went out and filled my super work horse dual cab Chevy Silverado with a full tank of gas at the local Circle K. The two passenger seats in the rear cab area were not for the overweight. When I returned home, I swept out the truck bed and then found an old quilt that we could place the mirror on so we didn't scratch its back as we drove. Plus, I had a lot of rope to use as a tie down to keep the mirror from shifting or sliding.

Both medicine men arrived around seven. Two Feathers was toting a large, unmarked box that I intuitively knew contained one-pound sticks of dynamite, or, as we called the stuff in Nam, C-4. I knew better than to ask how he obtained it. Better to leave some things unasked. Ray and I lugged the heavy mirror out to the truck while Two Feathers stood in the truck bed to facilitate sliding the heavy piece of Indian (or white settlers?) history into the bed. I then hopped up and spent several minutes tying it down to ensure it wouldn't move while we were on the road. Two Feathers had opened the rear cab's door and placed the C-4 under the seat located just behind the driver's seat. When I jumped down from the truck bed, I viewed it somewhat uneasily. Having used C-4 a couple of times in Nam so many years ago, I thought about what might happen if the box blew. But I knew if the box did blow as we drove, I wouldn't know what happened anyway.

We all boosted ourselves into the truck. Red Horse sat in the passenger seat while Ray and Two Feathers crammed themselves into the tight rear seat compartment. As I turned the ignition, Red Horse spoke.

"Jack, every so often keep an eye out on your side view mirror. Since The Ghost Mirror has magnetic powers, I think there is a good chance we will be followed. I believe the Spirit Woman will be drawn to us some way, so you probably will see her trailing us at a distance."

I nodded and said, "Okay! Let's see where we're going." Suddenly the Spirit Eagle landed on the front hood before I had a chance to pull away from the store. Red Horse motioned with his arm and pointed in a sweeping arc. With what appeared to be hardly any effort, the Spirit Eagle rose majestically off the hood, circled above us, and flew in a southerly direction.

"We go south," Red Horse commented.

So, I cranked up the engine and we were soon on I-25 South. After twenty-five miles, I noticed an old beat-up rattletrap of a truck that had positioned itself several hundred yards behind us. It always kept two or three cars between us. It didn't speed up, just lazily stayed in the lane behind us. I mentioned the truck to the three men. Red Horse leaned forward and looked at his side mirror while Ray and Two Feathers turned to survey the situation and then quickly turned back.

"I think Spirit Woman has found us," Red Horse commented. "We now should keep an eye out every few minutes. I suspect she knows that we know she's following us."

"Do you think she has evil intent toward us?" I asked Red Horse.

"No, I believe she wants to return to her time," he paused, "and we are leading her back to the cave. We will see how she makes a connection with us," he replied.

Every so often, the Spirit Eagle appeared in front of us, still headed south. On one occasion, when I checked my side mirror, I saw the eagle flying behind the Spirit Woman's truck. I wondered if she saw it or sensed its presence.

I had been driving down the interstate slowly, around sixty miles per hour, so we didn't jiggle The Ghost Mirror too much—or the C-4. I just tried to keep a steady pace. All of us sat in silence as we passed through Albuquerque and continued southward. About ninety minutes later, the eagle swooped down in front of us then skyrocketed like a Navy jet high off to the west. A mile later, we were at the Socorro exit leading to SR60, so I turned off and we were soon headed west on a fairly well-kept highway. By now, we'd been on the road for a bit over three hours.

Another hour passed. Red Horse dozed off and on, his head nodding up and down. For at least a half hour after I turned off onto SR60, I didn't see, or sense, the Spirit Woman's truck. Then, suddenly, it shot out of a side road in a cloud of yellowish dust about a quarter mile behind us. I mentioned her reappearance to everyone. Red Horse again looked in my side mirror and the other two men took a quick glance out my back window.

We soon approached the National Radio Astronomy Observatory located on the south side of the highway. Its numerous huge radio and astronomical telescope dishes pointed ominously in several directions to the heavens.

We were still in the desert, yet I had the feeling we had landed on some distant moon or planet, as those sentinels pointed forlornly to the sky. What kind of life were they attempting to listen to—or observe? Was there some sort of life out there? After what had happened to me over the past few days, I believed something was out there, although I couldn't quite grasp or much less define it. Shortly after leaving the observatory, as we approached Datil, New Mexico, our Spirit Eagle reappeared and headed south.

Arriving in Datil, we stopped at a beaten down, weathered trading post called Martins. The shabby place also advertised food and drink on a sign that had lost one of its two chain moorings so that it twisted and turned back and forth with the wind. We used the facilities and stocked up on five or six pre-made sandwiches of questionable appearance even though their labels displayed today's date. We didn't touch the donuts which looked at least five days old. We purchased a Styrofoam ice chest and ten pounds of ice, which we poured on top of the sodas we had purchased. We placed the sandwiches on top of the ice.

After walking around outside the premises for a few minutes, we loaded the cooler into the truck bed next to the lashed down Ghost Mirror. Then we climbed back into the Silverado and started south on Route 12, which turned out to be an incredibly narrow two-lane road with seemingly little room to pass any cars that might be heading toward us. To our southwest, the Tularosa Mountains loomed up some miles distant as we crossed the Plains of San Agustin. The

Spirit Woman had disappeared, I observed to the others, but I was sure she would pop up again in my rear-view mirror.

We traveled about twenty-five miles and entered Old Horse Springs, which consisted of nothing more than several abandoned houses. The buildings were not only dilapidated, but also looked as if they would lean over and collapse at any minute. The chimney on one had already tumbled down and a myriad of brick pieces were strewn across the front yard. The front door was gone, and all the former glass in the windows had been broken out. They looked like forlorn ghosts. Several miles after we passed through Old Horse Springs, our guiding Spirit Eagle reappeared and soared off to the south.

A mile later we came upon a gravel and dirt road, which was mostly dirt. As I turned left onto it, the road stretched south in front of us and paralleled the Tularosa mountains now off to our right. After driving a few miles, I spotted a cloud of dust behind us and intuitively knew that it was Spirit Woman. But her truck strangely appeared and disappeared in the dust. One second I could see it and the next it was either swallowed up or it simply evaporated into the dirty red sand colored cloud of dust.

I commented to the men about this phenomenon and that she seemed to be closing the gap between us. Red Horse observed, "She knows we are getting close, but she won't get too near us until we are not far from the cave, then she'll appear."

After a mile or so, the Spirit Eagle swooped low over the truck and flew off to the west toward the mountains. A hundred yards farther on, a really nasty looking dirt road shot off to the right. I pulled up and looked ahead. I saw lots of gullies and deep ruts and an opening to a canyon a mile or two west of us with red sandstone cliffs rising beside the entrance. Time to put the Chevy into four-wheel drive.

Our progress was slow—perhaps 5-10 miles an hour. I tried to drive down the middle crest of the ruts on each side and we all bounced around a lot in the cab. I hoped The Ghost Mirror wouldn't be damaged with all the shaking. The canyon stayed straight ahead in front of us as we wound and twisted our way to it. We climbed several rock-strewn inclines and dodged numerous large boulders for over a mile. I hadn't had time to look back to see if the Spirit Woman had chosen to follow us, but when I did, she and her truck had disappeared.

Finally, after an hour and a half, we reached the opening to the canyon and the going got a little better. The Spirit Eagle hovered constantly in front of us riding the thermals, calmly floating with the wind like one does in his swimming pool or at the beach. About a quarter mile into the canyon, the eagle landed on our hood. I stopped the truck.

"Well, Red Horse, do you think," I asked, "this is the place?"

"We will soon see," he grunted as he, and the rest of us, climbed out of the truck onto sandy ground. Erosion over the millennia had left a fine reddish sand that had spread over the canyon's floor where we now stood.

"What about the Spirit Woman?" Ray asked as he stretched his arms upward to the get the kinks out. "I don't see her or her truck. Have we lost her after she dogged us for so long?"

"I think not," Red Horse said.

Two Feathers spoke up. "No, she is near—or already here. We just can't see her, but I will know when she's close. I will feel her coming."

Since it was close to two in the afternoon, we decided to break out the food and drinks. All four of us sat in the shade cast off on the left side of the Chevy and silently ate. As we sat against the Silverado, the wind inside of the canyon picked up ever so slightly and gently blew eastward. About a hundred yards off toward the canyon's mouth, the breeze formed a small dust tornado. We watched as it twisted, turned, and danced across the landscape before suddenly vanishing.

"What next, Red Horse?" I queried as we all looked at the scene before us.

"I think we wait, Mr. Ward. I sense something is going to happen." He stood dead still, like a rock column, facing west up the canyon. Two Feathers strode over and stood with him but turned to face the canyon's mouth.

We all stood gazing at the sheer and smooth canyon walls which soared over us, looming, as if to warn us of some unknown insidious and impending danger. I had lowered the Chevy's tailgate and sat down swinging my legs. Ray soon joined me, while the medicine men appeared to have turned to stone as they gazed off into the distance. It was hot and sweat dripped off all our faces.

At first, I sensed something. The hairs on the back of my neck stood up. Someone or something was nearby. Then, I saw it. The largest rattlesnake I had ever seen much less encountered was slithering toward both medicine men.

"Red Horse and Two Feathers, you have a rattler coming your way," I said as calmly as I could manage, trying to keep any panic out of my voice.

Both men nodded but did not move. They were frozen to the ground. The snake moved between the standing shamans and coiled. From fifteen feet away, I could see its tongue flickering. The main part of its body was as thick as my arm. *Boy!* I thought. *I bet that animal can sure pack a punch!* I had no sooner said that to myself than the rattler started shaking its tail. We all were dead quiet as the sound of the rattles pierced the afternoon calm. Yet, it didn't appear aggressive in any way, but Ray and I were on super alert.

"Is this some kind or sign or omen?" I whispered to Ray.

"Don't know, but they will tell us in due time," he said pointing to the Indians.

No one moved for about ten minutes. Sweat just poured off my face and body, trickling down to my chest. I didn't particularly care for snakes. I saw them occasionally when I was in Nam. The deadly ones were kraits, of which there were two types according to the rumors—a three-stepper and a five-stepper. Meaning if one or the other nailed you, you would walk either three or five steps and then meet your maker. Whether or not that was true, I had no idea, but my machete was always handy, and I managed to dispatch several during my brief tour. But I spared the pythons we encountered on our treks tramping through the thick jungle. After all, their bite wouldn't kill you, but their massive coils would, so we bypassed them at a respectful distance whenever they appeared.

Without saying a word, Red Horse turned and looked down at the viper. The rattles stopped and the snake looked up at the medicine man. He slowly lowered his body and squatted in front of the huge rattler, which seemed mesmerized by this shaman so close to it. Red Horse said a few words in a language I again couldn't understand. Then he reached out and laid his hand on the body of the coiled serpent before him. He said something else, and in a flash the Spirit Eagle appeared, swooped down, grabbed the serpent with its talons, and then soared skyward before vanishing off to the south. Ray and I stood with mouths agape, not believing what we had just seen.

Ray and I just stared as Red Horse and Two Feathers walked over to my truck.

"What...?" I started to ask, but Red Horse held his hand up to silence my question.

"That was the spirit snake we saw in the mirror," he stated. "It needed peace, so I sent it back to its world of many moons ago."

Ray and I were stunned. I wanted to ask how it had escaped the mirror but decided against doing so. After all, I had absolutely no clue what was going on.

"So," I tentatively asked, "was that the omen you thought might occur?"

"No, that was the evil which we needed to rid ourselves from. I am still not sure," Red Horse answered, "but I think we need to wait a while yet for the omen."

Two Feathers spoke up saying, "And we still have to deal with the Spirit Woman. She will come."

We all drank a few more sodas. I glanced at my watch. It was four in the afternoon. *Are we going to get out of here by nightfall?* I wondered. I didn't relish the prospect of trying to drive the Silverado back to the "good" gravel road in the darkness. *But*, I inwardly sighed, *I'm probably going to do it.* The wind had picked up.

"Don't worry, Jack," Red Horse intruded into my thoughts so unexpectedly that I almost jumped before he continued. "We will have especially bright moonlight when we leave here." *How in the world*, I thought, *does he know what I am thinking? He must have some sort of ESP.*

The Spirit Eagle appeared and hovered in the air about fifty feet above us. It gave a high screech and took off to the west, disappearing within seconds. The wind coming down the canyon seemed to pick up with the eagle's departure. I looked at some cottonwoods growing up against the sides of the canyon's walls some fifty yards away. As I looked at the trees, blowing gently back and forth, Ray turned his head and looked the same way.

"Look," Ray pointed, "there's a great horned owl in the middle tree." The shamans turned and we all saw the bird of wisdom staring right back at us.

"Ah, my fellow travelers," Red Horse spoke with a grave voice, "we have our sign, at last. He is sacred to us and will show us what comes next. Now we wait."

All four of us leaned against the sides of the Chevy and watched the owl, which was perched on a branch about three fourths up the tree. Time seemed to creep by as we waited with anticipation for the owl to lead us somewhere. After a few minutes, as the shadows began to creep across the canyon's floor, the owl launched itself and briefly circled overhead. It then glided with the wind back alongside the canyon wall and flew beside the red cliffs for a hundred yards or so before it vanished.

Following the owl on foot, we made sure to keep a lookout for rattlers along the way, to the last place we'd seen the bird. As we rounded a jutting rock fold in the canyon wall, we found a three-foot-wide passageway in the wall. The owl was perched on a ledge next to a slit in the wall about ten feet above our heads.

As soon as it saw us, the owl glided off down the slit. We followed. After fifteen or twenty steps, we emerged into a round bowl-like area between fifty and sixty feet in diameter. It was as if we had stumbled into some sort of cathedral. Deadly quiet. There was no wind—nothing stirred. Our owl was resting on a ledge against the far wall. It gave a hoot that resounded off the walls for several seconds before dying down.

Red Horse crossed the vacant area of this hidden side canyon to stand under the owl. As we watched, he stooped a bit and vanished.

We rushed over to the area where he was last standing. As we neared the far wall, we immediately saw a curtain of rock, which we couldn't distinguish from where we had stood, with a dark area behind it. Red Horse emerged smiling.

"This is the place where the mirror once resided," Red Horse spoke with relief in his voice. "There are some signs inside, figures on the walls, which are Apache warning petroglyphs," he continued.

"Can we go in?" Ray asked.

Red Horse nodded. Two Feathers went first and returned after a minute or so. Ray and I followed singly. Being the last to enter, I found that it was, indeed, a small space. Red petroglyph warning figures seemed to glow in the semi-darkness of the small cave. I stayed only twenty-to-thirty seconds and turned to leave it, thinking to myself that the cavern will be easy to seal up. *Hell*, I thought, *I might end up causing the entire cave to collapse on top of it when I blow the C-4 to enclose the mirror. Ahh*, I thought as I came out into the light, *all we have left now is the denouement. Where is Spirit Woman?*

Two Feathers looked at me as I exited, as if he could intuit what was on my mind, "Spirit Woman is close. I feel her presence. Let's get the mirror and bring it here."

We quickly returned to the Chevy, untied and unloaded the mirror, which we stood up and leaned against the side of the truck. I glanced at my watch. It was getting close to six. Shadows were beginning to creep down the canyon's sides as the sun began its descent to the west.

As all four of us stood looking at the mirror, I began to hear a high-pitched ringing in my ears. When I glanced over to the other three men, it appeared they were experiencing the same thing. There was a loud electric zapping sound in the air over and around us. I looked up, but all I saw was clear blue sky. But, as I looked back down, I saw a whirling grey cylinder between us and the mirror. We all stepped back a foot. Then … there she was! Spirit Woman materialized right before our eyes and the cylinder disappeared. There she stood, still a translucent figure, with a ragged and torn almost see-through dress, which looked ancient on her thin body.

She gave a bow to both Red Horse and Two Feathers. Two Feathers greeted her, again in a language I didn't understand. She replied for over a minute as both shamans nodded during her speech. Then Red Horse pointed to me and Spirit Woman turned toward me and spoke.

"Mr. Ward," she said, "I'm sorry for bringing you to this place in such a confusing manner. I have been wandering for many moons unsettled and alone. I come from a world of many years ago. I knew the location of the mirror as I had observed the Apache hiding it in the first place.

"In my first life, I was a medicine woman. One day, I was gathering herbs and roots when I saw the Apache entering the canyon carrying the mirror. I hid and prayed they wouldn't notice my footprints. Just as I did so, the wind sprang up and, within seconds, it had erased my footprints. I knew this was a sign, but not what kind of sign it was. As I continued to watch, they next entered the side canyon, where you have just been. After an hour or so, they left. I waited a whole day before I dared come out. I walked into the side canyon, but, when I arrived at the bowl, I saw nothing. So, I looked for their footprints, found them, and quickly located the crevice."

She paused, and we all seemed to take a huge breath and let it out slowly before she continued. "Entering the small cave, I saw the mirror and wondered both how the Apache had acquired it and why had they taken such pains to hide it when they could have just chopped it up and burned it. Then I saw the red symbols and knew I shouldn't have been there."

She sighed before continuing, "I was young. I didn't feel threatened, so I approached the mirror in the dimly lit cave. I felt something like magnetism pulling me inexorably toward it. About two feet away, I tripped and stumbled toward the mirror, so I put my hand out to grab the wooded frame, but my arm slid onto the surface, and suddenly I felt my body falling into and through the glass."

She hesitated, wiped her head, then started to speak again, "I landed in the sand. There was desert all around me. Saguaros surrounded me. I had no idea where I was. In the distance I saw an abandoned wagon train, so I walked toward it. As I approached, an eerie silence surrounded the area. I was drawn to the rear of one of the wagons where I saw a strange pile of black ashes. Although there was a breeze, the wind didn't move those ashes. I instinctively knew I was in an evil place, so I turned and left."

Taking in a couple of deep breaths, when she let them out, the air whistled through her teeth. "I wandered for many days, but I never got hungry or wanted water. The days turned into months and years and still I didn't eat, drink, or meet anyone else. I could not feel myself aging in any way. My skin remained the same with no spots or wrinkles. I knew I had entered Ghost Land, where we go when we die. I didn't feel as if I had gone to our Indian heaven though. Perhaps, I prayed, I was in an in-between land of life and death. I thought that, maybe, I might be able to find my way back to life."

"Sometimes, after I had slept," she continued, "I would awaken in a new and different place. I would explore the new area, hoping that it might lead me back home. It never did. I continued to roam for many moons in each strange place the spirit world took me. With each new landscape, I never gave up hope, though, as I realized the Gods must have a purpose in mind for me."

She stopped talking as tears ran down her cheeks. She wiped them away with her hand. "Finally," she sniffled, "I found myself back in my land. The landmarks of my early life appeared again, and I realized I had found my home, but it seemed different and strange at the same time. I was so happy that I wept for many hours. But a voice within me told me I had to find the mirror again because by locating it I would be led back to my family and friends. So, I began my quest to locate the mirror and its hiding place."

The sun had begun to slide down past the rim of the canyon bringing a coolness that surrounded us. Ray and I stood amazed at what she was telling us, while Red Horse and Two Feathers simply nodded every so often at different points in her story.

Spirit Woman picked up her tale again and continued, "One day, I found myself on the outskirts of a what you call a city. I had never seen such a huge pueblo—it spread out all over the land. Yet, it wasn't like any sort of pueblo that I was familiar with because its thousands of houses didn't look like pueblo homes. Also, there were roads everywhere with strange objects moving on them without horses or cattle pulling them. I quickly realized that I wasn't back in my time, yet the mountains and land seemed familiar. I knew I was getting closer to my home. I wandered around for several weeks, still not feeling hungry or thirsty. When I walked, I encountered people for the first time since I found myself in this new in-between world, but, strangely, they appeared not to see me. I was invisible."

She paused to wipe the tears that were running down her cheeks. "One day I stumbled somewhat mysteriously upon your store, Mr. Ward, and I knew somehow that when I found The Ghost Mirror I should bring it to you because then I would be close to someone who could help me find my people."

"Why did you think that?" I asked.

She looked at me and answered, "Because I felt an unknown hand pushing, or drawing, me toward your gallery. It was similar to the feeling I experienced when I first located the mirror so many years ago in the cave. I knew I had to bait the trap so that if you took it then it would draw someone to it who could help me return to my people."

"Where did you find the truck? And who taught you how to drive?" Ray asked while the two shamans stood silently by absorbing Spirit Woman's tale.

"That, in itself, is another strange tale," she answered, "Several hundred yards away from Mr. Ward's store, there was an old, beaten down, rusty and reddish colored dilapidated truck. The tires were flat and it looked as if it had been sitting in that vacant lot, having been abandoned, for many years. I decided it would be a good place for me to sleep, even though as I peeked in a window, I saw that the seats were old, moldy, and cracked with stuffing spilling out of them. Because it seemed I was invisible, I guessed that if someone came along and looked inside, they wouldn't see me. Then, just as I was ready to try opening a door, I heard the hoot of an owl."

"I looked around and saw a palo verde tree about fifteen steps away toward the back of the overgrown and weedy vacant lot. In it was perched a great horned owl staring directly at me. I immediately and intuitively sensed that this was my spirit owl. By looking directly at me, I knew he could see me!" she exclaimed and smiled. "He would help me find the mirror! Then I tried to open the passenger door. I really had to pull on it, but, several seconds later, it gave a loud creak and swung open. I climbed in and soon fell asleep at peace, knowing I was now on my quest to find the mirror."

"In the morning when I woke up," she continued, "I sensed something different had occurred while I was asleep. I sat up, stretched, and looked around. Somehow the inside of the truck had changed. It looked clean, the dust was gone, and the seats were mended. The stuffing had disappeared. I exited the truck and saw that it now had old balding tires. But, strangely, standing outside the vehicle, I realized that it was translucent—I could see right through it! I looked at the tree and my spirit owl was still there staring at me. He hadn't moved all night. Then, I felt an invisible hand propelling me toward the driver's side door. I grasped the handle and the door opened without a squeak. So I hopped in, shut the door, and saw that a key was in the ignition."

She paused, "Suddenly, the spirit owl landed on the truck's hood right in front of me. It spread its wings and appeared to imperceptibly nod at me. I felt a sense of wonderment and joy flow into and out of my body. I instinctively knew I could drive this thing without having to worry about horses or cattle pulling it! So, I started the truck and a powerful force led me out on the highway."

"Well, I'll be," I commented to everyone, "I always wondered about that old rattletrap and what had happened to it. Here one day and gone the next—just disappeared. Now I know."

Spirit Woman looked at each of us, then nodded at what I had just said before taking up her amazing, almost unbelievable, tale again. "I was afraid the landscape would change while I was sleeping, so I always slept in the truck at night. Awakening each morning, I saw the spirit owl nearby and knew he was my guardian spirit and would prevent the landscape from shape shifting to another place."

"Even though I knew I was in the area of my homeland, it still took me almost two more years to locate this canyon. I was back in my own land, but I still had difficulty recognizing the changes nature had done over time. I began to hunt, driving down roads and up into canyons until one morning this silent force within me steered me up to where we are now standing. It took me all of ten minutes to find the slit leading into the bowl area. I located the hidden entrance to the cave and reentered it. I saw the red petroglyphs glowing on the walls and there was the mirror. Still intact!"

Tears streamed down her face again as she recounted this last statement to us. The sunlight had vanished from the tops of the cliffs, but it still shone on the far eastern walls of the canyon.

"Because The Ghost Mirror was too heavy for me to carry any distance, I had to set it down every so often, until I finally reached the truck. I loaded it into the truck bed and immediately left for the big pueblo, which, I had learned in my travels was called Santa Fe. Time flew as if I were sailing through the skies. I drove directly to your shop, and you, Mr. Ward, know what happened while you had it."

"What did you think might happen?" I asked.

She replied, "I wasn't sure. I just knew someone powerful would come," she nodded in Red Horse's direction, "and he would understand what needed to be done with the mirror."

Red Horse spoke for the first time in over an hour, "You are correct Spirit Woman. I knew from the beginning the mirror had to be returned to its special place. The spirits had sent me a message to wait for Two Feathers to come to my home. They also told me you were nearby and were lost between worlds. We will," he pronounced, "return you to your fathers, but now we must wait for tomorrow."

Turning to me, Red Horse spoke, "I know I told you we would leave tonight, Jack, but we need daylight to return Spirit Woman to her people."

I had several blankets in my large Husky tailgate cross box located in the truck bed just behind the passenger's seat. I hopped up onto the bed, opened my storage box, and doled out the blankets. I started to hand one to Spirit Woman, but she just shook her head and walked away into the quickly descending darkness. I looked at Red Horse with a question on my lips, but he interrupted my thought before I could speak.

"She will be fine. She will return to us in the morning," he stated with certainty in his voice, before continuing, "Spirit Woman has returned to her truck, wherever it is."

We lay the blankets on the sand around the Silverado. I had four flashlights from the storage compartment which I handed out to the other three, keeping the last one for myself. Two Feathers and Red Horse took theirs and walked off toward the back of the canyon. They soon returned with armfuls of twigs and wood. Ray and I left, walked up the canyon for several hundred feet until we found an old and dry arroyo which contained a lot of wood that had been washed down the creek bed during the sporadic rains which filled the canyon every so often. I surmised that some of the wood came from trees high up on top of the cliffs that had died, rotted, and eventually had rolled over the cliff's edge to fall onto the canyon's sandy floor. Ray and I returned to the Chevy to find that both shamans had started a fire. We piled our wood on top of their pile.

After several minutes, while we stared at the flames, Red Horse spoke, "Early tomorrow morning, both Two Feathers and I will go to the cave and prepare it."

Ray and I just nodded. I wondered what he meant but felt asking would be too intrusive. After all, I knew from living in New Mexico for the past thirty some years that Indians had their own rites and perhaps these two shamans were, in some way, going to purify the cave before we placed The Ghost Mirror within it and then implode the entrance.

We all soon dozed off as the flames flickered back and forth. I had an uneasy sleep. I sensed that during the night one or the other of the two shamans had risen and fed the fire to keep it alive during the pitch-black darkness that surrounded us.

I awakened at dawn just as the eastern sky began to light up. Then the sun peeked over the horizon and threw its yellow beams toward the canyon flooding it with daylight. Two Feathers and Red Horse were gone. Ray and I grabbed a soda from the Styrofoam ice chest and sat on the tailgate. We quietly sipped our drinks awaiting the return of Red Horse and Two Feathers.

"I wonder where Spirit Woman is?" I said out loud.

"She's nearby. I sense her," Ray stated.

So, we waited patiently, and around six, the two shamans emerged from the slit crack with Spirit Woman following them. We watched them come toward us, walking in a solemn manner.

When they arrived, Red Horse spoke first in staccato sentences, "It is done. We have prepared the cave. It is cleansed. Time now for Spirit Woman to go."

Ray and I looked quizzically at each other and then at the three Indians.

The Ghost Mirror was still propped against the side of the Silverado where we had placed it last evening after unloading it. Red Horse and Two Feathers walked over to it and ushered Spirit Woman to stand between them and the mirror. Not knowing what was about to happen, both Ray and I stood off to a distance and watched.

Both shamans began to chant and slowly stamp their feet into the sand. Spirit Woman stood with her arms clasped. After several minutes the chanting stopped. Two Feathers spoke something unintelligible and placed his right hand on Spirit Woman's left arm. Red Horse spoke what appeared to be a short blessing. He stopped and looked skyward. As the Spirit Eagle circled above us, we heard an owl hoot once. Red Horse placed his left hand on Spirit Woman's right arm. Then he looked at Two Feathers and almost imperceptibly nodded just before both men pushed Spirit Woman's back against the mirror's surface.

Ray and I looked on, our mouths agape, as Spirit Woman's body melted into the silvery surface inch by inch. Both Red Horse's and Two Feathers' hands disappeared into the mirror as they slowly pushed Spirit Woman into whatever world she was destined for. The shamans withdrew their hands at the same time.

"Now," Red Horse proclaimed, "we take the mirror to the cave, and Jack, then you can work your magic with the explosives."

Ray and I walked over to the mirror and laid it gently onto the ground. We positioned ourselves so that I was in the rear with him at the front. As we lifted it off the sand, the mirror mysteriously rose in our grip and seemed to be floating. It was light as a feather! Ray turned and looked at me, and I him. We both shook our heads at this supposed miracle. The medicine men started off to the slit canyon while Ray and I leisurely followed.

We got the mirror through the slit and walked it across the bowl to where Red Horse and Two Feathers were standing in front of the rock curtain hiding the entrance to the cave. We turned the mirror sideways and ducked into the cave. The red petroglyphs had all but disappeared. In their place were other symbols in yellow which illuminated the interior of the cavern. The two shamans followed us inside.

"Place the mirror over there to the back, standing up," Red Horse commanded us. After we quickly did his bidding, he continued, "Now stand apart. Do not touch anything or anyone. Be silent." Two or three minutes passed as we stood in silence before Red Horse mumbled something.

"It is done," he said, "now let's leave here." So we filed out without saying a word. Outside, Red Horse continued, "Jack, please prepare the opening to be sealed."

The C-4 box was on the ground behind him. *Geeze,* I wondered, *how did that get here?* I hadn't heard the shaman lifting the box out of the Chevy earlier this morning. Neither had I seen anyone tote it into the bowl area.

With Ray helping me, I carefully removed each stick of C-4. I placed each piece at strategic points around and over the rock curtained entrance. I then instructed Ray to take the plunger box and reel out the det cord (RDX, an explosive agent) through the slit and out into the canyon. Five minutes later he returned. I had laid out each detonator and separated them three or four inches apart on a green cloth I found in the dynamite box.

"Red Horse, would you and Two Feathers go out to the box and make sure nothing blows or falls into the plunger?" The two men nodded in unison and silently departed. I gave them about five minutes, to insure they had reached the box. After a few minutes, I heard a screech and looked up. It was the Spirit Eagle. It looked at us, flapped its wings, and with another high-pitched screech, zoomed off in the direction of the canyon. I figured that was a sign from Red Horse telling us they were in place.

"Okay, Ray. This is the dangerous part. We've got to be careful or we'll be joining Spirit Woman in her world sooner than we expected," he nodded then continued, "I'm going to wire each detonator, hand it to you, and you stick it in the end of each C-4 stick."

I placed fourteen or fifteen sticks of C-4 strategically around the entrance. I figured that would be more than enough to seal up the cave. Plus, it would bring down tons of rock from the cliff wall above it. Ray moved slowly and cautiously as I handed each wired detonator to him. It took us about a half an hour to get everything in place. By the time we finished, sweat was rolling down our faces and dripping to the ground.

"Okay, Ray, you can leave. I'm going to give an eyeball check to everything once you're out of here." He nodded and walked purposely out of the bowl.

I took a good ten minutes to eyeball each stick of C-4. Satisfied, I turned, left the bowl, and soon found the other three outside in the main canyon about sixty feet away from the slit canyon's entrance.

I walked over to the plunger box. "Okay guys, it's show time! I suggest each of you return to the truck. I'll blow it when you get there."

They walked off. When they reached the Silverado, I primed the box turning a round crank on its side, lifted the plunger up, and then jammed it down hard. I waited, it seemed forever, but probably only a second or two passed until I heard a "WHOOMP" come from the bowl. Seconds later dust spewed out from the slit canyon. I turned and waved for the three men to come back. After they returned, we chatted for ten minutes or so to let the dust subside in both the slit and the bowl.

"Well, let's go take a look see," I commented. I led and we cautiously walked into the slit. When we got to its end, I peeked around the corner. About three quarters of the bowl had filled with red rock. We emerged into what was left of the bowl and stared. It was hard to figure out exactly where the cave entrance had been as thousands of tons of rock had cascaded down and out, sprawling across the bowl's floor leaving a twenty-foot-high scree slope. After a few minutes, we silently filed out and returned to the truck.

"Well I hope we were successful and Spirit Woman is back in her world now," I observed.

I had no sooner finished my last statement than we all heard a high screech. Looking up, we saw the Spirit Eagle circling high overhead. It caught a thermal and rose before flying off toward the five-hundred-foot cliff face to our north.

"What?" I gasped as I pointed my index finger upward. The tiny figure of Spirit Woman stood on top of the cliff and the eagle landed on her right shoulder. Ray and I watched, stunned at what we were seeing. Red Horse and Two Feathers appeared unmoved by what was unfolding in front of us. Red Horse raised his right arm, palm facing Spirit Woman. She, in turn, raised her left arm palm facing us.

Ray and I watched mesmerized and then, *"Poof!"* She and the eagle vanished.

Red Horse turned to me, "Jack, we can depart now. She is back with her people."

I nodded. While I closed the tail gate, the others hopped into the truck. I climbed up onto the driver's seat and fired up the engine. I noted that the clock in my instrument panel showed it was only nine in the morning.

It took us six hours to get home. I pulled into the store's parking lot and we all exited the truck. Ray and I bid both shamans goodbye and watched as they walked away.

"Well, I guess we can open up for a few hours," Ray observed. I nodded in agreement as we turned and headed for our front doors. As soon as I unlocked mine and walked inside, I felt absolutely drained, exhausted over the events of the last few days. I called Ray and told him, "I'm not opening. I'm taking a hot shower and going to bed." I locked the front door and turned the sign to "Closed."

I walked back my office, straightened up some papers on my desk, filed some, threw others in my overflowing trash can before trudging back to my primitive living quarters. I took a long hot shower. While doing so, I wondered about what had really happened during the last twenty-four hours. Did it actually occur? *Maybe I was in some sort of hypnotized state and dreamt all this*, I thought. I shook my head in total disbelief as the hot water started to peter out. Stepping out of the shower, I toweled off and fell naked into my unmade bed.

I awoke around ten that evening surrounded by stillness. All was quiet and calm. I could hear the wind blowing against the building, which gave off creaking and rattling noises. As I turned over, I realized I could see a light from my showroom area. I knew I hadn't left anything on. So, I stood up, grabbed my tattered grey robe off my bedside chair, tied the cloth belt and traipsed out to the show room. But, as I quickly discerned, the light was coming from my office. I wandered into it and saw that someone had left my desk lamp on, but all the remaining papers on it were still neatly arranged just as I had left them. As I scratched my head I wondered if Ray had dropped in to get something, Then my eyes saw it and zeroed in on the desktop. Sitting in the middle of my desk's green felt pad lay an eagle's feather with a small blue band on its shaft.

I sat down, picked up the feather and twirled it in my fingers, frowning, not sure what it meant. As I sat there holding it, I reflected on my life so far—taking stock. I sensed an internal change creeping through my mind but couldn't quite formulate what it was. After a few more minutes of contemplation, I was jolted by the realization that the events of the past few days had deeply affected my thinking about the plight of American Indians. *How could I help them?* I wondered.

Due to my expertise in selling American Indian art, I had a little proficiency in teaching art history. Off and on for the past ten years,

I offered art history classes at a local community college, relying heavily on H. W. Janson's *History of Art*, which was prolifically used throughout the U.S. college system for the past fifty years. *Perhaps, I thought, I could put my teaching skills to further use by going to the nearby Hopi Reservation and offer to teach different courses—Asian History, U.S. History, Art, etc.* After all, most people knew that education on the "Rez" was abysmal and that most teenage Indians dropped out of high school. Maybe I could teach something that would inspire them—I could focus on how the expansion west, Manifest Destiny, deeply affected and changed Indian culture.

I returned to bed and resolved to ask Ray in the morning to contact both Red Horse and Two Feathers to set up a meeting so I could pitch my proposal. If I could convince the two shamans, they might possibly be able to put in a good word for me with the tribal elders, which might ease my way onto the reservation.

Two days later, both Red Horse and Two Feathers, along with Ray, sat in my office as I discussed my idea. Both shamans liked my proposal and agreed they would talk to the Council of tribal elders. Five months later, after the Council's approval, and a myriad of U.S. government forms, many of which had to be signed and notarized, plus an extensive FBI background check and interview, I stepped into a classroom at the Hopi reservation high school to teach "U.S.-Indian Relations from 1600 to the Present." I specifically designed the course. After a lot of research, I ended up writing more than two hundred typewritten pages of lecture for the class.

Much to my, and the tribe's, surprise, it soon became one of the most popular elective courses among the school's teenagers, especially for those who decided to attend college. I prided myself in that maybe, just maybe, I made a difference in their lives. As years passed, I expanded the course to include the Spanish exploration of both Americas, and I ended up turning it into a two-semester course.

Each night, I returned home after class with a smile on my face and the realization that I was finally doing something worthwhile: I knew I was making a difference in the teenagers' lives.

I finally realized that not only was I at peace, but I also discovered another passion and purpose in my life. Teaching is a gift with uncountable rewards. Pleased and gratified by what I was now accomplishing with my life, I knew my helping students gave them hope. I knew this change was due to my exploit concerning the mirror and its convoluted return from the present into the past.

I AM GOING

When I'm Ready to Take That Final Trip
Across the River Styx -
Please Don't Prolong My Going -
Give Me Medicine
To Prevent the Excruciating Pain -
Just Make Me Comfortable -
But Don't Use Life Support

To Put Off the Inevitable -

Just to Give Me a Few More Hours -

or Days.

After All . . . It Is My Life

God Knows I'm Coming

Why Would You Delay My Seeing Him?

Let Me Go . . .

The Boat Is Waiting -

And Charon Grows Restless.

THE SHIP

The red-tailed hawk lazily circled the pinkish-red sandstone mesa, riding the hot, late afternoon thermals that pushed upward from the sunbaked desert floor far below. The feathers on the bird of prey's underside were pale, as if bleached by the desert sun's relentless presence in this desolate landscape. The bird's sharp eyes searched for movement below. Other than insects, it hadn't caught anything since the early morning and was now getting hungry. A vague, almost indistinct road meandered its way across the valley's floor toward the ancient rock sentinel that the hawk continued to circle as it looked for its evening meal. To the west, the blood red orb of the sun began to sink behind a low-lying purplish mountain range.

Off in the distance, the hawk's eye caught a flash of reflected light. A plume of dust followed a dirty and dust covered sandstone colored Ford pickup truck that slowly wound its way across the desert floor toward the mesa's rock-strewn base. The alert hawk followed the truck's lurching movements as it slowed for numerous potholes in the barely discernable dirt road and crawled across the sand beds of several dry arroyos.

An older gray-haired man in his late sixties with a deep tan wearing a dirty white shirt, his left arm hanging onto the driver's side mirror, slowly guided the rusty vehicle to the foot of the mesa where the road petered out. Killing the motor, he steered the Ford FWD 250 to a stop as rocks crunched underneath its new Michelin tires. In front of him was the lone sandstone pinnacle—in the Southwest it was sometimes referred to as a hoodoo. Except, this rock tower looked more like a Greek Ionic column than a hoodoo. The hawk had been circling this column when it first espied his approach. About two feet in diameter, the stone pillar rose to a height of about a hundred feet and, indeed, stood as an unmistakable sentinel.

The man opened the door, which protested loudly in the form of a high-pitched squeak the farther out he pushed it. Climbing out of the truck, he turned, reached back inside onto the front seat and grabbed a sweat stained straw hat that he pushed down onto his head. He ambled a few paces away from the older model Ford where he stood and relieved himself on a nearby bush.

Walking to the back of the truck, he unlatched the tailgate. It dropped with a resounding thud in the late afternoon silence. Sitting on the tailgate, the grey-haired man pulled a Marlboro cigarette from his shirt pocket, lit it, and inhaled deeply. A thermal updraft caught the smoke and whisked it skyward dissipating it within seconds. Finishing the cigarette, the man flicked the butt off into a cairn of nearby rocks that someone had gathered at some point in the distant past. He glanced at his watch. It was close to six o'clock as the blood red sun began to drop in the eggshell blue western sky. A shadow crossed the ground in front of him. Looking up, he saw the hawk circling above where he was sitting.

The hawk, curious as to what the human beneath him was doing, circled lower to investigate. He saw the man look up. For a millisecond their eyes locked on each other, then the red-feathered bird caught an updraft and, in a matter of seconds, was lifted several hundred feet higher until he was nothing more than a speck in the sky. The man stared at the vanishing bird and consulted his watch again. In three days' time, at about this hour, he would learn if his research was correct.

John Upshur Rushton was a history professor at a small church-affiliated university in Virginia's Shenandoah Valley, which is sometimes referred to as the breadbasket of the Confederacy, as it was an exceedingly fertile area. His father, John Sr., had been a medical doctor—a pathologist. Their middle names reflected that of a far distant cousin, Secretary of State Abel P. Upshur, who had died on February 28, 1844, during a pleasure cruise for dignitaries up and down the Potomac River, outside of Washington, D.C., on the Navy ship, *USS Princeton*. President John Tyler was also on board with former First Lady Dolley Madison and four hundred other guests.[14]

The captain of the *Princeton*, Robert F. Stockton, to please and impress his important guests, was demonstrating the ship's two largest cannons which he had designed, when the one known as

---

[14] "USS Princeton (1843)," Wikipedia, last modified July 10, 2022, https://en.wikipedia.org/wiki/USS_Princeton (1843).

the "Peacemaker," built in Liverpool, England, exploded killing Upshur, along with Secretary of the Navy Thomas Walker Gilmer and four others.[15]

Between sixteen and twenty people were injured, including Stockton and Senator Thomas Hart Benton. This calamitous disaster killed more U.S. government officials in a single day than any other catastrophe in American history. Fortunately, Tyler, along with most of his guests, was below deck when the explosion came and was not hurt.[16]

Lying on his deathbed in 1994, John Sr. related to his son a disjointed and somewhat incredible—almost unimaginable—story. It was so fantastic that, at first, John almost didn't believe the old man. John Sr. had to have been delirious. But then, hours from dying, the suddenly lucid old man swore to John that he was telling the truth.

Many years before, the old man related to John Jr. that he had performed an autopsy on a strange alien type being. He told John Jr. that in late June of 1947, two years after John had been born, there had been some newspaper stories about a civilian pilot, Kenneth Arnold, who had seen "Flying Saucers" on June 24, 1947, while flying near Mount Rainier. This preposterous tale became the origin for the UFO craze across the U.S.[17]

Meanwhile, John Sr. said, "Three weeks earlier on June 14, 1947, a rancher, W. W. "Mac" Brazel, who lived on his remote ranch with no phone or radio, outside of Corona, New Mexico—a small town of less than five hundred souls—had recovered unidentifiable debris scattered over a square mile of his ranch. It consisted of tinfoil, rubber strips, and thin wooden sticks."[18]

---

[15] Ibid.

[16] Ibid.

[17] "Kenneth Arnold UFO Sighting," Wikipedia, last modified June 25, 2022, Https:// en.wikipedia.org/wiki/Kenneth_Arnold_UFO_sighting.

[18] Webster, Donovan. "In 1947, A High-Altitude Balloon Crash Landed in Roswell. The Aliens Never Left." Smithsonian Magazine. July 5, 2017.

"Brazel," John Sr. continued, "took his find to the Roswell sheriff, who, in turn, contacted the Roswell Army Air Field (RAAF), which assigned Major Jesse Marcel, an intelligence officer, to inspect the 'crash' site. This turned out to be the origin of what later became known as the 'Roswell Incident'," his father explained as he coughed. "In early July," the dying man haltingly continued, "Brazel led the major and the sheriff to his ranch where they gathered up more pieces of the mysterious debris. In a July 8, 1947, military press release," John Sr. further related to his son as his voice started to give way and his breaths came in gasps, "it was stated that personnel from the 509th Operations Group, based at the RAAF, had recovered a 'flying saucer,' which," his father grunted, "had landed on a ranch near Roswell."[19]

With a death rattling gasp, John Sr. said, "Eventually, the military mysteriously backpedaled and the War Department debunked the story by stating it had identified the debris as that of a 'weather balloon,' but by that time, the news was out leading to myriad UFO stories that a flying saucer had been found near Roswell. A small city of thirty-one thousand people in 1947, Roswell saw a chance to put its name on the map and started hyping up the news of an alien spaceship, quickly expropriating the story for their own," John Sr. coughed and laughed, "despite the fact that Corona was located ninety miles northwest of Roswell!"[20]

The old man, who had been working at the University of Chicago's medical school, was a well-known and respected forensic scientist with an international reputation. "Out of the blue," John Sr. rasped, "an FBI agent knocked on my office door late one afternoon and informed me that my expertise was needed for a top secret government project."

---

[19] Webster, Donovan. "In 1947, A High-Altitude Balloon Crash Landed in Roswell. The Aliens Never Left." Smithsonian Magazine. July 5, 2017.

[20] "Roswell Incident." Encyclopedia Britannica (Encyclopedia Britannica, inc.), accessed July 1, 2021, https://www.britannica.com/event/Roswell-incident.

"Would you be interested?" the agent inquired.

"Of course!" the old man had heartedly replied. After signing an oath of secrecy, John Sr. told his son, "I was escorted by the FBI agent and flown to Los Alamos, New Mexico, on a private and unmarked U.S. government plane." The dying man paused and then told his son, "I met with two other men in my field—Irvin Westaway and Martin Isaacs, both of whom I already knew. Like me, the others were also sworn to secrecy."

Changing into medical attire, the three men were led to a windowless refrigerated room where a badly mangled, half-burnt body lay on a stainless steel operating table. "The creature, and indeed it was once some sort of living being," John Sr. declared forcefully in his dying voice, "was not like anything we three men had ever encountered before in our lives. It had a huge bulging head with large sunken eyes. The internal organs, we agreed, were nothing like any humanoid or animal we had ever seen in any of our forensic research." The being, John's father told him, had been dressed in some sort of wire-like clothing that had, apparently, at one time, enclosed the alien's entire body like a cocoon. They used wire cutters to strip the thing.

"As we cut the being's clothing off," the dying man related, "a small round flat object fell out of the sleeve I was removing with my wire cutters. It fell onto the table. Without thinking, I picked it up and slipped it into my pocket, reminding myself to leave it with the alien's clothes once we cut them off and set them aside. After removing the clothing, we put the remnants on a nearby shelf. I became so absorbed in dissecting this creature and the subsequent autopsy that I totally forgot about the object."

The old man paused, coughed, and then continued. "After the autopsy, they told us to shower. As I stripped off my clothes, which they told us would be incinerated to prevent any contamination we might have picked up, I felt the object in my pocket. I took it out and scrutinized the round silvery medal. It was about the size of a silver dollar, but not as thick. It was smooth on both sides. I decided to keep it as a memento and secreted it in a side pocket of my vest. When I returned home, I waited until I was alone in my office to further examine the object."

John Sr. paused at this point. His breathing came in half gasps as the cancer prepared to make its final assault. He told John Jr. where he had hidden the object all these years—in some hollowed out pages of a well-worn copy of H. G. Wells' *The Invisible Man.* "Look for it after I'm gone," he instructed his son.

"For years, I've wondered what this silver object was—what clues it might have held to the dead creature's origin," the dying man continued. "I kept it at home. Every so often, I would take it out, rub it, and look for a hidden spring—all to no avail. Then, one afternoon, while sitting at my desk, I dozed off—accidentally leaving the coin on my desktop. By that time," he wheezed then a violent coughing spell that lasted for over forty seconds seized him before he could continue, "I had come to call the silver disc a coin for lack of a better term."

John Sr. coughed several more times before resuming his almost unbelievable tale, "When I awoke about an hour later, as the setting sun stretched its light across the top of my desk, the silver object was glowing. I looked down at it and could see some type of writing. There were three sentences on the upturned face—the first one in a language with symbols I never was able to decipher. It may have been the being's own language. The second sentence was in English and the third in Spanish."

The old man gave off some deep hacks as the cancer now had him in a final death grip. "Fearing the lines might quickly vanish," he continued, "I copied them down. After deciphering the last sentence, I moved the silver disc out of the sunlight and the writing quickly disappeared. Placing the disc back into the sunlight, the writing slowly materialized, but this time the second set of three sentences was completely different! I, again, copied each line down. I realized the second set of inscriptions were in three different languages—German, Russian, and Chinese. On my third try, the original inscriptions reappeared."

"I had found what appeared to be something akin to the Rosetta Stone from 196 B.C., which had been discovered in 1799 by a French officer during Napoleon's campaign in Egypt. Later on," the old man continued, "I realized each line duplicated the English inscription."

At this point, the old man was racked by a terrible coughing spell. When he was able to continue, his voice was hoarse. "John," he said, "I don't have much time now. Listen closely. I flipped the shiny disc over and left the other side in the dying sunlight. Figures and symbols I didn't recognize materialized. I copied them down and moved the disc out of the sunlight, but the same figures reappeared. Over the years, I took the disc out and laid it in the sunlight, and the same symbols always materialized."

"What was the translation, Dad?" John had asked.

"I put the translations inside the binding of Paul Wellman's book, *Glory, God, and Gold*," the old man uttered just before he sunk into a final coma. Several weeks after the old man's death in late 1994, John searched for both books. Wellman's was easy to find among a separate collection of Western histories, but John had to search for a few days before locating *The Invisible Man*, which his father had stashed on a shelf behind some medical books. Opening the paperback novel, he found the smooth silver object tightly embedded in a hole his father had cut out of the book's pages.

John remembered the first time he opened the tightly folded paper he had pulled from the binding of Wellman's book. The first sentence read "113/25/18Δ36/30/41Δ221Δ1922." The second sentence read as follows: "Every 5 annuals only during a full moon." The last sentence read, "Use reverse, reflect moon, & transmit from August 8, 1956, onward."

John puzzled over the meaning of the three sentences for several months. Then he put the cryptic paper aside as more important things intruded, especially teaching with all its attendant problems and demands. Somehow, the years flew by without his contemplating the silver disc and its meaning. In 2010, he retired from teaching Asian history at the university and moved to Elkton, Virginia, a small town of some 2,800 people that nestled on the western edge of the Blue Ridge Mountain chain. After settling in, he had more time to complete projects that he'd put off for many years. He resurrected the coin from the book where it had been hidden and the mysterious paper notations his father had made.

For months John puzzled over the meaning of the first sentence. The other two sentences seemed fairly easy to decipher. He believed the second meant every five years when there was a full moon, while the third directed the silver disc's owner to use the other side as a sort of a signal. But what on earth did the figures in first sentence mean? It had to be a location of some sorts.

But where? Where? he wondered. On numerous occasions he placed the coin in direct sunlight and reread the first sentence over and over to make sure his father had indeed copied down the correct message.

Finally, during an exceptionally warm spring day, he casually asked one of his friends, who sailed a lot not only on the Chesapeake Bay but also took the intercoastal waterway south to Florida and then on into the Caribbean, how a person could locate a specific place on Earth? John received an instant lesson in longitude and latitude. Bingo! He immediately realized what the first part of the sentence meant! Half of the line was solved—113/25/18 meant 113 degrees, 25 minutes, 18 seconds longitude and the other figure, 36/30/41, stood for a latitude location.

Later on that afternoon he drove over to the university library, a beautiful brick faced building with a high bell tower that overlooked a serene lake. Locating an atlas there, John looked up the coördinates. It appeared the place was located in the remote northwestern corner of Mohave County, Arizona. From his historical research during his graduate student days, John knew he would be able to pinpoint the area much more accurately with a U.S. Geological Survey (USGS) map. Going to the government documents section of the library, he soon found an address and telephone number for the USGS in Washington. He figured he would call them in a few days and find out how much it would cost to get a USGS map for that section of Arizona.

Yet, he had only solved half of the top line's puzzling numbers. John pondered over what the 221 and the 1922 figures represented. Several weeks passed. He failed to decipher the riddle. Then one morning in May, John was flipping through his Day Timer appointment book when figures at the top of the page for May 16 suddenly jumped out at him. The line read 136th Day, 229 Days left.

He walked back to his home office and entered the small but tidily organized room. John quickly went to his desk and sat down. Pulling out a drawer on the lower right side of the roll-top where he kept his year's supply of Day Timers, John removed the August booklet from its small gray plastic storage case and flipped to August 8. It said 220th Day, 145 Days left. "Damn!" John groaned. He thought he'd solved the riddle, but a cloud of gloom settled over him. Then it hit him—of course! Leap year! He flipped open his Day Timers. Inside the front cover there were always three years displayed. He found that in two years' time there would be a leap year and counted the days until August 8. It was the 221st day!

The 1922 figure, John realized, had to be the time. Vaguely, in the back of his mind, he remembered that the military used some sort of different time, but he couldn't remember exactly how they did it. He pulled out his campus phone book and looked up the chairman of the ROTC department. Colonel Theodore Archibald Kingman was more than happy to tell him how the military timetable worked. Each day, the Colonel explained, was divided into hours in terms of 100s starting at midnight. One in the morning was 0100 hours. So, in civilian terms, 1922 would be 7:22 p.m.

At last the puzzle was solved, or at least John thought he had correctly decoded the first sentence. *Now all I have to do*, he thought, *is find out when there's a full moon every five years from August 8, 1956, onward and which one of those years is a leap year.* Using the library's facilities, John learned that only one past date matched the required time. It occurred in 1976. The next date would be in 2012. *I have two years to prepare*, he thought pensively.

After eight months, John started making plans and preparations for his trip to the Arizona Triangle, as that part of the state was nicknamed. He needed camping equipment and supplies. Leaving early one morning, he took Route 33 East passing over the 2,365-foot Swift Run Gap in the Blue Ridge Mountains, drove through Stanardsville, the county seat of Greene County, and, after several miles, soon connected with Route 29 South, which he followed into Charlottesville.

He quickly located Blue Ridge Outdoors, a business that catered to campers, canoers, and kayakers. He purchased a significant amount of outdoor equipment—a North Face tent, both a Coleman stove and two lanterns, MREs (Meals Ready to Eat), ropes, multiple two-gallon water containers and a 100-quart Igloo ice chest. Once home with his purchases and supplies, he called L. L. Bean and ordered a pair of GORE-TEX hiking boots and a flannel sleeping bag good to forty degrees. He knew he didn't have to worry about cold nights. Where he was going, he would be lucky if the temperatures dropped below a hundred during the hot August nights he would encounter.

The next day, John ordered survey maps from the USGS for the entire northwestern area of Arizona, plus Utah and Arizona state road maps, which he obtained via each state's Board of Tourism. With the help of AAA, he mapped every stop along the way where camping was allowed.

Finally, six months before his departure for Arizona, he took his truck to his favorite garage repair shop in Harrisonburg, where he talked to his friend Randy Timberlake, the businesses owner, proprietor, and chief bottlewasher of the car repair business.

"Randy, I'm going to need a full rehab of my truck," he told the mechanic. "I'm headed out west to Arizona and will be going on some unpaved roads or trails out in the middle of bumf*ck nowhere. Keep it as long as you need and replace or repair anything you find. I sure as hell don't want to break down in the middle of a desert," he smiled and chuckled, "and not be found until the crows and varmints have picked my carcass dry." Both men laughed.

Randy assured John that, by the time he finished with it, John would have an almost new vehicle. "Plus, John," he added, "I think you ought to have it repainted. That way we can sand down the metal and fill in all of the rust spots."

John agreed by nodding his head vigorously while Randy was speaking and gave him a thumbs up.

"Now, what color do you want? The original or what?" Randy asked.

"Let's go with a sandstone design. That way it'll blend into the southwestern terrain where it'll be difficult for anyone to spot me," John replied.

Six weeks later Randy called John and told him to come get his newly rehabbed pickup truck. John called an Uber, which picked him up within a short time and drove him to Harrisonburg. Arriving at the shop, he saw his Ford, now painted with colors to match the desert hues. *Hmmm*, he thought rather gleefully, *that's gonna be great camouflage!*

John left Elkton on July 15, on what would have been his mother's 103rd birthday had she lived that long, but, unfortunately, she died of cancer when John was only six years old. He wanted to take his time crossing the country to arrive at the "purported" site no less than three-to-five days ahead of time. He headed south on I-81 through the Shenandoah Valley. When he reached Lexington, John exited onto I-64 West, which was a straight shot to St. Louis, where it terminated. He then shifted over to I-44, heading southwest until he picked up turnpikes in Oklahoma, leading him to Oklahoma City where he easily hopped onto I-40 West.

From there John headed directly west until he arrived in Amarillo, Texas where, at Exit 75, he took the off ramp to have dinner at The Big Texan—a world-famous restaurant with a nationwide reputation for its seventy-two-ounce steak challenge. If a customer accepted the steak challenge, he had to eat a seventy-two-ounce steak plus a shrimp cocktail, baked potato, salad, with a roll and butter—all within one hour! The challengers paid a hundred dollars up front. If the customer won, the Big Texan refunded their money. If he failed to complete the challenge however, he owed the Big Texan seventy-two dollars. The challengers sat at one of six tables, which rested on a raised eight inch high twenty-by-twenty-foot platform area above the main dining floor. On the wall above to the tables was a large time clock for each separate challenger.

John was seated on the six-foot wide second floor which wound around the open main floor level, giving every customer a view overlooking the challenge area. As John took his seat, he observed one customer taking the challenge who had about seventeen minutes left on his clock. *That guy's not going to make it*, John thought. Two more men, who were the size of pro football players, accepted the challenge and were seated. John lingered over his meal while he eyed the two newcomers. When one of the men won the challenge in thirty-four minutes, John paid his check and left. Time to hit the road again. The Big Texan had been a nice interval.

After spending the night in Amarillo, John headed west on I-40 through northern New Mexico and Arizona. He stopped for the night in Winslow, Arizona, where he had made a prior reservation for one night's stay at the well-known posh La Posada Hotel. After having an absolutely fabulous dinner that evening, followed by a scrumptious breakfast the next morning, he hit the road west again. Continuing on I-40 to Williams, Arizona, he left the interstate and took Route 93 north to Las Vegas. Spending the night in Vegas without gambling a cent, he headed north on I-15. More than two hours later, he entered the spectacular Virgin River Corridor.

Most of the northwestern corner of Arizona is an extremely remote, narrow, deep, and mostly uninhabited gorge carved during millennia by the fifteen-mile passage of the Virgin River. It was so rugged that travel through it either by horse or on foot was nearly impossible. Yet, over nine years, from 1964 to 1973, construction crews labored to complete Interstate 15, which curved and twisted along the river's steep slopes for twenty-nine miles from the Nevada to Utah state lines. The Arizona Department of Transportation had to reroute the Virgin River twelve times to fit the highway design. That section of highway is now called the Virgin River Corridor. To that date it had been the most expensive rural interstate construction project in the U.S.[21]

---

[21] Herrmann, Tom and Wegner, Grant. "Road Trip: The I-15 Virgin River Corridor is a hidden engineering marvel." ADOT. July 12, 2022.

The steep incline and curved road through the gorge amazed him by the engineering feats that it had taken to carve the highway through this inhospitable rock terrain with cliffs rising straight up for hundreds of feet alongside the pavement. He noticed that at the bottom of most cliffs, there was a six-foot-high mesh wire fence, which had been erected to catch any "small" rocks that occasionally tumbled off from the high escarpments. The ever-winding uphill road of the Virgin River Corridor had some splendid sights, most of which John missed because he was focused on the road to avoid ending up in the river gorge below off to his right.

As he climbed upward, John realized this section of road had to be extremely dangerous for the hundreds of eighteen-wheeler drivers who used the highway every day on their way to and from either Salt Lake City or Las Vegas. If their brakes failed, there was nowhere to pullover and, most likely, they would eventually end up in the gorge—not a fate anyone wanted to see or happen. This was, indeed, John concluded, an extremely dangerous section of highway. After a quick forty minutes, John emerged from the gorge, leveled off, and headed into St. George, Utah, where he found a motel and spent the night.

The next morning John rose early, found a nearby Waffle House restaurant, and ate a hasty breakfast. Fortuitously, next to the restaurant was a Circle K gas station with a Quik Stop store. After filling his tank, he entered the Quik Stop and purchased six ten-pound bags of ice, which he poured into the Igloo ice chest he had purchased back in Virginia. When the ice chest was two-thirds full, he loaded Cokes, Sprites, and other sodas he purchased in the Quik Stop on the top of the ice. After that brief stop, he took I-15 South for four miles, until he could exit onto Route 7 East where the Port of Entry Utah tourist center was located. Stopping at the tourist center, John picked up a few maps and pamphlets.

Continuing a few more miles on Route 7, John saw the entrance to the newly constructed St. George Airport, which had just opened the year before in 2011, as a replacement for a much smaller land locked airport that had originally been located atop a mesa in the middle of St. George. To kick off the inauguration of the airport, St. George had arranged for an air show by the Navy's Blue Angels. According to one of the leaflets he picked up at the tourist center, the show had been spectacular.

"Wish I'd seen that show," John mused aloud. "It must have been an amazing sight for the spectators when the blue jets popped up from behind the various mesas which dot the airport's surrounding landscape."

Soon after the turnoff to the airport, John found the exit to County Highway 5, a rugged unpaved road with a faded and peeling U.S. Forestry Service sign with what had once proclaimed in now almost indistinct green letters the route to both the Grand Canyon-Parashant Monument and the north rim of the Grand Canyon National Park. Turning onto the dirt road, John headed south into the desolate Arizona Triangle. Driving slowly and carefully on the dirt packed road, it took John almost two hours before he arrived at the intersection of County Road 103.

At the intersection, John pulled off to the side and parked. Like Highway 5, Country Road 103 was another unpaved road heading off to the southwest where, eventually, as John saw on his USGS map, it ended up at the north rim of the Grand Canyon. As he exited his truck to take a stretch and relieve his bladder he noticed a faded sign with an arrow pointing to the east which indicated that the massif to his left was Diamond Butte with an elevation of 6,325 feet.

Well, he thought, *I'm almost there*. He took out his portable GPS (Global Positioning System), opened it up, and switched it on. He had previously preset the final coördinates into the instrument. The reading indicated that he had a few more miles to go on 103 before he reached a right hand turnoff leading in a northwesterly direction. Leaning against the side of the Ford, John sipped on a Sprite, which he'd pulled out of a small ice chest that he kept on the front seat. It was August 5. "Only three more days," he chuckled aloud to himself, "until I find out whether or not I've been on a wild goose chase or not."

Taking his time as he headed down the poorly maintained southwesterly artery, with the USGS map next to him, John slowly drove down the unpaved 103 roadway for several miles until he found an unmarked turnoff on the right side of the dusty and seldom traveled road. He stopped again, fired up his GPS and saw that he was headed in the right direction.

The going was exceedingly difficult, but his 4WD Ford was able to handle the rocky and bumpy terrain. The track was deeply rutted from years of windblown erosion and the occasional rare flash floods that swept across the arid sunbaked desert. Every so often, the road followed an arroyo for a few hundred yards before climbing out. Fortunately, at some time in the past, someone had delineated the sides of the faint track across the various arroyos with four-or-five-foot pieces of rebar, each surrounded at the bottom by a two-to-three-foot cairn of rocks.

At several of the dry gulches, John had to exit his truck and move large branches which had been deposited on the faint track during the rare floods that filled the arroyos. At every few miles, he paused and checked his GPS. Finally, in the distance he saw his destination, a mesa with a rock sandstone column rising from the desert floor next to it. It took him another hour to reach his objective before he pulled to a stop with the ancient sandstone monolith towering over the front of his truck. It was now late afternoon.

At the bottom of the red sandstone sentinel was a small scree slope, where, over millennia, rubble had clipped off the column. After finishing his cigarette and drinking a soda, he rested for several minutes before deciding to walk around the monolith. *Well,* he thought, as he circumvented the pillar, *this certainly would be a place and marker for what, I hope, will happen in three days' time.* Upon completing his inspection of the upright monument and because the blood red sun was beginning to set in the west behind the purplish mountain range, he decided he should set up camp. Looking around, he espied a slight overhang about fifty yards away on the side of the sandstone mesa that loomed up before him.

Great place for my camp! he thought.

After moving his Ford over to the camping spot he chose, John began to unpack and set up camp. After smoothing out a sleeping area, he erected his two-person sized North Face tent. Next, he toted out both his Coleman lantern and stove along with the Igloo ice chest. Using the ice chest as a table, he placed his stove on top of it. After unloading his other camping paraphernalia and setting it up, he started building his fire pit.

Surrounding and scattered around the overhang area were a plethora of five-to-ten-pound sandstone rocks that, over hundreds of thousands of years, had spalled off the mesa's sides due to the rare rains and snow that had dropped and collected into the mesa's small cracks and crevices. During the winter, any remaining water that hadn't evaporated would freeze and expand causing further cracks. Because sandstone is somewhat porous and fragile, the expanding ice would, from time to time, pop off a piece of stone, or talus, which then tumbled down to the ground below.

Having established his campsite, John decided to fix a quick dinner from the MREs he purchased in Charlottesville. He had plenty of water to boil because while at Blue Ridge Outdoors he'd purchased five two-gallon water containers. In the desert, you can never have enough water. Plus, he also had water from the melting ice in his Igloo chest. Although he had planned to be here three or four days at the most, John realized that being in a forbidding and arid climate meant he needed to keep his body hydrated.

He spent August 6 and 7 exploring the area around the sandstone sentinel. On the afternoon of August 7, about two hundred yards from his campsite, he discovered a pathway leading up to the top of the mesa. The pathway was probably made over time by migrating animals, such as mule deer, antelopes, or coyotes. Taking the track, John found that it wound back and forth for several hundred yards until he emerged on the top of the mesa after an easy fifteen-minute climb.

From his highpoint position on the mesa's flat tabletop, he could see for seventy-five or a hundred miles in all directions, and, looking downward, he observed that his campsite lay directly below. As he took his time revolving in a complete circle, taking stock of his surroundings, John noticed the top of the sandstone column was only several feet higher. And a red-tailed hawk was perched on top of it looking directly at him from approximately two hundred feet.

"I wonder," John said aloud to himself, "if the hawk is some sort of omen, or, maybe, a guardian spirit?" At this point, John was not about to discount anything he encountered or experienced. He hoped and prayed that he had correctly deciphered the silver disc.

No sooner had John spoken than the hawk rose off the top of the column and began to circle it in ever widening loops until it varied from its flight and hovered directly over him. The changing updraft from the desert floor caused the red tail to float up and down with the wind like a rowboat bobbing in the water. But, ever so slowly, the hawk began to drop closer and closer to John who continued to look up at it as it quietly descended. John eyed the red-tail's cautious descent with some wariness and awe. *I wonder*, he thought, *if I extend my arm out … maybe he'll land on it?*

So, he slowly stretched his arm out parallel to the top of the mesa. The red tail continued dropping and then, with a quick flourish of its wings, settled on John's arm. John intuitively knew something he could not fathom was happening. The hawk's talons gripped his arm for balance, but not too tightly, and stared into John's eyes before chirping, "Kee! Kee! Kee!" John stared back and raised his outstretched arm ever so slowly. The feathered animal quickly moved down his arm until it perched on his right shoulder. After a few minutes, John decided to see if the hawk would stay on his shoulder while he walked around the mesa's flat top.

"Well, my friend," John uttered, "shall we walk around the mesa?" John suddenly thought, with some amusement, *What am I doing talking to a hawk?* He then wondered aloud, "I must be going gaga!"

The red-tail gave a high-pitched sound—"Kee! Kee! Kee!" Taking that as a positive answer—or an agreement that he was, indeed, loco—John ambled around and explored the mesa's top. After a few minutes, he found a small cairn of sandstone rocks, about five to six inches high. *That's interesting*, he thought. *I'll have to check that cairn's location with my GPS.* Every so often he would stop, pause, and look into the hawk's eyes which always turned its head and stared directly back into John's eyes. After fifteen or twenty minutes, John decided to return down the pathway to his campsite.

"I'm going back down now to my campsite," John said aloud before taking a swig of water from his water bottle, which had hung from his belt. Next, he poured a small amount into the palm of his left hand and slowly offered it to the hawk. With no hesitation, the red tail sipped at the water until it was almost gone. Lowering his hand, John started to descend the pathway while the bird sat contentedly on his shoulder all the way down until he reached his campsite. John sat on the Ford's tailgate with the bird still perched on his shoulder and gulped down the remaining liquid in his water bottle. As soon as he poured the last sip of water down his throat, without warning, the bird stretched its wings, let go its grip on his shoulder, gave a "Kee! Kee! Kee!" sound then rose several feet into the air before it caught an updraft and slowly rose before it dashed off out of sight over the mesa's top.

"Had to be some sort of an omen," John muttered to himself, "or guardian spirit. I think this definitely has something to do with the coin." Sliding off the tailgate, he walked to the passenger side of his truck, opened the door, reached in, and retrieved his GPS. After turning it on, he input the coordinates of the mysterious silver disc, which he had pulled out of his pocket and turned toward the setting sun to double check his memory, as to what he had discovered. The machine showed that the exact position he wanted was on top of the mesa he had just explored with the red-tailed hawk.

That evening, as he ate another MRE for his supper and sipped on a soda, John reflected on both his discovery from the information contained on the silver disc and on the story his father had related on his deathbed. He was excited—and nervous—at what unknown experience might possibly await him on the morrow. *Surely,* he thought, *the red-tailed hawk had some part to play. But what part? Was it a harbinger of what might or might not happen tomorrow?*

In mythology, John remembered, hawks were associated with the sun gods. From historical research during his teaching years, he recalled that in ancient Egypt they were deemed royal birds. From Greek mythology, John also had a vague recollection that they were related to the goddess and enchantress, Circe, who had a vast knowledge of herbs and magic potions and had lived with, and bore children by, the mythical figure Ulysses. He also mulled over the fact that hawks were also messengers for the sun god Apollo, who just happened to be the god of oracles.

John began to ponder his situation. He had a lot of unanswered questions. Was the red-tailed hawk going to lead him somewhere tomorrow? Was the hawk magical—or somehow an oracle? What connection did it have to the silver disc? Or was there any connection? Was he going to encounter some sort of god or alien? Or was this trip totally in vain? Was anything really going to happen tomorrow evening at 7:22? John knew that he needed sleep. Plus, he wanted to wake around 5:00 in the morning so he'd have a full day to prepare for the unknown tomorrow evening.

His sleep that night was fitful. John kept awakening and falling back to sleep due to his anticipation as to what might, or might not, happen on the evening of August 8. Finally, after a night of intermittent sleep, he arose at 4:30 in the morning. After preparing a quick breakfast and having several cups of coffee, he sat down on the Igloo container with his small memo book and listed everything he might need while on top of the mesa: the GPS, two two-gallon water containers, a lightweight jacket for the evening chill, camera, and about ten other items.

After checking over his list several times, John decided he would have to make at least two trips to the top of the mesa. Since it was still cool in the early morning, as the sun began its ascent over the eastern horizon, he decided to bring the heavier items, such as water, on his first trip. Arriving on top of the mesa, John found a small niche where he could place the two water containers out of the direct sunlight. During the coming day, it would be hot on the mesa's tabletop and the water, although shaded, would warm up considerably. But, at least, he would have it close by in case he needed it.

After his first trip to the mesa's tabletop to stash the heavier items, John spent the rest of the morning tidying up his campsite and packing items in the truck that he no longer needed. Whatever happens tonight, I'll leave at first light in the morning, he thought.

Or, maybe, he surmised grimly, *if what I think might happen, perhaps, due to unforeseen circumstances, I won't even be alive to return to Virginia. After all, I'm so far off the grid here, if I'm badly hurt or injured—or dead—no one's gonna find my bones—or my sandstone camouflaged truck—for years.* He nonchalantly shrugged, as he continued to think, *Well, it's not like I have a wife or kids that I'd be leaving in the lurch.*

The day was unusually warm. According to the temperature reading on his GPS, the land heated up to 110 degrees by noon and hit 125 degrees in the late afternoon. Underneath the overhang, he relaxed and read a biographical history book—*The Kool-Aid Kid*—by a local Charlottesville author detailing the man's combat experiences as a medic in Vietnam. He always enjoyed reading about people's personal experiences during various and sundry wars. In particular, Bernard Fall's Vietnam books, especially *Hell in A Very Small Place*, detailing the 1954 French defeat at Điên Biên Phù, were rather appealing to John's desire to learn more about certain historical events.

Around 5:30, the late afternoon oppressive August heat began to abate. Closing his book, he thought, *Well, I'd better be going.* Standing, he checked his vest pocket to ensure the silver disc was still there. Off to the west he could see some dark gray clouds marching slowly toward him. *Hmmm,* he thought, *I sure hope there's no lightning in those clouds—not much cover up on top of the mesa.* Gathering up the rest of the items he planned to take to the tabletop above, he started out toward the path. After six or seven minutes he arrived at the starting point of the upward switchback path.

No sooner had John taken his first step onto the trail than he heard a loud "Kee! Kee! Kee!" The hawk's trill echoed over him and he quickly glanced upward. The red tail was landing on the stone monolith that had overshadowed his camp these past few days.

Well, I guess I don't have to worry, John thought, *my guardian hawk is back—if it is a guardian and not an ominous spirit bent on doing anything evil to me!* He started his ascent and wondered what might happen at 7:22, or was he just on a wild goose chase?

As John stepped onto the stone tabletop, he could see the dark purplish clouds off in the distance as they leisurely marched toward the mesa. *So far, so good,* John thought as he didn't see any lightning bolts coming out of the approaching darkness. He checked his watch. It was 6:16. Only 66 minutes to go. Now, he realized, isn't that a kind of coincidence? Not exactly a good number. Almost the mark of the beast—666. Hmmm, wonder why my arrival just happened to be at precisely this time? Is this another omen? As he dug into his side pocket and brought the GPS out, he heard an almost imperceptible rush of feathers before the red-tailed hawk landed on his right shoulder.

"Well, hello again, old friend," John commented as he reached up and stroked the bird's back. "Good to see you!"

"Kee! Kee! Kee!" The hawk replied.

"Well," he said aloud, "surely that must be a good sign—at least I hope it is!"

"I'm checking my GPS to precisely locate the coördinates," John informed the bird perched on his shoulder. The bird just stared at him but bobbed its head twice as if it actually understood him. John shook his head back and forth thinking, *Here I go again, talking to the bird. I really must be senile. Geeze!*

It took seconds for the GPS to identify his position and show the precise location of the longitude and latitude point he was searching for. It led John directly to the small rock cairn he had discovered the prior day. Nearby was a small low rock outcropping in the shape of a seat, that John decided to use as his viewpoint.

He walked over to the covered niche where he'd stored the water, and brought one bottle over to the stone bench, which was about 25 feet away from the cairn. Sitting down, he realized he could still see the top of the stone column that the red tail used as a perch. *Was the pinnacle some sort of mysterious lookout for the bird? Or was it a navigation point for what might happen at 7:22?*

The time seemed to inch along. The dark purple cloud soon hung over the mesa as wind from the west picked up and blew it eastward. John took out the silver disc and rubbed it. Nothing. *Well, what did I expect it to do?* he thought. *After all, with the cloud overhead, there's no sun to bring out the writing or the numbers.* The hawk bent down and tapped the coin with its beak. Suddenly, the numbers and writing materialized! John was momentarily startled and almost jumped up.

What in the hell is going on? he asked himself. *Okay,* he realized, *the bird either knows something or is part of something!* John quickly checked his watch: 7:07, only fifteen minutes to go … until what? Sitting back, he tried to remain calm, but, inside, John's stomach was churning. He could feel sweat pouring down both his face and armpits. John couldn't decide if he was nervous or in the beginnings of panic mode. *Calm down,* he kept repeating to himself, *what happens, will happen!*

Placing the silver disc on his thigh, John took a large swig of water. Next, he poured some into his left palm and proffered it to the hawk, which leaned down and, in a few seconds, sipped up every single drop. Replacing the top to the water container, John picked up the coin resting on his leg and kept it in his hand. According to the disc's instructions he was supposed to use it to reflect the moon, when, or if, something happened.

The cloud seemed to have suddenly stopped directly over the mesa. John glanced up at it. It appeared to him that the entire misty mass had, indeed, frozen in place in the night sky and was now simply hovering in position over the mesa. *That's strange,* John thought. *Wonder what that means?* He wiped the sweat from his face, glanced at his watch. It was 7:21. The hovering cloud mysteriously opened, like the lens of an old camera, and allowed the moon to quickly emerge through a small round opening. Suddenly, he felt the hawk's talons tighten on his shoulder. Remembering the coin's third line about a signal, John held it in his open hand, just in case it emitted some type of invisible and silent transmission—or was it some sort of homing device using the moon's light?

Schroom! A white shaft of light, perhaps two feet in diameter, shot out of another part of the darkened cloud illuminating the top of the sandstone tower surprising John, who involuntarily flinched at the sudden sound and light.

"Kee! Kee! Kee!" The hawk loudly trilled.

Holding the coin in his hand, John stood, remaining as still as he could. He let his eyes do a 270 degree sweep of the area, not taking them away from the spotlight which bathed the top of the sandstone column. He dared not turn to see what was behind him. Anyway, if there was something behind him, he hoped the red tail would give him some sort of warning.

As he stood staring at the illuminated monolith's top, John sensed something as the hair on the back of his neck started to tingle. Holding the coin in his open hand, he took a quick glance back and forth, but couldn't discern anything. He checked his watch. It was 7:22. John glanced over to the cairn. He thought he could see something shimmering over top of it, but it was so indistinct that he was still able to see the desert terrain behind it. Then a faint, almost inaudible, motor-like hum reached his ears. He didn't want to turn away from the cairn but felt compelled to take a quick three-sixty sweep ... but saw nothing! He rapidly turned back to view the cairn area.

Suddenly the heavenly spotlight winked out leaving the sandstone column in semi-darkness. The overhead cloud immediately closed the small hole which the moon had peeked through and totally obscured the lunar light. Then, slowly, the shimmering faded away and John stared in absolute awe at what was materializing right in front of him. It was a ten-foot round silver cylinder about fifty feet tall with a flat top. The overhanging cloud seemed to darken taking away the lustrous shine of the object that had materialized in front of him. He felt the hawk loosen its grip on his shoulder.

"Okay," John muttered to himself, "Am I f*cked bird, or what?"

The red tail gave a muted "Kee! Kee! Kee!" as if muttering to itself.

Despite the slight cooling wind that had sprung up as the cylinder had landed, John could still feel sweat pouring down his face. Pocketing the coin in his vest pocket, which he had tightly held onto for the past few minutes, he decided to sit down on his stone bench and wait.

"Obviously," he spoke aloud, "whoever or whatever is inside knows full well I'm out here. Hmmm ... wonder what's next?"

After several minutes, on the side of the silver cylinder facing him, an invisible three-by-six-foot door whisked silently upward. A set of steps appeared then rolled out and downward to the stone surface below making not a sound as it descended and touched the sandstone rock. As John peered into the ink black space behind the door, he thought he saw some movement.

"John Upshur Rushton, thank you for coming," a voice clearly said from out of the air directly in front of where John was seated.

Shocked at the mysterious voice, he automatically scooted back a few inches on the stone bench. "Give me a few more moments," the voice said, "and I'll be with you shortly."

John sat mesmerized, stunned at what was happening to him, at what he was hearing, seeing, and experiencing. There was nothing logical, he realized, that could explain this phenomenon. "Okay," he said in a low voice to himself, "it's time to suspend reality and just go along with this miracle." Feeling antsy again, he stood. The red tail shifted its weight accordingly.

Several more minutes passed before John saw a nebulous form emerge from the cylinder's door. Vague at first, as it descended the steps, the form took the shape of an ordinary man wearing blue jeans and a loose nondescript green shirt. John felt the red tail lift off from his shoulder. It flew over and landed on the being's shoulder. The alien—what else could it be?—reached up and stroked the hawk's back feathers. Whoever or whatever it was approached John, who stood perfectly still as the man-like being neared. John extended his hand. The man took his hand and lightly shook it.

"I am glad to meet you, John." The being's voice had a slight metallic tinge to it. "My name, despite my appearance, is Mel-El. Please, do not be afraid. I have no intention of harming you. Come, let us sit down and talk a while," Mel-El said as he gestured toward the stone bench. "I am sure you have questions, and I will try to answer what I can."

Both men sat looking at each other. John felt so tongue-tied, he hardly knew what to say or even ask. He was too dumbfounded and wondered if this was just a dream. The red tail shifted its position on Mel-El's shoulder and looked directly at John. A faint light appeared around Mel-El's body as he sat.

"Let me begin," Mel-El offered. "Perhaps I can fill in some of the blanks for you."

John nodded his head saying, "Thank you."

Mel-El continued, "I come from a world that would take your present-day space probes over one hundred thousand years to reach. Our world, in your language, is called Zero57A. After millions of years of development, our technology is far superior to anything you have on this planet. We travel the entire universe looking for other humanoid occupants and developing worlds. Some of those worlds, we have colonized. Others, like yours, we merely watch. We come at set times every so often to take a measure of your development. For short periods of time, we insert members of our planet onto Earth to listen, read, or observe what is happening on your world."

"If I may interrupt, Mel-El," John interjected, "your technology must make ours look as if it's in the Stone Age, so you obviously have the capability to destroy our planet. Am I correct?"

"Yes, we do," Mel-El replied and nodded before continuing. "At this time, however, we have no wish to do so. Yet, we are becoming fearful, as your Earth has developed horrible weapons of mass destruction with your atomic and nuclear warheads. During the past thirty or forty years we have been watching your world more closely and will not, I emphasize, *will not* allow you to destroy either yourselves or this viable planet Earth. We will most likely have to step in and save you from yourselves in your near future."

"Alright," John inquired, "leaving that behind, what can you tell me as to what actually happened in Roswell, New Mexico, over sixty-five years ago? Was that someone from Zero57A?"

"We lost one of our scouts," Mel-El replied. "We are not exactly sure what happened. We suspect some sort of radiation interfered with his ship's navigation system. We now believe it was perhaps from your testing of atomic bombs in Nevada, to the west of where we are now sitting. Several days passed after his transmissions ceased, so we sent an explorer ship and recovery crew who arrived and quickly ascertained that your military had already found the scout's body. Under cover of darkness, our explorer ship and its crew cleaned up as much of the debris as possible and left. It dumped the remains in deep outer space because the parts were so badly damaged and burnt beyond recognition that it was almost impossible to determine what exactly caused the scout ship to crash."

"Why," John asked, "didn't you try to retrieve the body?"

"We thought that such an act would raise more questions among your people," Mel-El answered. "We knew from intercepted military transmissions that the mere existence of our scout's body would bring about the utmost absolute secrecy and coverup by the highest echelons of your government. Your military knew that no one would believe the story that a deceased alien had been discovered on Earth. The panic that might ensue could possibly lead to an atomic or nuclear war. We didn't want to take that chance."

"Can you tell me about this silver disc?" John reached into his vest's pocket and extracted the silver coin before continuing, "Its instructions directed me to keep it out to reflect the moon. And," he continued, "do you want it returned?" as he extended it to Mel-El.

Mel-El took John's hand and folded his fingers over the silver disc before continuing, "No, John, you are to keep it. Every one of us from Zero57A carry similar discs. Depending on the world or star we are surveying, each disc is made specifically for that celestial orb with the most common languages of that world entered on it. By holding it in your palm as it reflected the moon's light, it confirmed to me that you were here."

"But how did you know who had possession of the disc?" John queried.

"Each disc," Mel-El answered, "sends out a constant transmission reporting its location, so if one of our scouts or crewmen is killed, it will be found by an Earthling. Hopefully, like you, that person may be able to decipher it and attempt, as you have, to contact us."

"If there have been similar tragedies here on Earth," John inquired, "how many discs have been found by someone on Earth and how many finders were successful at solving the cipher?"

"Over the past five hundred years, we've only lost one other disc, and it wasn't recoverable because our ship was lost in your Pacific Ocean's seven-mile-deep Mariana Trench," Mel-El replied. "We still monitor its location as your inventors and scientists on Earth continue to develop more and more sophisticated and capable deep sea exploration vehicles," he added.

"So, then, why even make me aware of your existence?" John asked, "You could have not even shown up tonight, and I wouldn't have known a thing. I'm in my late sixties now. I would have returned home, chucked the disc in a desk drawer, and forgotten it. Obviously, Mel-El, you have a purpose in revealing yourself to me. So, how can I be of help you? There is absolutely not one person on Earth who would believe me, if—IF," John stressed, "I told them about the disc or tonight's events."

"John, by finding your way here, you have more than proved that you are an extraordinary individual," Mel-El replied. "Please keep the disc as it will guide a special man to your home. After that man arrives, we ask that you mentor him for a time. Also, we request that you give our man an appropriate name, so he will fit into your society. You can teach him the ins and outs of your world. When he is ready to leave, give him the disc."

Mel-El paused before continuing, "You see, we on Zero57A now believe your world needs to be more speedily infiltrated by more of our people who can keep an eye on and warn us if your countries are drawing too close to war, which may happen in your year of 2022. Such a nuclear war would destroy all life, both flora and fauna along with mankind. We on Zero57A do not want that to occur."

"Why not just invade Earth?" John commented before adding, "With your superior technology that would appear to be, what we call, a slam dunk conquest."

"We believe," Mel-El replied, "that would lead to the destruction of at least half the earth as your United States, Russia, and China, along with India or Pakistan, and perhaps Iran, would most likely respond by launching their nuclear weapons against their longtime enemies who, they would presume, are behind such a takeover.

"At this time, we believe that a more subtle approach may be possible." Mel-El continued, "While you are the only individual to solve the riddle of our disc, there are thousands of similarly minded persons, like yourself, throughout the 195 different countries of your world. We believe we can discreetly approach those individuals and ascertain if they, too, will help mentor the hundreds of Zero57A occupants we intend for migration, infiltration, or insertion onto your planet."

John nodded and thought about what Mel-El had asked him to do. "Yes, Mel-El, I will help. I certainly would not wish to see Earth be completely destroyed during my lifetime—or at any time in the future!"

"Thank you, John," Mel-El replied.

"Mel-El," John queried, "may I ask you a few more questions?"

Mel-El nodded and shifted on the stone bench to look more directly at John. The hawk on his shoulder turned its head and continued to stare at John.

"In Arizona, there is a native American Indian tribe called the Navajo. In their lore," John continued, "they believe in people, or supernatural beings, known as shapeshifters—entities who can change their shape at will. My father described the individual he autopsied as having an entirely different bodily shape than yours. Do you and the people on Zero57A have that ability?"

"Yes, John, we do," Mel-El answered. He paused briefly before continuing, "We have the ability to assume any form that is called for on whatever world, or star, we are visiting. In that way, we can appear to be like the other beings on that particular world. It is our way of being less frightening, or threatening, to any of the lifeforms we encounter."

"But, what about Roswell?" John queried.

"Sadly," Mel-El replied, "when one of us dies on a foreign world, our lifeform reverts to its original state."

"But, what happens," John pointed out, "say on Earth, which you now plan to infiltrate, if one of your people dies? Wouldn't the discovery of such a body form cause a massive and hysterical panic?"

"Yes, John, it certainly might," Mel-El answered. "Since Roswell, however, we have developed a failsafe precaution. The disc, which all of us now carry, has been programmed to detect the immediate cessation of life in its carrier. The disc causes the body to immediately incinerate itself and vanish within seconds, leaving no trace whatsoever. Only the disc would remain unscathed in our hope that someone like you might find and decipher it. That person would, obviously, be another fairly trustworthy contact."

John nodded. "That leads me to a further question, mostly out of curiosity. How long do you live on Zero57A?"

"John," Mel-El replied, "we live between ten and twelve thousand years. You see, there are no diseases on Zero57A. We have eliminated all pathogens, so have no fear of sickness or disease. I, for example, am soon to be 8,763 years old, counting by your 365-day year. Toward the end, our bodies begin to break down and our system fails to function properly. Death happens quickly in one or two days."

"What can you tell me about your time travel?" John asked, "For instance, how long did it take you to arrive here from Zero57A?"

"John, we have developed a system. In your language it is known as warp speed and is somewhat similar to what was depicted on your TV show *Star Trek*. Our type of speed would be incomprehensible to you or anyone else on Earth. On Zero57A, once our ship is ready for liftoff, we enter the coördinates of that part of the universe we intend to visit. We're then transported through time and speed instantaneously. In all, it took me about thirty seconds in your time to arrive here."

"Are there women on Zero57A?" John asked.

"Yes," Mel-El replied, "we have the equivalent of what you call women. Our breeding ability, which I won't get into, is such that we can specifically choose whatever sex we want for the child. But," Mel-El paused, "to prevent a disproportionate ratio, or unequal quantity, of one sex over the other, we are regulated and must wait for a higher authority's approval. Our women do not travel unless we decide to establish a permanent presence on whatever planet, or star, we have decided to infiltrate."

John sat back, somewhat stunned by all that he had heard. "All this information," he said to Mel-El, "is, for me, incredibly difficult to absorb. But, despite what logic tells me, I have no problem whatsoever believing all you've told me."

Mel-El nodded, leaned over toward John and placed his hand on John's knee before speaking, "Yes, I imagine what you have learned tonight is overwhelming, but I truly believe you can be of assistance to us."

The moon broke through the clouds, which seemed to melt away and disappear around it. John glanced at his watch. It was nearing midnight! He couldn't believe that the time had passed so quickly. The glow around Mel-El's body seemed to fade as the moonlight beamed down on both of the men.

"Would you please tell me about the hawk? Is it real, or what?" John asked.

Mel-El reached up and stroked the back feathers of the red-tail before replying, "Yes, in its appearance to you, the hawk is real. But he is actually one of the animal forms that we have constructed on our world of Zero57A. He is our scout, our eyes and ears on this planet."

"His hearing," Mel-El continued, "is so sensitive that he can perch on any building and overhear whatever one particular person is saying deep inside the bowels of any edifice—no matter how thick the floor or walls. He is programmed to transmit that information to us on Zero57A in, to use words you will understand, nanosecond radio bursts that are totally undetectable by your now existing scientific inventions. We have already inserted many similar birds throughout your planet."

"Because you had the disc, he was able to follow you all the way here from Virginia," Mel-El paused, "We will send him to you once our man, whom we want you to mentor, arrives at your home. You will know that the hawk is ours because one of its tail feathers will be blue in color, like this," He stroked the red-tail's back again, letting his fingers linger on one tail feather which, with the faint glow surrounding Mel-El, changed to blue before John's eyes.

"Well, Mel-El," John stated, "I will try my best to teach, or guide, whoever you send to me, and I'll work to inculcate them into the ways of our society and world."

"That is all we can ask of you, John," Mel-El replied. "And now," he continued, "it is time for me to depart."

The two men rose and shook hands. The red tail leapt from Mel-El's to John's shoulder.

John watched as Mel-El walked over to the silver cylinder's steps. He mounted and started to ascend when, halfway up, he turned and waved at John before disappearing inside. Seconds later the steps retracted and the door closed soundlessly leaving no trace of its location on the curving cylinder's rounded sides. After several minutes, John could again detect an almost inaudible sound of humming. Then, a beam of light, similar to the one that had come out of the clouds prior to Mel-El's arrival, burst out from the silver cylinder's flat top ascending over a few hundred yards before disappearing into the inky black night sky. Then, two more beams, parallel to the mesa's top, shot out from the sides of the ship several feet below the ship's rounded top.

John stepped back until his calves rubbed up against the edge of the stone bench. He was startled to see the shape of a Christian cross in front of him.

Have I, he wondered in awe, *encountered God? No, I guess not, but Mel-El certainly appeared to be godlike.*

The ship hummed a bit louder then started to shimmer in the night, and in a nanosecond, vanished along with its crucifix shaped light beams. John gathered up the items he had carried to the top of the mesa, placing them in a backpack he had brought along. He decided to leave the two large water containers in the niche where he had originally stowed them. *Maybe,* he thought, *if they last, sometime in the future, someone may discover them at a crucial time when they, too, will need water.*

The red tail sat motionless on his shoulder as John, using one of the flashlights he had brought along, made a slow and careful descent to the desert floor. As soon as he touched the desert floor, the hawk screeched, "Kee! Kee! Kee!" Flapping its wings, it launched itself off his shoulder, disappearing into the ink black night.

After his long night's excursion to the mesa's top, John realized he was totally drained and exceedingly tired. Arriving at his campsite, he crawled into his tent and immediately fell asleep on top of his sleeping bag. When he awoke around 7:00 the next morning, he ate a hasty breakfast, and started breaking camp. By 8:15, he was all packed up with everything stowed away in his truck. It had, he realized, been an interesting few days. One part of him didn't want to believe what had happened, but a stronger part implicitly believed and accepted the event as unalterably true. *But, he wondered, what had the cross represented?* John shook his head and mused, *Or, is that just another unsolvable mystery?*

John decided to take a leisurely ten-day return trip to Elkton. Once home, it took him a few days to return to his normal routine. Knowing that his visitor might turn up at any time, John cleaned and straightened up one of his spare bedrooms. As he finished that chore, he realized that the house needed to be neatened up, so he spent the next two days turning a slightly disorderly home into a tidy one.

Several weeks later, just after John had returned from a trip to the local Piggly Wiggly grocery store and was getting ready to sit down in his La-Z-Boy, the doorbell rang. He seldom had visitors, unless they were Mormons or Seventh Day Adventists trying to get him to join their slightly eccentric religious sects. As he rose and walked to the front door, John had a premonition as to whom his visitor might be. In opening his front door, he saw a twenty-something young man.

"Mr. Rushton?" the young man inquired.

"Yes, I am," John answered, before continuing, "I believe you are the visitor I was told to expect?"

"Yes, sir. My name is Bar-Kel," the young man answered as he extended his hand to greet John, "but I was instructed that you would find a more appropriate name for me."

"Yes, yes, please do come in," John motioned with his arm as he also extended his hand to shake Bar-Kel's hand.

Just before he closed the front door, John saw a blur, and then noticed a red-tailed hawk, with a blue tail feather, had materialized and settled onto a limb of John's dogwood tree, which was located in his front yard near the street's sidewalk. *Guess my guardian angel's back,* John thought, as he led the young man into his sitting room and motioned him to sit down on the divan opposite his chair.

The two men discussed various and sundry matters for thirty to forty minutes before John, as instructed by Mel-El, decided to tell the young man what name he had selected for him.

"Bar-Kel, since we live in the southern part of the U.S., I've chosen what I believe will be an appropriate name for you to use while you're here. It will be Madison Lee Stuart. James Madison was our fourth president and is known as the 'Father of the Constitution,' our governing document. Robert E. Lee is the name of a famous Civil War general from Virginia, and Jeb Stuart was one of his dashing and most effective cavalrymen. Lee wasn't victorious in his struggle and Stuart died in a battle. You can call yourself Madison L. Stuart, or just Madison Stuart if you so choose. But, with such a name, you will have absolutely no trouble blending in to our Southern society."

Bar-Kel nodded his head and said, "Thank you, Mr. Rushton. It is now committed to memory and Bar-Kel is no more when we are outside this house."

"Then, Madison," John intoned, "I insist you call me John during your time here. Please feel free to look over anything in my house and ask me any questions you might have. As you can see, I have over three thousand books in my private library, so feel free to read anything you like."

"Thanks, John. I will," Bar-Kel answered as he picked up a nearby book lying beside him on the divan. Opening it, Bar-Kel turned the pages in such a blur that John couldn't see him reading. In less than a minute, he closed the book and set it aside. Looking at him, John raised an eyebrow in a doubting manner.

"As you can see, John, I have an eidetic mind," Bar-Kel commented as he looked around the room at the various books.

"If you read every book in my library, they will teach you a lot about many subjects, although I tend to lean toward historical accounts," John informed the young man.

Over the next two years, John taught Bar-Kel everything he could think of that might help the young man to assimilate into American society. Bar-Kel surprised him by reading all the books, more than three thousand, in the house in a matter of four months.

One day, shortly after he finished reading John's entire library, Bar-Kel told him that by using his own unique silver disc he had the ability to transmit everything he had read or learned back to Zero57A in nanoseconds. Reaching into his pocket to demonstrate,

Bar-Kel removed his disc, held it between two fingers for several seconds, and then returned it to his pocket.

"By doing that," Bar-Kel commented, "I just transmitted everything I've read or learned since arriving here. The scientists on Zero57A will not only incorporate that information into the coins of those who will follow me, but will also input it into the minds of our future Earth settlers."

John looked at Bar-Kel in awe then he nodded. *Will wonders never cease?* He thought. *Wow!*

In addition, John took the young man on various field trips not only around the South but also all over the U.S. Every so often John quizzed the young man on some facet of history, societal norms, politics, or places they had toured and was always astounded by Bar-Kel's memory. It seemed to John that Bar-Kel was an alter ego of Seymour Cray, who, before he died in 1996, had invented the world's first supercomputer. Following them everywhere, the red tail kept its distance, so it didn't appear to be trailing them. Occasionally, John caught a quick glimpse of the bird.

Finally, one day, about twenty-five months after Bar-Kel's arrival, the young man came into John's sitting room, sat down on the divan, and said, "John, it is time for me to go. I am most appreciative of all your help during these past two years."

"Well, Bar-Kel, it was my pleasure," John replied before continuing as he pulled his silver disc out of a vest pocket. "Mel-El instructed me to give this disc to you upon your departure."

Bar-Kel leaned over and took the disc from John's hand. He then pinched it with two fingers and offered it back to John.

"You are to keep it," Bar-Kel replied. "As previously instructed, I have reprogrammed the disc so that now it is uniquely yours. From time to time, you might want to check the symbols and numbers in case someone from Zero57A needs to contact you."

John stared at the silver disc, rubbed his fingers over it, and returned it to his pocket. The two men stood, hugged, and patted each other on the back.

"Go with God, Bar-Kel. Best wishes on your journey," John said, his voice cracking. He knew he would never see the young man again.

Bar-Kel turned, walked to the front door, opened and stepped through it. Then he nodded to John and quietly closed the door. John walked to the front window so he could watch Bar-Kel walk down the steps and take his brick-patterned walkway to the street. Pulling the window curtain aside, he saw no one. Bar-Kel had vanished. And so had the ever-present red-tailed hawk.

I SAW DEATH WALKING DOWN THE STREET

I Saw Death Walking Down the Street

And I Cried Out to Him,

But He Continued Onward.

I Ran and Caught Up to Him

And We Walked Hand in Hand

Down the Street of Chaos.

I Stumbled over the Trash Bins,

So, I Kicked the Garbage Cans

Out of My Way

But We Kept On.

Fire Raged All Around Us

And Buildings Tumbled Down.

The Wind Blew Hard Against Us

But I Kept Pace.

The Snow Was Deep and Cold

Yet, We Trudged Slowly Onward.

Not A Word Did He Speak

And I Was Content.

We Climbed the Hill

And Watched the Filthy Gutters Overflow.

The Sun Beat Down upon Us,

But I Kept Pace with Him.

He Moved a Little Slower Now,

So, I, Too, Slowed My Pace.

He Seemed To Hesitate

As We Reached the Top.

I Reached Out My Hand,

But He Flung It Back.

We Neared the End of the Street
And He Stopped -
Turned and Pointed,
And I Looked Back.
Floods of Joy Overcame Me
As I Realized What I Had Seen.
There Was Beauty in That Chaotic Mess,
And I Turned to Tell Him So.
But He Was Gone.

THE WINDOW

t was another hot, humid day in The Nam. The jungle exuded a smell of dampness combined with an overpowering stench of decay. The soldier, struggling through shoulder-high elephant grass, put his right arm up to signal a halt and stopped to wipe his sweating brow with a faded green towel draped around his neck. John Rayner, a point man for Bravo Company, 2/8 First Air Cavalry Division, Blackfoot Platoon, cautiously looked around. The wood line was still a few hundred yards away, but with the wind in his face, Rayner could smell the malodorous fetor of the jungle in front of him. Like some amorphous ghoul, it loomed ahead as if expecting the American patrol to dare and breech its confines and enter its lair.

It had been a good morning so far. They had eaten a C ration breakfast, saddled up at eight, and moved out at an easy pace, taking their time to inspect any man-made objects they had encountered. Rayner was a combat rifleman—an 11 Bravo in army lingo—but he was also his infantry company's chief point man. Over the past five months in-country he had developed a sixth sense about unseen dangers and could almost feel when an enemy's eyes were watching him.

All his life he had been a hunter. His dad, dead five years now from an accident in a southwest Virginia coal mine, had first taken him deer hunting at age five. At age seven, Rayner had shot his first deer, an eight-point buck that had stepped out of the woods not thirty feet away. It had paused to drink from a small stream in front of the excited curly-haired redhead.

Rayner shifted his sixty-pound rucksack, trying to make it conform more evenly to the sweaty contours of his already sore back. In The Nam your back was always hurting from the rough metal edges of the ruck's frame and the weight of fifty-to-sixty pounds of supplies—C-Rats, a few dirty and sweat smelling clothes, sixteen to eighteen fully loaded eighteen round clips of M16 ammo, the bandolier of M60 machine gun ammo that everyone was required to carry, and the ever present heavy between five and seven quarts of water every infantryman carried.

The sun was hotter than hell this morning. Roger Palmer, his second in line, moved up beside him. Rayner glanced at his watch. It was little past ten. Although it seemed much longer, they had only been moving for a little more than two hours. He absently noted that his arm was bloody with little cuts from contact with the sharp-bladed elephant grass.

"Hotter than a mother f*ck," Palmer whispered, almost spitting his words out due to a dry throat from the jungle heat.

"Yeah," Rayner commented somewhat hoarsely, clearing his throat as quietly as he could. His mouth felt like it had cotton in it. "See that break in the wood line," he pointed, "just to the left of that dead tree?"

"Uh-huh," Roger grunted, squinting his eyes and using his hand as a shield from the harsh morning sun that beamed down unmercifully on the infantrymen who were standing in the grassy savanna-like field. Beads of sweat rolled off their dirt encrusted foreheads. They hadn't bathed in weeks. Charley would have no problem smelling them, just as the GIs knew when they smelled sardines, the gooks were hellishly close.

"There's something there. Something that just don't look right to me." Rayner jabbed his hand for emphasis. "See that shimmering. Comes and goes. Like some kind of reflection or sum'thin. I'm gonna check it out."

"Be real careful, John," Palmer whispered. "I'll be on your left about fifteen yards out. I'll tell Iceman to move up on your right." In Nam everyone seemed to have a nickname. Rarely did they call each other by their real names. Or, if they did, only by their last names. It was the infantryman's way of not getting too close to anyone. After all, here today, dead tomorrow. In this case, the Iceman's real name was Ned Niceman, whose father, they had all learned, was an Army colonel who had been hopping mad when his only son chose not to go to officer candidate school. The Iceman, a surfer from Hawaii, told them that he preferred to be a regular guy and not some candy ass second lieutenant kissing some captain's rear end.

"OK," Rayner agreed, "let's do it. But slow and easy, bud. Radio back to the captain that I got a bad feeling about this one. We'll move out in two minutes. Pass the word for the guys to put their rifles on rock and roll and stay at least fifteen feet apart." As Roger disappeared back into the elephant grass, Rayner unclipped his camouflage-green plastic canteen from a C-ring attached to his rucksack, unscrewed the top, and took a short swig of the chemically treated warm water the army flew out to them every three to four days. Before swallowing the foul-tasting liquid, he swirled it around in his mouth with a grimace. *God!* he thought. *That f*cking shit tastes terrible.* He spit out the remainder without letting his eyes leave the distant tree line.

He thought briefly about home. Father dead. Mother working … sometimes. She worked when the local clothing factory needed extra hands. The rest of the time she was on welfare because the small ten-man coal mine, where her now deceased husband worked and eventually died, went bankrupt leaving her with no widow's pension. *Even if there had been a pension*, Rayner thought ruefully, *it wouldn't have been enough to feed all of us.* Their house, not much more than a three-room shack on the side of a mountain facing New River, was falling down from old age and the harsh West Virginia winters.

There wasn't much to go back to. Nothing, as far as he was concerned, to look forward to if he returned. There was no girl eagerly awaiting his return. All the ones he'd known in high school had either dropped out, gotten pregnant, or married. Besides, his momma had troubles enough of her own. There was a five-year-old brother and twelve-year-old sister who needed to be fed. No jobs awaited Rayner upon his return. West Virginia people were always poor or out of work because the coalfields sporadically opened, or closed, depending on which coal baron owned them.

In his senior year, he dropped out of high school and moved to Bristol, Virginia, looking for a job. He worked in a diner there that catered to railroad workers and sent some of his meager wages back to his momma when an Army recruiter entered one day and persuaded him to join the Army. He figured that joining would both show his patriotism and, beyond the benefits, including life insurance, he would earn enough to send more money home.

Hell, he thought grimly, *at least if I get killed, Mom'll get the proceeds from my life insurance policy. She could at least buy a used car.* His father's mid-50s truck had died long ago and now sat rusting on cinder blocks in their front yard while the black paint peeled off its twelve-year-old frame. *I'd be better off dead*, he thought rather grimly. *If I die in a combat zone, box me up and ship me home*. Rayner hummed the popular phrase to himself. THE WORLD, what the grunts called home because the jungle war in Southeast Asia was so far away from home, enabled everyone in Nam to pretend they were actually on another planet instead of in some godforsaken country known as Vietnam.

Shaking off these sobering thoughts, he cautiously turned his head to see if Palmer was deploying the rest of the five man point team behind him. He was. The point team usually moved a good fifty yards ahead of the rest of the infantry column. Over the top of the elephant grass, Rayner could barely make out the bobbing heads of the rest of Bravo Company as they moved up to watch and wait. Only sixty men strong, they couldn't help him a bit with what he and the rest of the point members now had to do. With a sigh that infantrymen have known through the ages, he glanced back at the foreboding jungle.

Shit! he thought to himself, *that weird shimmering's still there. What in the f*ck is it?* he wondered. His survival instincts, honed to a sharp edge by nineteen years of survival in the hardscrabble mountains of Virginia and West Virginia and a five-month eternity in Southeast Asia, warned him now to be extremely careful. Hunkering down, Rayner pulled a topo map from a deep pocket in his fatigue pants and stared at it. It showed that the patch of jungle in front of him was about a half mile wide. There was a small river snaking back and forth behind it. *Good place for a gook hospital,* he thought. Stuffing the topo map back into his fatigue pants, he glanced at his watch.

The two minutes were about up. *Well, I better get the show on the road,* he thought with some resignation. *At least it's a bright sunshiny day for dying,* Rayner grimly reminded himself because he firmly believed that he had nothing to live for.

If he died, his momma might miss him but, if he returned home, he'd just be one more mouth for her to feed—unless he got a job in the coal mines. Rayner knew she couldn't afford an extra mouth to feed. He'd probably end up on welfare, too, if he returned to his West Virginia homeland, or he'd work in a coal mine and eventually come down with black lung disease.

After all, he reminded himself, *this was The Nam and 11 Bravos weren't expected to survive their twelve-month tour of hell anyway.* Hefting his M16, he slapped the bottom of the magazine to make sure it was seated properly, flipped the rifle's safety off, and shifted another button to full automatic—what grunts called the "rock and roll" position. If Charley was waiting up ahead, Rayner wanted to make sure that his first burst would be strong enough to lay down a suppressing fire giving him time to find cover. But, he intuitively knew, being in elephant grass meant there really wasn't any cover. *Of course,* he thought rather ruefully, *the only damn cover I'll probably find will be a blade of grass. People back in The World would be amazed,* he mused smiling grimly to himself, *how big a blade of grass really is!*

Wiping the sweat from his brow one last time, Rayner tucked the towel's soaked ends inside his drab olive t-shirt, sighed, stood slowly, and started walking in a zigzag line toward the tree line. Almost immediately, a large anthill appeared to his right. Approaching cautiously to make sure no one was hiding behind it, he passed to its right and kept moving. About ten minutes later, he stopped within fifty feet of the jungle's edge and the eerie shimmering spot—his eyes searching out every opening in the thick jungle wall ahead of him. Nothing stirred. Even the wind had mysteriously died. Beads of sweat poured down his neck and his adrenaline surged the closer he approached the tree line and that mysteriously wavering thing that lay just ahead in front of him.

The shimmering beckoned him onward. It had rounded edges about five feet wide and seven or eight feet tall. *Must be a mirage or something*, he thought. Oddly, Rayner realized, he could see right through it, although what was on the other side appeared somewhat vague and blurred. *Where was the jungle?* he wondered. He moved cautiously toward it, every instinct alert, his eyes searching for telltale footprints, trip wires, or reflections off something metallic like a trigger for a deadly "Bouncing Betty" land mine, anything to give him a clue as to what was happening in front of him. But there was nothing, just the foreboding quiet of the shimmering whatever it was, and the evil odor of the nearby jungle spreading out before him as he warily approached it. The lush green trees and snakelike vines seemed as if they wanted to reach out, grab him, and pull him inside their green depths. He edged closer, not sure what he was encountering.

Unexpectedly, the hairs on the back of his neck began to bristle. *It's there!* his senses screamed. *Something is in there.* But he couldn't quite put his finger on what it was. Rayner's senses screamed at him to be wary. Dropping into a half crouch, he moved toward the shimmering area. The elephant grass began to peter out. He found himself on the edge of an open space some twenty yards wide between the elephant grass and the wood line. For some unknown reason, the vegetation seemed to have mysteriously dried up. *Maybe*, Rayner thought, *they sprayed Agent Orange here*. The desolate stretch was a perfect killing zone. He felt totally exposed and defenseless. If he wanted, Charley would be able to pick him off easily. If this was an ambush, he was as good as dead, Rayner knew.

Rayner strained his ears for any sound or sign of movement. Nothing. Looked again. Still nothing. He felt an overpowering urge to piss in his pants but suppressed it. Every fiber in his body told him to stay where he was, but the break in the jungle's screen enticed and beckoned him onward like a siren's call. Besides, they'd received orders from battalion to check out this patch of jungle and the river behind it. Supposedly, they were searching for a gook base camp and hospital.

Fat chance of that ever happening, he thought dubiously. Still, Rayner felt that an invisible hand was propelling him involuntarily forward. Moving closer to the shimmering he thought he saw something move within the area. Raising his rifle, Rayner shook his head and again looked at the pulsating waves that seemed to seductively undulate before him. An eternity passed in a heartbeat.

Suddenly, there was a microburst flash of light and Rayner saw a group of men in strange uniforms walking toward him. Although he knew at once they were soldiers, some inner voice told him not to feel threatened by them. He instinctively held his fire. Dressed in shades of grey and brown, with black leather belts and other unusual accoutrements, they carried odd-looking rifles tipped with long silvery bayonets. The men were strangely familiar, like some figures out of a diorama Rayner vaguely remembered from his youth. Most remarkably though, they were not oriental but white men like himself. One of them even had a full beard and gray hair under a crumpled brown slouch hat pulled down low over his eyes. Then, as suddenly as they had appeared, the figures vanished. Rayner shook his head not quite believing the image he had just seen.

What the hell is going on? Rayner wondered. "I must be hallucinating," he whispered to himself. Frozen to the ground in a half-crouch, he was afraid to look around. Afraid to check on the position of his buddies behind him. Afraid to take his eyes off the wavy screen in front of him and the lurking jungle looming sinisterly behind it for even a second. Yet, something eerily beckoned and coaxed him onward. Like a sultry temptress, the shimmering screen seemed to pull him strongly toward its wavy undulating mist. Rayner felt as if he was within the grasp of some invisible beast that was irresistibly sucking him toward its maw. The image of a deer frozen long ago in the headlights of his father's used '55 Ford truck flashed crazily through his mind.

"I gotta get out of here," Rayner mumbled to himself as he ran a slightly shaking hand across his brow. "When we stand down next week, I'm going to go to Saigon for a little R & R. I definitely need some boom boom time." The image of a Saigon bar girl, her white *ao-dai* gathered up around her waist as she waited for him to take her upstairs, flashed across his mind. He remembered her soft naked body and her flat stomach. She had been so young—probably several years younger than him. He shook his head, hoping to clear his mind both of the bar girl's memory and the invisible cobwebs that seemed to tug mysteriously at him.

Like Scylla and Charybdis, the shimmering waves seemed to reach out like a magnet, pulling him forward to consume him. Not taking his eyes off the looming wood line, Rayner slowly inched forward, carefully measuring out each step of his advance. He was now clear of the elephant grass. He knew he was in the killing zone—a perfect target. Finally, about twelve feet away from the shimmering, he stopped. It was the weirdest thing he had ever encountered during his tour in Nam. He felt as if he could see through the wavy illusion, or whatever the hell it was. Yet, it had grayish pulsating edges but there was no jungle between those wavering sides.

Rayner wondered if he was going nuts. Another microburst suddenly jolted him. What he could see on the other side of the shimmering wasn't jungle. It was a small meandering river. The scene vanished in a microsecond. But now something was wrong. He just knew it. With a start he realized he could no longer hear the incessant buzz of insects—an ever-present sound in The Nam that was always with you in the jungle, no matter where you went. Crack! Crack! Crack! The distinctive fire from an AK-47 exploded from the jungle off to his left.

Rayner recognized the distinctive "Crack! Crack! Crack!" sound at once—it was a sound one never forgets after a combat tour in Vietnam. "Ambush," Rayner yelled as he dove, hitting the rock-hard sunbaked ground, with the weight of his sixty-pound rucksack painfully jolting his entire body. His now unbuckled helmet slipped off, bounced on the ground, started to spin, and rolled a few feet away out of his reach. Flattening himself behind a dried-up tuft of elephant grass, he automatically returned fire. Although he saw no one, he emptied his M16 in seconds in the direction of the distinctive AK-47's sound. Ejecting the empty clip, Rayner clumsily groped for a new magazine and once found inserted it into his weapon while he frantically searched the jungle for targets. He was totally exposed and he knew it.

Bullets slammed into the ground to his left, stitching a path in his direction and splattering him with pieces of dirt and dead pieces of elephant grass. Rayner, knowing he was probably a goner, frantically struggled to edge away from the danger. Crawling to his right, he realized his rucksack's bulk maddeningly prevented him from rolling over. Another string of explosions abruptly tore at the soil to his right. *Shit! I'm boxed in*, he thought. *This is it! I'm a dead mother f*cker for sure now*, he realized.

He froze, knowing in every fiber of his being that Charley was adjusting his fire and he had only seconds left to live. The next burst of crossfire would surely get him if he stayed put. He pawed at the confining rucksack straps, but they refused to slip off. With no memory of rising, Rayner's adrenaline kicked in. Suddenly, he was on his feet charging forward with his weapon blazing, spraying the jungle in front of him. All he could remember from his infantry training at Fort Polk, Louisiana, flooded back to him. When in doubt, take the offensive and lay down a suppressing fire as you charge the enemy's position.

Stumbling crazily from the shifting weight of the rucksack, he raced madly toward the jungle screen as more bullets whizzed by his ears and plucked at his clothes. He felt a bullet slam into the rucksack's metal frame with shocking intensity. The force of the AK round spun him toward his left. With nowhere else to go, Rayner—desperately cried, "Shit!"—dove directly into the shimmering curtain landing with a bone jarring thud on the other side.

The firing abruptly ended. Rayner quickly looked up. A sudden and grateful silence greeted his gasps for breath and still pounding heart. "What the f*ck?" he said aloud. He was no longer in the jungle. He looked behind him. There was a thick forest instead of the open field he had just crossed. Shaking his head, he looked from side to side. Gentle hills, tilled with fields of what appeared to be corn and wheat edged by split rail fences and neat country lanes met his gaze. Dotted here and there were inviting groves of shade trees and quaint farmhouses with barns. In the late afternoon's light, the rich land rolled away toward a line of higher peaks, made blue and purple by the haze of distance and the threat of rain. There was a deadly silence, save for the serene trickling sounds of a river, which meandered off to his left.

I'm dead, he immediately thought. Slipping off the rucksack straps, he stood and dusted off his clothes. *I sure don't feel dead!* he mused, chuckling to himself. *What in the hell is going on?* he wondered. *Where is everybody? And where the f*ck am I?* Questions flooded his mind. Rayner shook his head and blinked his eyes in disbelief.

The impossible scene, however, did not change. A steep-banked river, perhaps thirty or forty yards wide, flowed slowly past the small rise on which he stood. About a hundred yards off to his left, a triple-arched stone bridge spanned it. Behind the bridge, a rocky bluff loomed ominously over the river. Rayner's mind raced. Impossible as it was to believe, he knew this place. He *knew* it! He had been here as a kid while vacationing with his family. But that was a long time ago and half a world away. How could he possibly be here now? Idly, he wondered if he really was dead.

Startled by this grim thought, he again checked himself over, taking personal inventory. His helmet was gone, but then he remembered it rolling away in the elephant grass just a few minutes ago—or was it hours? He still had his rifle and eight fully loaded clips of ammo nestled in the olive-colored cloth bandolier around his neck and chest. His clothes though, were torn and bloodstained and amazingly still damp with his sweat!

He shivered. With the sun now all but gone, the air was decidedly chilly. *But how could that be?* he wondered. *It was morning just a few minutes ago. Have I been unconscious?* Again, he looked around in disbelief. *Where are the guys? What the hell is going on?* He felt totally disoriented. The late afternoon chill caused him to shiver. Bending over, he pulled his rolled-up fatigue jacket out of the rucksack and put it on. After the searing heat of Nam, it now felt like he had stepped into early fall.

Rayner suddenly realized there were bodies spread across the ground on both sides of the bridge. Some were dressed in blue, but others were in grey. It was hard to be sure in the rapidly failing light, but he thought he could see at least a dozen lying scattered between him and the entrance to the twelve-foot-wide bridge. More lifeless bodies lay floating in the river's gentle current. In the distance he could hear firing. *That sounds like cannons*, he thought. *Naw, it couldn't be.* Again, he wondered if he was dead.

Bending over, he grabbed the rucksack and, in one fluid well-practiced motion, swung it into the air and over one shoulder. The straps bit into his sore shoulders as he readjusted the cumbersome equipment. In the process, he nicked his hand on the torn metal tubing where the AK round had ripped into the metal frame. Licking the small cut in his right palm, he dusted his hands off on his fatigue pants by switching his rifle from one hand to the other. Mechanically, he reloaded his M16 with a fresh clip, flipped the rifle's safety on, and walked slowly over to the nearest body.

The man was very young and very dead. Dressed in light blue pants and a darker blue jacket, he lay face up, his eyes staring sightlessly at the now blood-red sky as the sun began to sink in the western sky. The dead man's chest was exposed. Someone, or perhaps the victim himself, had ripped open his clothes to reveal the terrible wound that had killed him. Having already encountered enough dead and rotting corpses in Nam, Rayner's practiced eye and nose told him that the soldier had been dead about a day.

Next to the body lay a small black book. Lifting the volume, Rayner opened it to a blood-smeared page and read the words: "Even though I walk through the valley of the shadow of death, I will fear no evil, for you are with me."[22] Upon the fly-leaf, written in ink by a delicate hand, he also read: "I hope and pray that Providence will permit you to return to me when this cruel war is over." The note was signed: "Your beloved, Lucy."

Rayner gently replaced the Bible where it belonged and stood uncommonly still for a few moments, stunned by what his mind

---

[22] ESV Study Bible (English Standard Version). Wheaton 22[IL]: Crossway, 2008. Psalms 23:6, 966.

was telling him. The dead man was undeniably a Union soldier—a veteran of a war that had ended over a hundred years ago and some twelve thousand miles away from where Rayner was supposed to be. Madness trickled at the edges of his mind.

He found himself repeating the biblical verse he had just read, "Yeah, though I walk through the valley of the shadow of death, I will fear no evil; for Thou art with me," to which he tacked on another phrase—"For I am the meanest son of a bitch in the valley!" He chuckled grimly to himself, thinking about how he and myriad other Vietnam vets had distorted and popularized the Bible's original lines.

His hand automatically went to his neck where he fingered a chain holding a two-inch-long crucifix with Christ on it. His friend, schoolmate, and neighbor, Mary Eubanks, who was a die-hard Catholic, had given it to him before he left for Nam. Although brought up as a Baptist, he believed the crucifix was some sort of a talisman that, hopefully, would get him back to THE WORLD.

Trying not to think, Rayner slowly made his way toward the old stone bridge. The profusion of broken rifles and discarded equipment littering the ground, as well as the freshly torn condition of the soil, indicated that a sizable battle had recently been waged here. Yet, the comparatively small number of bodies, however, as well as their condition, suggested that at least hours, perhaps as much as a day, had passed since blood had been shed over this patch of ground.

There were no wounded soldiers left—only dead ones. Those who were still breathing had obviously already been collected for the surgeons. Even some of the dead had been visibly attended to, as evidenced by one line of six corpses neatly laid out beside the road leading away from the bridge. *Perhaps*, he pondered, *these six men survived the battle and were readied for evacuation but succumbed before transportation arrived. At least in Nam,* he thought, *we have Medevac choppers that can evacuate us within thirty minutes of being wounded.*

The bridge, especially, showed signs of a fierce battle—its once pristine stonework, now heavily pitted and cratered by bullets and shells, was splashed with dark stains that could only be blood. Bodies, two and three deep in places, lay scattered along the narrow confines of the twelve-foot-wide span. Stepping over corpses, Rayner quickly approached the bridge. Whereas before all the dead had been Union soldiers, many were now obviously Rebels, clad mostly in coarse shades of reddish-brown or grey. Some even wore drab items of civilian clothes, and a surprising number, Rayner noted, were barefoot.

The sound of galloping horses abruptly broke the spell. Looking up and turning to his right, Rayner saw three riders approaching from the edge of a wooded area about a hundred yards downstream. Once exiting the woods, they drew to a temporary halt, looked around, and spotted him in the fading light. Spreading out, in what appeared to be a well-practiced maneuver, they rapidly galloped toward the bewildered Vietnam vet, closing the distance until they drew to a halt about twenty-five feet away. As dusk was rapidly approaching, it was too dark to tell what colors they wore since they were between him and the setting sun. He stared at them and they at him.

Rayner waved. The three men dismounted and cautiously approached him until they halted with their horses about eight feet away. Unsure of what else to do, Rayner decided to act as friendly as possible until the three soldiers made their intentions known.

"Hi! Name's John Rayner. I ..." he paused, hesitated, and smiled somewhat nervously before continuing, "I'm lost. Could you tell me where I am and who you are?" Feeling a trickle of blood seep down the side of his face, Rayner reached up and wiped the side of his head. His hand came away bloody. *I must have scratched my face,* he thought, *when I hit the ground after the AKs went off.*

The lead rider, older and more grizzled than the others, was obviously in charge. From the stripes on his sleeves, Rayner also recognized him as a sergeant—although he still could not see well enough in the fading light to tell which army the man belonged to. The man placed his hands on his hips and spat a wad of tobacco juice out of his heavily mustachioed mouth. It landed squarely on Rayner's right boot.

"What the hell kind of getup outfit is that yew got on, boy?" the beefy sergeant asked. "Them's strange clothes yore wearing. Yew some kind of newly outfitted Johnny Reb or somethun?"

"Well, sarge … uh, not exactly," Rayner tentatively replied as he tried to figure out where the now decidedly unfriendly conversation was headed.

"Where yew from, boy?" the man demanded as he spat another wad of juice that connected this time with Rayner's left boot.

"I'm from Bristol, Virginia," Rayner replied flatly, becoming more irritated by the man's obvious rudeness. He suppressed the urge to wipe off the stains because it would mean taking his eyes off the three men and their relative positions in front of him.

"Well, I guess that makes you a damn Johnny Reb, don't it? Yew a deserter, or a spy too, boy?" the man demanded. "You pickin' over dese bodies? Robbin' from the dead?" he asked, sweeping his right arm toward the river.

"Uh no, Sarge, I don't even know where the hell I am," Rayner answered as he furtively checked with his finger to make sure his M16's safety was off. He didn't like where this conversation was going.

"Well, boy, I think yer a deserter. That's what I think. And ya know what we do to deserters? We shoot 'em. That's what we do. Don't make no never mind ta us whether you be North or South. Yer still a damn deserter. And ah damn grave robber too." The man was visibly working himself up. "Yew see all these dead boys?" he continued sweeping his arm in an arc across the killing ground as if to divert Rayner's attention, but Rayner kept his eyes on the man's face. "Well, they're a result of you damn Rebs. We lost a lot of good men here yestediddy 'cause of you mother f*ckin' secesh trash." The man nodded to his companions, who drew their pistols and started to spread out. "Now you just stand still boy. Gimme that damn rifle yew got an' raise your hands."

As the sergeant started forward to reach for his rifle, Rayner stepped back and, in a blast that sounded enormously loud in the fading light of day, fired in a sweeping motion. All three men, as well as two of the horses standing behind them, went down in a crashing melee during the three second burst. The remaining horse galloped off. The two remaining horses, crying piteously, thrashed and struggled to get to their feet, as blood streamed down their flanks. Rayner efficiently put a bullet into each animal's head. He then walked over to the downed men and deliberately kicked each one in the ribs with his boot. When the sergeant grunted and opened his eyes, Rayner gave him a *coup de grâce* in the head as well.

Rayner stood quietly, aware only of his breathing and a ringing in his ears from the reverberation of the exploding M16 rounds. The smell of cordite wafted through the cool evening air as adrenaline still surged through his body like an anodyne. The smell of blood rose with the slight westerly breeze and assaulted his nostrils. Like so many times before, it took him a few moments to regain control and start thinking again. And when he finally did, also like so many times before, he was appalled at what he had done.

There had been no thought involved in the killing. He just did it. The whole incident had been nothing more than an automatic reaction that had been ingrained in him during his infantry training back in the States—when in doubt, fire first and ask questions later. Otherwise, you're going to end up dead. He hated what he had become but had no idea what to do about it. Slowly, like air bubbles rising from a steaming hot spring, Rayner grew aware of other sounds around him. Voices called out to each other, startled by the unexpected uproar. Off in the distance he could hear scurrying type noises, which seemed to come closer in the fast-approaching night.

I gotta get out of here! he thought as he turned back toward the bridge. The cloying smell of the newly shed blood blew past him in the fresh night air. Picking his way across the bridge, the stench of death from the multitude of decomposing bodies assaulted his nostrils. Rayner fought to keep his sanity. *What happened? Where are my buddies? How could I possibly be here? Am I dead or just dreaming? Maybe,* he thought, *I was knocked unconscious by an AK bullet.* His tortured mind tried to make sense of the recent events.

After climbing over several piles of bodies, he finally made his way to the west side of the bridge. What appeared to be a farm lane angled to the left up the steep bluff that faced the bridge. The main road appeared to follow the river downstream. Rayner chose the farm road. Moving as fast and as silently as he could, Rayner climbed the overgrown road. He now noticed that many of the bodies on this side of the river were clad in grey and homespun. Most were already bloated and had begun to rot.

Breathing heavily, Rayner finally reached the top of the bluff. The red bulb sun lay low on the distant Western horizon. At the hill's summit, he turned to look back into the little valley that he had just left. It appeared that several dozen men with torches were searching the area around the bridge's east side. They seemed reluctant to cross the bridge. Since he was several hundred yards away, he didn't worry about pursuit. He paused, sat down on a nearby log, and changed the magazine in his rifle. Taking out his canteen, he unscrewed the cap and took a long swallow. The water was cool and sweet tasting—not at all like the purified Army supplied water he'd been used to drinking.

What is going on here? he wondered, staring at his canteen. Not twenty minutes ago, when he had last taken a sip, the water had been hot and foul tasting. He looked at his watch. It read 7:02 in the evening. When he had last looked at his watch, seemingly not twenty-five minutes ago, it had read a little after 10:00 in the morning. He shook his head and looked at the watch again. It still read 7:02. *Either I'm hallucinating, or I'm dead,* he thought, *Shit, none of this makes any f*cking sense.*

After resting for about a quarter of an hour, Rayner decided to keep moving. Some unknown force—maybe it was his intuition—told him to head south and west, away from the river. For the first half mile or so the landscape resembled a torn and shattered wasteland. More dead bodies were strewn across the battlefield. Rifles, their bayonets gleaming in the fading sunlight, lay everywhere, but some of them had a darker color. *Most likely, dried blood,* he thought as he moved through and over the battered twisted pieces of war.

Shattered tree branches dangled from their limbs or lay scattered about on the ground. Some trees had no leaves at all. Although it was early evening, a murder of crows perched upon the dead, feasting, their caws resonating in the deathly silent gloom. Rayner saw some papers fluttering near a body dressed in grey. Squatting down, he picked up the paper and unfolded it. It was a newspaper, dated September 15, 1862, from Sharpsburg, Maryland. Tilting the paper toward the remaining sunlight, Rayner eyed the headline which screamed, "REBELS INVADE!"

A sub-title noted, "Lee Crosses the Potomac; Frederick Falls."

Unclipping his flashlight from an "O" ring on his rucksack, Rayner used it to read on for a few more minutes before dropping the paper, which fluttered away in the night breeze. He shook his head. He couldn't believe this was happening to him. *How the hell did I end up in the f*cking Civil War?* he wondered with exasperation, *I'm in the middle of the battle of Antietam. F*cking ANTIETAM! Shit!*

Moving out, he continued walking in a southwesterly direction. The moon had now risen but was mistily clouded over. Before long, Rayner started to feel raindrops. The rain soon drenched everything and turned the ground slimy. Shivering, Rayner stopped and shrugged off his rucksack. After a brief search of its depths, he retrieved his poncho. Delving deeper, he located his soft cloth boonyrat hat and placed it on his head to keep the drizzling water out of his eyes.

After an interminable period of cautious movement in the eerie darkness, staying close to the edges of woods whenever possible, he reached a farm road. Although reluctant to move out in the open, he weighed the risk and decided to follow it. Staying to one side of the deeply furrowed farm track in case he had to dive into the woods for cover, Rayner cautiously edged into the open space. Machine-like, he slogged along, hunched inward against the rain, placing one foot in front of the other, over and over again, totally submerged in the simple act of moving. After a long while, he felt as if he was sleep walking with no conception of time or place—lost in an uneasy haze that required no conscious thought or decision.

With a start, after what seemed an eternity, Rayner suddenly found himself standing at the top of yet another hill, looking down on a much larger river. The rain had finally stopped. The moon, reappearing from behind the clouds, illuminated the flowing water so that it looked like a shiny silver ribbon knifing its way through in the darkness. Unlike the river by the bridge, however, this one was two-to-three-hundred yards across, swift-running and deep. A quarter of a mile away, looking like a giant worm writhing on the earth, thousands of men and wagons filed down and into the river, emerging on the other side. Mounted sentinels with flaming torches lined their route, guiding them to and over the ford. He could also see a lot of activity around what appeared to be an old mill dam on the far bank.

Instinctively, Rayner knew that these men were Confederate soldiers. Robert E. Lee's fabled Army of Northern Virginia was retreating back to Virginia after the battle of Antietam Creek, the bloodiest single day in the War Between the States, or, as the Yankees called it—the Civil War. Not far over the hills behind them, the Yankee Army of the Potomac, led by the woefully incompetent and ever fearfully hesitant General George B. McClellan, slept, totally unaware that its prey was escaping in the rain and the dark. Impossible as it was to believe, Rayner had somehow been transported back to the night of September 18, 1862, and was actually watching men who should have been dead for the better part of a century moving across the Potomac River at a place called Boteler's Ford.

Long lost names suddenly bubbled up in his mind like water erupting from a hillside spring. After all, he had heard the stories his entire life. His family had fought in the war and had proudly worn the gray in defense of the Confederacy, even though the western counties of Virginia had broken away from Virginia and had been accepted by the Yanks as an additional independent state of the Union. Indeed, his great-great grandfather had even fought in this exact battle, serving under the great Stonewall Jackson himself. Perhaps his ancestor was down there right now, waiting his turn to cross back into Virginia.

Rayner continued to watch the retreating column for some time, not daring to turn his eyes away for fear that what he was seeing might disappear. *After all, this was a dream, wasn't it? Or maybe*, he mused, *he really was dead, and this experience, in some perverse way, was meant to soften his passage to heaven ... or hell.*

Finally, with a sigh of resignation that soldiers have known for ages Rayner shrugged his shoulders, took a deep breath, arched his back to readjust the rucksack and descended the hill. He walked slowly toward the ford, letting his legs take over for his mind. The moon had disappeared behind another cloud and the soft drizzle had begun anew. He passed between several groups of riders huddled atop their horses against the rain. Although a few looked his way, no one challenged him, evidently assuming that he was merely another straggler rejoining the retreating column. Indeed, he was now so covered with mud that it would have been hard telling otherwise in the dark even if the sentinels had been more alert.

Keeping to himself, Rayner stopped at the edge of the road and watched a column consisting of between fifty-to-sixty men move down to the water. Wagon after wagon creaked by, an occasional groan or a muffled shriek escaping from wounded soldiers inside. Most of the men, though, were quiet, shuffling past like resigned souls in a weary underworld. Many walked like zombies, staring straight ahead, neither caring where they stepped nor concerned where they were headed just as long as they got there, wherever there might be. They had a look that was, what Rayner had learned to call in his war, the thousand-yard stare. Other groups stood aside, patiently awaiting their turn to join the procession. Now and then, tired voices would call out either names or regimental numbers, trying to locate lost friends or units. One nearby group, thus identifying itself as from Virginia, attracted Rayner's attention. When it finally stepped forward into a brief opening in the column, he decided to join them. None of the men even looked at him as he found a place in the ranks.

As he carefully edged down the slippery bank to the ford, Rayner suddenly realized that his heavy rucksack would weigh him down in the water. It might even drown him, strapped to his back like an anchor, if he lost his footing. But, since it contained all that remained from his former world, he was loathe to part with it. Slipping it off his back, he looped both its straps over one shoulder so he could drop it if he was forced to do so. Then, holding his M16 high in one hand with his other free for balance, he entered the river. The water was swift, dragging at his legs and cold for September. Soon hip deep, it took his breath away and numbed his feet as they crunched along the rocky bottom. The falling drizzle made the watery crossing all that more miserable. After a few minutes, though, he emerged on the other bank, dripping wet, but safe.

Pausing briefly, Rayner leaned against the three-foot-high embankment that flanked the road leading down to the Potomac. Checking his rifle to ensure the barrel was clear of any debris he might have picked up along the way, he lightly wiped it down with the oil cloth he always kept in one of his trouser pockets. Although other men had also stopped to rest nearby, no one said anything to him.

Everyone was simply in shock—or just too tired to talk. Also, since other soldiers were checking their weapons as well, his actions did not appear unusual enough to stand out in the dim moonlight that filtered through the fast-moving clouds above Lee's withdrawal. Having ensured his weapon was serviceable in case he needed to use it again, Rayner swung his rucksack over his shoulders. Next, he readjusted his poncho so that it hid most of his rucksack's features. Then he stood and rejoined the southward retreat.

After a few hundred yards, he entered a little village, which, he noted from a dilapidated sign, was Shepherdstown, Virginia. Every house was lit with lantern light that spilled out into the road. A number of villagers stood outside, offering kind words of encouragement to the foot weary soldiers and also offering their homes to the wounded. By listening carefully to a conversation between a mounted officer in an ink black waterproof type of coat and a civilian hunched under a dripping umbrella, Rayner learned that the retreating army was heading toward Martinsburg.

Some of the townspeople offered refreshments to the soldiers as well. Without thinking, Rayner stopped with some other men before an old woman dressed in black, who was pouring something into a cup. When his turn came, he smelled the buttermilk and drank it down greedily. It tasted unbelievably good. When he handed back the cup and thanked her, Rayner realized that the black-clad woman was intently staring at him. With a start he suddenly realized that, by moving into the light emitted by the open doorway of her house, his strange appearance was no longer hidden by the darkness.

Slowly backing up and hoping to lose himself within the depths of the column, Rayner casually turned and nonchalantly moved away from the woman. He fought an urge to run. Extremely sensitive once again about how unusual he looked, about how totally out of place he was, he walked away in a hunched over position with his M16 pointed downward, holding it tightly against his right leg under the poncho so it wouldn't draw more notice or scrutiny. Tugging his cloth hat down over his eyes as far as it would go, he finally risked a glance backward at the old woman. She was animatedly talking with the mounted man Rayner had noticed earlier and pointing in the direction of the retreating column. Staring his way, they tried to pick him out of the mass of soldiers struggling southward.

Rayner's stomach sank, the buttermilk now tasting like acid. His mind raced with thoughts of escape. Inwardly he cursed himself for being so foolish. He looked around for a place to hide, but the column was still within the brightly lit town, the road crowded tightly between buildings on both sides. There was nothing else to do for the moment but walk on and hope the anonymity of numbers would protect him until he could slip away unnoticed once the retreating column reached the countryside's darkness. As he walked, his eyes firmly fixed on the back of the man in front of him, the fingers of his right hand unconsciously found their way once again around the comforting handgrip of his M16.

Nothing happened for what seemed a long time. As the column finally cleared the town and the comforting folds of a darkness returned to obscure its ranks, Rayner gradually allowed himself to relax. *Maybe, just maybe, they forgot me*, he thought. But, the unmistakable sound, however, of clopping hooves soon dashed his hopes. Glancing backward, Rayner saw the mounted man in his black coat was riding slowly along the far edge of the column to his right. He appeared to be scrutinizing the soldiers as if looking for someone. Passing by, the rider then spurred his horse through an opening ahead and trotted back along the near side. From his silhouette, Rayner could tell that he was closely examining every soldier he passed.

Sensitive to his looks and dress, Rayner kept his M16 partially covered with his poncho. Pointing the lethal rifle downward and holding it close to his body, he hoped the unusual weapon wouldn't draw too much attention—or scrutiny—from the approaching horseman. Although the Potomac had washed off some of the dried blood on his face, Rayner could feel the remaining cracked and congealed blood. It helped him blend in until the man on the horse drew alongside of him. Looking up, Rayner realized the man was a major due to the insignia on his cavalry hat.

With no other choice, Rayner awaited the inevitable.

"Mighty unusual outfit you got on, son," the major's soft voice commented—his tone, deep and slow, betrayed no emotion, but hinted at more than casual curiosity. "Where did you get those clothes?"

"It's a long story, sir, but I didn't steal them, if that's what you're asking," Rayner replied.

"No, son. That's not it. It's just that I never seen that kind of uniform before. The only troops I've ever seen that wore green were Berden's Yankee Sharpshooters. I don't know of any of our boys who wear green." Leaning over in his saddle, the man touched Rayner's sleeve. "Feels awfully thin and flimsy too. What kind of material is that? I'll bet it doesn't keep you warm."

"Yeah, well," Rayner shrugged and replied, shivering in spite of himself, "it is kind of cool, especially when wading across rivers." Rayner grinned up at the man, inwardly praying that he would just ride on.

The man grinned back. "Where are you from, son?"

"Bristol, Virginia, sir." Rayner replied truthfully and smiled at the major. In spite of his fears, he was beginning to take a liking to this officer. Off to his left, Rayner could see the first light of dawn peeking over the horizon. *Thank goodness*, he thought, *it's still dark enough so this guy can't really see what I look like in full daylight.*

"I didn't think you were a Yankee—but that's what Mrs. Talliaferro thought you were. You know the woman back in town, dressed in black—the one who was passin' out buttermilk? But I don't think so. You don't talk or sound like one." He continued to stare at Rayner for a few moments more, as if he was trying to come to some sort of a decision.

"Well," he finally sighed, sitting back in his saddle, "you better see the supply sergeant and get him to find you a warmer set of ...."

At that moment, Rayner, who was still looking up at the mounted officer as he continued walking, tripped on something in the road. He stumbled into the soldier walking in front of him. As he fought to regain his balance, his unwieldy rucksack started to drag him sideways and down. Without thinking, Rayner automatically swung his M16 out from underneath his poncho and, grasping the muzzle, jabbed its butt into the ground to arrest his downward descent. He prevented a nasty fall, but his poncho, slipping to one side, exposed most of Rayner's rucksack. The first of the sun's rays chose that moment to begin their daily streak across the morning sky.

The officer reined in his horse, instantly alert and staring hard at Rayner's now exposed equipment. "Wait a minute, here," the major said, his voice suddenly hard and more businesslike. "What kind of rifle is that, soldier?" the officer asked as he spied Rayner's M16. "I've never seen anything like that before in my life."

Rayner, as the conversation had continued, had begun to feel more and more relaxed. He had even felt himself growing to trust the polite manners and genteel style of the officer. Now, though, the man had spotted his M16. Rayner suddenly felt trapped. *Shit*, he thought grimly, *I'm in for it now.*

"Oh," Rayner said, trying to sound casual as he struggled to tug the poncho back across his rucksack, "it's a new kind of rifle I was issued down in..." All he could think of was Fort Benning, where he had taken his basic infantry training. "Uh, Georgia," he finished lamely. Rayner could feel sweat beads beginning to pop out on his forehead. *How the f*ck am I ever going to get out of this?* he silently wondered.

"Give it to me, son," the man demanded.

"Sorry, sir. No way."

Now all business, the officer spurred his horse and swung it around in front of Rayner, blocking any escape. The column of tired and weary men, up to now oblivious to the scene, came to a halt as the two men confronted each other.

"Give me the rifle," the man repeated. "That's an order, soldier." His steely grey eyes seemed to bore right through Rayner's body. He extended his arm, as if to grasp the weapon when Rayner handed it to him, and motioned with his fingers for Rayner give him the M16.

"With all due respect, sir," Rayner replied firmly, surreptitiously flipping the M16's switch to semi-automatic as he spoke. "I can't do that. Please don't make me hurt you."

The man looked at Rayner oddly, withdrew his hand, and rested it on top of his black leather holster. "If you are one of us," he finally said in a furious tone, "you will give me that weapon. The only reason you wouldn't do so is because you're not one of us." He paused for what was clearly his last time. "Now, I've given you a direct order, soldier. Hand over that weapon … or else." He unbuttoned the flap to his holster. The snap of the buttons parting sounded like a gunshot in the fresh morning air.

Sadly, Rayner shook his head. He heard, sensed, the men around him begin to back away. No one wanted to get accidently shot in the coming violent, perhaps deadly, confrontation.

The officer started to pull his pistol from its holster.

"Don't do that, sir," Rayner warned, "or you'll regret it! I'll just go away. Nobody has to get hurt."

"You threatening me, boy? the enraged man shouted, his hand surging upward with his pistol.

"You damn little Yankee bastard!" The man's arm straightened and arced downward toward Rayner, who raised his M16 and efficiently shot the Confederate officer between the eyes. The man, not comprehending that he was already dead, that half his brains had been blown out the back of his head, stared at Rayner in surprised disbelief for a long moment, and then toppled slowly off the back of his horse. The nearby soldiers scattered at the sound of the M16. Rayner quickly grabbed the animal's reins before it could bolt. Pulling the horse toward him, he stuck his foot into a stirrup and, straining against the awkward weight of his heavy rucksack, swung clumsily up onto the vacant saddle.

The soldiers who witnessed the killing looked dumbly at him, momentarily in shock. Several of them began to realize what had just happened and started to raise their own weapons. With adrenaline coursing through his veins, Rayner kicked the horse into sudden movement, and hung on for dear life as a rugged volley crackled through the air all around him. He felt a slight burning sensation in his left thigh. Urging the terrified animal to its fastest pace across a muddy field, he guided it into a nearby tree line and plunged into the woods. Branches hit him in the face, so Rayner rode low in the saddle, ruthlessly goading the horse onward.

After a hard five-minute run, he slowed the chestnut-colored steed to a walk and began to pick his way through the thick forest. It was now early morning, and the sun began to filter through the treetops. Every so often during the next half hour or so, he reined in, paused, and listened for sounds of pursuit. Hearing nothing, Rayner continued to move deeper into the thinning forest whose leaves, he noted, were beginning to die and drop with the approach of fall.

He was tired, sore, and hungry, and his left leg had a stinging throb. Looking down Rayner saw that a bullet must have grazed his thigh. Part of his pants leg had been ripped open by the passing Minié ball. He could see blood welling up from a thin furrow that stretched six to eight inches across his skin. Pausing again, Rayner dismounted rather clumsily, and tied the horse's reins to a nearby tree. Pulling off his rucksack he searched for and quickly found his first aid bandages. Slipping his pants down to his knees, he studied the wound before wrapping one of the gauze bandages around his injured leg.

Remounting—it was hell pulling himself back up on the horse's back with his burdensome rucksack dragging him down—he pointed the horse in a southerly direction. After traveling an hour or so through the dense woods, he encountered a fast-flowing stream between nine and twelve feet wide. Fearing that someone might try to track him, Rayner gave his chestnut a pat on the shoulder and guided the stocky horse into the rocky stream. Keeping to the water for over an hour, he carefully picked his way upstream until he came upon a well-used ford. There were lots of hoof prints along with some wagon ruts on both sides of the stream. After exiting the water, Rayner paused, dismounted, and refilled his canteen. Making sure to erase his footprints, he remounted and followed the washed-out track which seemed to lead in a westerly direction. After traveling about a half mile, he veered off into the woods, heading south again.

Rayner, who had been a hunter all his life, now searched for a place to hole up for the rest of the day. He and the horse picked their way through the forest until mid-afternoon when they came upon a small glade near a cliff. Over the years, as erosion had eaten away at the cliff, trees had fallen from the top of the incline to the bottom, forming a massively tangled deadfall. After unsaddling and hobbling his horse, which contentedly nibbled on the grass in the glen, Rayner fixed a small fire next to the base of the cliff and heated up some C rations—pork and beans. *I've only got three days' worth of food*, he thought, *and then I'm going to be up shit's creek.*

Maybe, he reflected further, *I'll wake up in the morning and find out all this is a bad dream. God, I sure hope so!*

As he finished off the pork and beans, Rayner mulled over the events of the past day and a half. He felt as if he was actively participating in some sort of never-ending nightmare. Nothing whatsoever made any sense to the confused soldier. Unexpectedly, he visualized himself inside a dark, gloomy room in an unfamiliar house. Suddenly, across the room, a lone window materialized. The sun's bright yellow rays streamed in—almost blinding him by their ferocious intensity. Some unknown force seemed to propel him across the room. Standing in front of the window, he pushed up the sash and sat down on the sill. A mysteriously invisible hand suddenly shoved him to the ground outside.

Picking himself up off the hard dusty earth, he imagined that by slipping through the window he had somehow entered a new and different world. When he looked around for the house, it had vanished.

He remembered reading H. G. Wells book, *The Time Machine*, in high school and wondered if he had, indeed, entered some sort of time machine that had mysteriously propelled him back into the past during the time of the Civil War. Shaking his head, Rayner came out of his reverie and decided to get some sleep before he started to hallucinate again. Glancing at his watch, he realized that over an hour had passed since he started to eat the pork and beans. It had seemed like just a few minutes. He idly wondered why time in this world seemed to be so distorted.

Using the massive deadfall as a wind break, Rayner set up a small campsite underneath the tangled tree limbs. Gathering up many of the old and broken limbs, he effectively hid his position. Next, he dragged the heavy leather saddle into his concealed position to use as a headrest. By now he was dead tired. He reckoned if this wasn't a dream, or he wasn't really dead that he had been awake for close to thirty-six hours.

Of course, in Vietnam, he had often gone two and three days without sleep. Once he had even gone five days. While he had learned to adjust under such circumstances, he had never really gotten used to it. The longer one went in Nam without sleep, the more one tended to act like a zombie. You just automatically went through the motions without fully realizing what you were actually engaged in, or what task you were performing at that particular moment in time. Having slept in the woods many times during his short lifespan of nineteen years, Rayner did not find it too difficult to get to sleep.

As he drifted off, he heard an owl's hoot off in the distance. Another hoot farther off seemed to answer it. The owl hoots reminded him of the Tokay Geckos back in Nam, whose nighttime mating call sounded like, "f*ck you! f*ck you! f*ck you!" when they chirped at each other. *That was another sound you never forgot,* he thought.

When he awoke, dawn was breaking and there was a light ground fog around the glade's edges. It was chilly and Rayner shivered as he broke out a small wad of C-4, lit it, and heated a cup of coffee. *I gotta get some more fresh water today,* he thought as he sipped the last of his coffee. Pulling a pack of Marlboros from his fatigue jacket, Rayner lit a cigarette, sat down on a knee-high log, and thought about what he should do. The smoke curled away from him in a lazy spiral. The sun's rays, barely touching the western fringes of the glade, caused the dew on the grass to sparkle.

Well, Rayner thought, *if I ain't dead, and this ain't a dream, then I am somehow back in the Civil War, which don't make no sense at all to me. I guess I jus' better keep moving south.* Gathering up his meager possessions, he prepared to break camp.

Removing the horse's hobbles, he saddled it and then tied his rucksack onto the back of the saddle. *From now on,* he silently thought, *the horse could carry the extra weight.* His shoulders still ached from carrying the equipment almost continuously for thirty-six hours. Plus, his wounded leg felt somewhat stiff. Holding his rifle in one hand, he managed to mount the horse using his good leg and headed out.

About an hour later, he reached the edge of the woods. Traveling slowly, he moved steadily south, avoiding all roads, or well-traveled trails. Occasionally, in the distance he saw people moving about on their farms. Whenever he saw anyone, no matter how far away, Rayner drifted into the nearest copse of woods and kept to the tree line as best he could. For the next several days, he ate sparingly and refilled his canteens, often at the numerous streams and creeks he encountered.

"Well," he said to himself at one point, "at least I had a million shots for a ton of all dem weird diseases before I got to Nam. I sure hope they still work, so I don't catch no bad germ from aller the crick water I been drinking."

He figured he was somewhere in the Shenandoah Valley, as there was a massive block of mountains to his right and a single mountain range to his left. The wound to his left leg had begun to bother him. It itched a lot. He washed it often and changed the dressing once a day, but now he was out of gauze. He figured it must have gotten infected.

By mid-afternoon on his third day of travel, he encountered a rather large muddy river which swept before him in a northeasterly direction. Following it south for several hours, he soon found a shallow point where he could ford the muddy stream. It was early evening when he and his horse plunged in and walked steadily across the hundred-yard-wide river. Rayner thought this was probably the best time to cross since the light was fading. That would mean there was less chance of anyone spotting him fording the river. The cool water felt good as it had been a hot and dusty day, but he felt a searing pain in his left leg as the water seeped into his wounded thigh. Plus, he was now beginning to feel slightly feverish. Once he reached the other side, he dismounted so he didn't become a silhouette when he reached the top of the embankment.

Using the chestnut both as a shield and a support since his wound had started to throb, he slowly climbed the steep embankment and suddenly came face-to-face with a young blond-haired girl. She was carrying a large wooden bucket with shiny metal straps around it at the top and bottom. They both froze, staring mutely at each other for a few seconds.

"Oh," Rayner, who was startled, said, "Hello there, miss." His eyes quickly scanned the area behind her for signs of other people who might be lurking in the wood line behind her. There was no one else. No sign of any habitation. He wondered where she had come from. "Who are you?" he inquired.

Cocking her head to one side, she stared at him a little longer, twiddling a piece of straw or grass—Rayner couldn't tell which—in her mouth. Her silence made him uneasy, so he again searched the immediate area for other people. His senses failed to detect anyone. *But then*, Rayner thought, *after what has happened to me, my sixth sense may be all screwed up.*

"My name's Maisie," the girl said after what seemed an eternity, which was really only a few seconds after he had first posed his question. Her voice had a sweet melodious sound, almost birdlike. Yet, the sound of her voice shocked him somewhat because he had been surrounded by silence during the past several days. He guessed she was about sixteen or seventeen.

"Uh, my name's John," Rayner said, trying to appear friendly. "Where do you live, Maisie?"

She stared at him for a few more moments, without answering, before pointing off to her left. He could just barely see a chimney to what, apparently, was a cabin nestled far back in the woods. A barely discernable path wound its way toward the wood line. *How the hell could I have missed seeing that when I first looked behind her?* he asked himself. *Jesus H. F*cking Christ! My fever must be getting worse if I missed seeing something that obvious*, he thought, becoming rather irritated with himself for making such a blatant blunder.

"I didn't mean to frighten you," he continued. "It's jus' that I ain't seen no one in a coupula of days."

The girl continued to stare at him. Her blue eyes seemed to bore right through his body as if tugging at his innermost soul. Rayner felt terribly uncomfortable and uneasy as he shifted his weight back and forth on his feet. His eyes tended to constantly scan the area around him and behind the girl. As he continued to watch her, Maisie seemed to fade away in the late afternoon light and then, just as quickly, she reappeared several feet closer to where he stood holding his horse in readiness to mount and flee should anything untoward develop.

"Well, I better git going. See you," he quickly mounted, kicked his horse, and started to move past the girl, who had stopped in the middle of the path leading to the river.

Maisie held up her right hand, the two middle fingers, slightly separated, pointed right at him, the thumb tucked into the palm under them, with the two outside fingers raised like horns. Rayner felt as if he had walked into an invisible brick wall. He and the horse came to a dead stop. He stared at the girl in front of him as the hairs on the back of his neck began to bristle. *What was going on here?* he asked himself.

"Come," Maisie said motioning with her left hand, "you need to see my momma." She turned and walked back toward the hidden cabin. Rayner followed, feeling as if an invisible hand had grabbed him and was now gently forcing him to follow the barefoot girl. For the first time he noticed that Maisie was rather tall and that she wore a blue and white checkered dress. A creamy white bow kept her waist-long hair pulled back at the neck, but it spread out in a lush blond triangle across her back.

He stopped the horse at the wood's edge and peered into the deepening gloom. The sun had almost sunk behind the far blue mountains, and its light filtered dimly across the valley. Maisie turned and spoke. "It's okay, just me and my momma live here." Her eyes, Rayner swore to himself, seemed to glow. She turned and walked ahead of him into a light mist. Rayner, still sensing some sort of a trap, reluctantly followed her. The trees seemed twisted and much denser than any he had so far encountered. They crowded up close to the path as if to block the passage of anyone who might try to force their way through the tangled growth. Rayner glanced back once or twice, but it seemed as if the woods had closed behind him forcing the path to vanish into the undergrowth.

After several minutes, they emerged into a small clearing. Across the open glade a tumbledown shack rested against a rock cliff. A thin tendril of smoke wafted from the chimney. The smell of hot food seemed to permeate the small clearing. An old woman emerged from the door as Rayner and Maisie drew close. *She looks like she is a thousand years old,* Rayner thought.

"No, I'm not that old, John Rayner," the woman chuckled. Rayner, who was midway toward dismounting, froze in mid-air staring at the woman whose face was lined with wrinkles. The shock of her words seemed to hold him there in suspension. He felt as if he was suddenly paralyzed, unable to either dismount or remount. A surge of fear ran throughout his body. He wanted to get away from these people, but a curtain of descending darkness held him there in limbo. Slowly, he lowered himself to the ground, holding on to his M16 so tight that he could see his knuckles turn white from the strain.

"Maisie, take his horse to the barn, child. You," pointing to Rayner, "come on inside."

Rayner, as if in the grip of some invisible jailor, limped over to the cabin's door. Entering, he saw that the shack was much larger inside than it looked from the outside. His eyes glanced quickly around the room. It was neat and tidy, but sparsely furnished. A cloth covered doorway off to his right seemed to lead into another room or, he thought, a cave in the cliff behind the cabin. *Probably leads to their bedroom*, he surmised. A solid rock chimney dominated the far wall. He smelled some sort of roasted meat slowly simmering in a pot before the fire.

"It's alright, John. You are safe here," the old woman intoned. "Put your weapon over there by the door," she commanded gesturing with a pointed and crooked finger in the general direction of the front door. Rayner, doing as she instructed, limped over to the cabin's entryway and hung his M16 on a peg next to it. As soon as his fingers let go of the weapon, a sense of great peace and contentment washed over him filling him with a deep sense of relief. Feeling as if a massive load had lifted from his shoulders, Rayner instinctively knew he was now in a safe place among friends. Almost imperceptibly, his fever seemed to mysteriously abate.

"Who, or what, are you?" Rayner asked, somewhat baffled, as he returned to the middle of the room and slumped into one of only three chairs that nestled against a four-legged wooden table. "How do you know who I am and what I'm thinking?"

"My name is Dora," she replied. "I have the second sight." She stirred the simmering pot, then turned and peered at him. Her coal black eyes seemed to penetrate Rayner's body deep down into his soul. He felt naked under her piercing gaze. She shuffled over and sat in a lone rocking chair close to the fireplace. "You have come here from far away, haven't you?" Looking into the flames, she waited for him to reply.

"Er … yes," he hesitated, not knowing just what to say. "Uh, a real long way." He looked around wondering when Maisie might return.

"Maisie will be here shortly. She has some chores to attend to," the old crone commented.

"Now," Dora stated, "you and I have to talk. You are from another time, aren't you?" *Damn!* Rayner thought, *She really is a mind reader.*

Rayner nodded dumbly and then, with tears streaming down his face, the words tumbled out as he told the wizened ancient what had befallen him. She nodded but did not interrupt as he related his experiences during the past several days. When he finished, a silence descended upon the room. Dora rocked back and forth.

Maisie glided silently into the room. Rayner felt her presence before he realized she had suddenly appeared beside him. He didn't remember hearing the cabin door open to admit her. She was just there, stroking his head with a soothing touch. *How long,* he thought, *since I've had a woman?* Then he quickly banished the thought and felt guilty because the old woman could read his mind. Rayner glanced quickly in Dora's direction, but she seemed far off.

Dora got up without a word and shuffled over to the steaming pot. She ladled out some food on three plates and gestured for them to sit at the table. They ate in silence as the warmth of the fire filled the room. Dora gave him a second helping, which he wolfed down. They drank dandelion wine that Rayner found to be especially tasty.

The meat, he knew from hunting back home, was venison. After dinner, Maisie cleared the table and washed the dishes in a small wooden tub. She joined Rayner and Dora as they sat before the fire.

"In the morning, John Rayner," Dora said, "you must leave here and walk back toward the river. You will find what you are seeking. You may sleep here before the fire," she gestured to a straw-filled mattress on the floor that had mysteriously appeared from out of thin air and now lay off to one side of the rock fireplace. "Now," she continued, "go over there and lie down. I need to look at your wound."

Rayner was tired. As if in a trance, he nodded and numbly obeyed the woman. He wondered if they had put some kind of sleeping potion in his food—or into the dandelion wine he had imbibed. He lay down. The mattress felt warm and comfortable. Rayner vaguely remembered watching the old woman shuffle over to the bed.

Dora knelt beside him and touched his forehead. His fever seemed to vanish in an instant. Then, she placed both hands on his left thigh directly over his wound. Within seconds, Rayner, who could now barely keep his eyelids open, felt as if her hands had somehow drawn the inflammation out of his body. Her touch felt cool, almost as if she were freezing the area around the festering and inflamed wound.

He glanced down and realized he was now naked below the waist. He had no memory as to how his pants had been removed, but there they were, hanging on a peg next to his head. Even though he didn't wear underwear, Rayner realized that he had no self-consciousness about being naked in front of either Dora or Maisie. It just seemed natural. Glancing down at the location of his wound, Rayner was shocked to observe that it was now nothing more than a vague scar. *How did she do that?* he wondered. But, by then, he was too tired to care and drifted off into a deep and peaceful sleep.

When he awoke, the room was shrouded in darkness except for the glow of embers from the fireplace. Somehow, during his sleep either Dora or Maisie had removed his sweat-stained and smelly T-shirt along with his green fatigue jacket. He lay naked on the straw filled mattress and Maisie lay beside him. She, too, had nothing on.

"What are...." He struggled to rise, but felt too weak to move.

"Shhhh," she whispered, gently pushing him back down on the mattress. She glided over on top of him. Her skin was incredibly smooth—almost silky. Rayner's hands moved over her body as he thought, *Gosh, it sure feels wonderful to touch a real woman again.* She straddled him and his whole body seemed to relax. An incredible sense of peace and joyous rapture flooded over and enveloped his body. He felt as if he was floating in the air suspended between dream and reality.

Afterward, they lay together for what seemed like hours as he drifted in and out of sleep. Not a word passed between them. At some point, she took her finger and traced a circle on his chest. Her fingernail burned his flesh. He flinched, but, somehow, endured the pain because he felt as if nothing he could do would stop her if he even wanted her to stop. Finally, in the early morning hours, she kissed him once and was gone. He felt powerless to stop her from leaving and drifted off into a heavy and deep sleep.

He awoke with a start. The morning light filtered through the lone cabin window landing right where Rayner had been sleeping. He looked around. Neither Maisie nor her mother seemed to be anywhere in the cabin. A grim silence permeated the room. The embers in the fireplace had all but died out. He glanced at the doorway to confirm that his rifle was still there. Standing, he quickly dressed, but couldn't find his green T-shirt anywhere. His fever had disappeared. His left leg no longer hurt. Yet, a thin red scar remained.

Tiptoeing across the room, he stopped in front of the cloth covered doorway. Pulling the curtain aside, he saw that it concealed nothing more than a shallow closet with six empty wooden shelves. A surprised mouse quickly scampered off, diving into a hole in the wall behind one of the empty shelves. He walked to the front door, grabbed his rifle, and stepped outside. His rucksack was propped up against the cabin next to the front door. He tramped over to the barn, but his horse was not inside. In fact, the barn looked as if it hadn't been used in ages. A fine mist had seeped into the clearing.

With sad resignation he saddled up, adjusted the rucksack on his shoulders and groaned at its weight. He peeked into the cabin one last time in hopes of finding the women but nothing stirred. The furniture, including his straw filled mattress, had vanished. The fireplace looked as if it hadn't been used in a hundred years. He could see dust on the floor in the early morning light and cobwebs proliferated throughout the cabin. The place now smelled of mold and had taken on an abandoned, somewhat dilapidated, appearance.

What had happened to him the previous night was like a dream. Moving across the clearing, he walked toward the wood line, where he thought he might find the path to the river. The trees seemed to move and part, almost as if they had stepped aside for him, and then the well-trodden path materialized right in front of him. Mist seemed to rise from the ground as he entered into the woods. He turned one last time to look back at the cabin, but it had vanished in the morning mist.

Mysteriously, his feet seemed to know the way though patches of fog that obscured the pathway every so often. Finally, he reached the open area between the tree line and the river which he could distinctly hear off in the distance. Emerging from the woods, he noted that the ground fog was especially thick. There was a definite chill to the morning air. He looked around, but fog had wiped away any trace of the path back to the cabin.

Rayner decided to take the old woman's advice and turned toward the river. The ground fog soon swallowed him, swirling above his head and caressing him as he forged ahead through the ever-deepening white gloom. He couldn't see more than two or three feet in front of him. Guiding himself by the sound of the rippling water, he approached the river with some trepidation and caution. A deadly silence surrounded him.

Walking alongside the river, Rayner felt someone's presence nearby. A vague figure suddenly loomed ahead of him, but whoever it was had their back turned to Rayner and could not see him. Just as suddenly as it had appeared, the ghostlike figure vanished in the fog's misty tendrils. He glanced around and thought he saw someone behind him, but then the mists swirled and that figure, too, was swallowed up in the fog. The chilliness of the Virginia morning suddenly changed to hot and humid. He trudged onward, sweat pouring down his back. Icicles of fear swept over his body. The smell of rotten vegetation and wet mud assaulted his nostrils.

One second he was in the fog and the next he was in an open area next to the river bank. A bamboo thicket rose up in front of him.

"Rayner! god damn! Where the hell have you been?" A voice behind him shattered the ominous silence.

Rayner quickly turned. It was Palmer. He was about fifteen feet behind Rayner along with the rest of the point team. Rayner stared at them as his mouth dropped wide open. His eyes darted to the tree line, but all he saw was impenetrable jungle. He immediately sensed that it was late afternoon, but how could that be? He had just left the cabin about ten minutes ago.

Palmer ran up to him and gave him a huge bear hug.

"Hot damn! You are one lucky son of a bitch! We thought you were dead after this morning's ambush," Palmer blubbered. "We looked all over for your body but couldn't find it. Thought the gooks had dragged it away. What happened to you?" He asked. "How the hell did you manage to link back up with us?"

"I, er ..." Rayner hesitated, struggling to find the right words before replying, "ah, escape and evasion, you know." He couldn't believe he had returned to The Nam—or had he really left? "I guess I just got lucky linking back up with your guys," Rayner replied as he wiped his sweaty brow. "It's been a long day."

"Hey, what happened to your chest man?" Palmer asked as he pointed and jabbed his finger into Rayner's torso, "Looks like a tattoo." Rayner looked down at his half-unbuttoned fatigue jacket. His eyes immediately caught the outline of a one-inch-wide red circle which seemed to have been burned into his flesh next to his heart.

"Ah," Rayner groped for words, "I guess I must have accidently placed my rifle barrel there after the firefight and got burned," he replied.

"Boy, am I glad we persuaded the CO to check out this river after the firefight," Palmer commented. "Otherwise, we might not have found your ass, Rayner!"

"That's for sure," Rayner replied, still puzzled and not quite sure how he had ended up back in Nam—if he had ever left.

But the red circle never did go away. Rayner never told anyone about his Civil War adventure. After all, he figured, who the hell would believe him—a country hick from the mountains of West

Virginia? He wasn't quite sure he believed it himself. It must have been a dream. Yet, enigmatically, the red circle said otherwise.

Toward the end of his tour Rayner received a letter from his mother. She wrote in big block letters that had been taught to students in the first or second grade. It was the only way she knew to write. Her parents forced her leave school in the fifth grade because they needed her for a multitude of chores around their wooden ramshackle hovel of a home to help with the six other babies her mother continued to pop out with some regularity, one every year or two.

Rayner's momma wrote: "Dear Sun, we hopes yer doin' OK. We dun got a new nex' door naybor, an oller woman named Dora Smith. She hab the sight and is a heeler. Also, she gots a dawher, name of Maisie, who has a bewfull baby girl named Raynell."

Rayner couldn't wait to get home. Six weeks later, he was climbing the dirt road leading to his momma's rustic cabin.

DEATH'S DARK COACHES COME MARCHING ON

The Laboring Swain Toils His Weary Way
Up the Long, Rock-Strewn Hill;
And Men of Honor Say
Its Soil Was Rich to Till.

High Up on That Promontory
He Sits Himself Slowly Down
To Ponder the Old Remembered Story
That for Years Went 'Round.

The God Zephyrus Sweetly Blows
As the Blood-Red Sun Slowly Sinks,
And His Tattered Clothes
To Sad Misfortune He Links.

O'er the Mountain in the West
Those Bright Rays Begin to Fade,
And the Swain Remembers That He Did His Best
As by God He Was Often Bade.

He Turns to View the Valley
Which Shadows of the Coming Night
Cover O'er the Lea,
And Silent Death Comes to Test His Fearful Might.

Some Mysterious Darkness Approaches,
Summoning His Pale White Sister - the Moon,
To Show the Way for Death's Dark Coaches
That Will Be Coming Soon.

From the Dark Forbidden Caves Emerge the Bats
To Herald the Near Advent of Mighty Death;
And from the Distant Swamp Rise Bothersome Gnats
To Fight Every Man's Breath.

Now Comes the Silent Fog
Which Covers the Moor
Rolling Silently O'er Many a Fallen Log,
And Obscuring Each Friendly Village Door.

To the Swain's Aged Eyes Come Tears
As He Gazed upon the Hamlet,
Where for Many Long Ago Years
Love Had Run the Gauntlet.

Ah, Yes, the Old Man Remembers Well
The Sad Tale of Two Lovers
Upon Whose Lives the Axe of Death Fell
Like the Land Which the Falling Snow Covers.

Their Love Was Spoke of Afar;
A True Romance 'Twas in Every Way
To Be Sure Nothing Could Mar
The Vows to Be Spoken on That Future Day.

But, Oh Beware the Unseen
Which Lurks at Every Corner
With Two Evil Eyes That Gleam
On Every Mourner.

Spring Arrived at the Village in Full Bloom,
And the Man Picked Many a Flower
Not Suspecting the Forthcoming Doom
As He Walked Her Back to Her Bower.

With Flowers Came Love Unending
And Every Good Night Kiss
Was Like Love Fully Blending
Each Time They Parted from Their Happy Bliss.

When They Strolled Around the Village Square
The Children Played as the Old Surveyed,
And She Plaited Long Love Knots in Her Hair
Walking in Pastures Where the Horses Neighed.

Many a Stroll They Took upon the Heath,
And Oftentimes They Rested by a Spring;
When (As Goes the Village Belief),
He Gave Her Their Engagement Ring.

The Story Was Oft Told
That, As They Rested by This Brook,
(Whose Sweet Waters Were Very Old)
They Gave Each Other Many a Loving Look.

As They Lay by That Slow Moving Stream
Squirrels and Birds Would Hop Around Them,
And They Were Kind To God's Lively Creatures - Not Mean
As Are Some Evil-Minded Men.

They Rested Here Very Often to Talk
Of Many Matters on Their Minds,
And No One in This Direction Would Walk
For Fear of Disturbing Such a Love That Binds.

It Was on Such Nights as This One
That Those Two Lovers Met at the Old Village Barn
To Talk of Love and Many Things They Had Done
While Listening to the Old Folks Spinning a Yarn.

For Love Is NEVER Lost
Tho' Lovers May Be Parted
On Seas That Are Tempest Tossed
Or on Lands Far from Each Departed.

The Man Was a Tall Strapping Youth
Who Worked at the Village Smithy;
And He NEVER Spoke an Unkind Word in Truth
To the One He Loved Who Was So Pretty.

He Loved Her with All His Heart,
And She with All of Hers Likewise.
Each Day He Met Her in the Village Mart
For, You See, Strong Love NEVER Dies.

Oh Sweet Love! How Long Do You Last?
Is It a Year . . . Month . . . Or Day
O'er Which Your Magic Spell Is Cast,
Or Does It Continue to the Last Words People Say?

She Was the Fairest Lass to Behold
Her Golden Hair Streamed Down Her Back,
And Her Face Was of Such a Beautiful Mold
That Not a Single Virtue Did She Lack.

All the Village Talked
Of the Day They Would Marry,
And Every Day in the Green Meadows They Walked
To Pass the Time and Tarry.

But Plans of Lovers by Unseen Hands Are Moved
And Evil Shall Step In
As Oft Has Been Proved;
And the Black Forces Will Not Stop Them.

Remembering These Long Forgotten Facts
The Swain Looks Down
And Now Clearly Sees Death's Tracks
Engraved upon the Ground.

The Dark Vaults of His Memory Are Opened,
And Pages of Time Unroll
From the Day They Were Penned
Up in His Mind's Scroll.

On Their Wedding Day the Sun Was Bright,
And Many Flowers Were in Bloom
So That Spring Could Be Smelt Every Night
To Mark the Dread Approach of Gloom.

No Happier Couple Was There in All the Land
As They Stood on God's Holy Ground,
And When the Village Pastor Joined Them Hand in Hand
The Village's Gaiety Was a Sound.

A Marriage Feast Was Held Nearby,
And the Food Was Plentiful
So That before Night Was to Draw Nigh
Everyone Was to Partake a Delicious Mouthful.

A Town of Some Considerable Size
Lay Near This Happy Village Life,
And There Many a Villager Had Won a Prize
For the Goods Raised on His Fief.

In This Lovely Town
They Were to Spend Their Honeymoon,
And the Story Went 'Round
They Were to Leave Late That Afternoon.

Oh, These Poor Unsuspecting People!
Can No One See the Horrible Approach of Death
That Lurks Behind Every Steeple
To Worry Every Man's Breath?

Why God Is Love to be So Short
That Was So Sweet?
As You Sit before That Great Judgment Court
Can You Not Stop Death So Fleet?

The Sun Has Headed to Bed
Before Dark Night Creeps Near;
And, As the Last Dying Rays Are Fled,
The Village Bids Adieu to the Lovers So Dear.

The Timely Coach Draws Up
Before the Village Inn Door
Where the Happy Couple Have Sup
So to Love Each Other More.

Hand in Hand the Ill-Fated Coach They Enter
As the Dark Mysterious
Prepares to Fully and Finally Splinter
This Wonderful Love So Glorious.

Not Many Miles Away
Lies Waiting in the Bush a Highwayman
Bent on Desire to Have Money That Day -
If - He Possibly Can.

The Coachmaster Drives His Horses Hard
For Coming Quickly Is an Inky Black Storm,
And, Now, Death Must Play His Final Card
According to Correct Form.

The Cold Rain Comes Pelting Down
While This Varlet Waits upon His Black Steed -
A Horse That Paws at the Muddy Ground
While His Master Waits to Commit This Heinous Deed.

Lightning Flashes Cover the Earth and Sky,
And It Seems Thor Is Displeased
And Throws His Yellow Bolts from on High
So His Temper Will Be Appeased.

But God No Longer Controls the Situation
For Death Has Its Work Cut Out,
And No Man - in Whatever Station -
Can Stop This Bout.

Oh God - How Can You Be So Cruel
As to Let Death Separate This Pair?
She Is the Fairest Jewel
That Ever Breathed This Mortal Air!

The Love Story Now Unravels
As the Highwayman Hears the Horse's Tread
That along the Road Travels
Like Something from the Dead.

He Draws His Pistol Now
And Cocks It with Sureness
And Waits So Long He Knows Not How
'Til He Hears Nearby the Horse's Harness.

Down He Rides upon the Stage
And Yells for the Driver
(A Man of Ancient Age)
To Stop or He'll Soon Be a Cadaver.

The Horses in the Coachman Quickly Reins -
For He Has No Wish to Die;
He'd Rather See This Rogue in Chains
Than from His Bullets Fly.

Dressed in Black the Robber Demands
All the Money the Travelers Own,
As Other Passengers Follow His Command;
The Lovers Are Left Alone.

The Devil Aims His Pistol
Straight at the Smith's Breast.
Soon Death's Bell Will Toll,
And Someone Will Be Laid to Rest.

Damn the Man Who'll Hurt the Innocent!
To Make a Few Pence Here and There,
Because He Thinks Life Isn't Worth a Cent;
And - That No One Will Care!

"Kind Sir," the Smith Begs, "Please Spare Us.
We Have So Little to Give
This Is Not Worth All This Fuss
For Which a Man, Like Yourself, Must Live."

"You Have 'Til the Count of Three
To Hand Over All You Possess,
Or, Soon, from Life You'll Be Free
From My Bullet in Your Chest."

The Lover Would Not Budge
As the Rain Now Fell Like Stones,
And Thor Did Now Indulge
In Lightning Which Cracked in Somber Tones.

Aeolus Let Loose His Stormy Winds
Which Blew the Rain in Torrents,
But - Death Always Wins
Over All the Tears Man Vents.

The Nearby Trees Sway
As If Moved by Some Unknown Hand,
For There Is to Be a Death This Day
Which Will Be Mourned Throughout the Land.

From Out of All This Tumult
Comes a Sharp Pistol Crack.
The Rogue Has Committed a Heinous Fault
On this Damned Night So Black.

The Elements Tried Their Best,
But Lo - What Is This Horrid Tragedy?
The One Who Was So Blest
Lies Now in Her Lover's Arms So Bloody!

Neither Wind, Nor Rain, Nor Lightning Could Defect
Black Death in His Planned Track
For She Had Leaped to Protect
Her Lover from the Bullet That Now Lodged in Her Back.

The Highwayman Has Seen His Mistake,
And He Stirs His Gallant Charger to Flee;
But No More Errors Will He Make;
The Lover Shoots Him Down with Avenging Glee.

Now, Suddenly Nature Ceases Her Violent Acts;
And the Lightning, Wind, and Rain Are Still
As Is a Virgin Forest before the First Settler's Axe,
Or after the Hunter Has Made His kill.

He Clasps Her Tightly in the Cradle of His Massive Arm
But Life Ebbs from Her Pretty Lip;
For Death Has Done His Wicked and Evil Harm,
And No More Breaths of Air Will She Sip.

Her Eyes Are Seen to Flutter,
And Her Lips Move Convulsively
As If Some Words They Wish to Utter.
"I Loved You," She Said, "Faithfully."

What More Is There to Say?
For She Is Now Gone,
And He Took Her Body Back That Black Day
To Lament Her for O So Long!

Death Comes Silently Down Every Street
And Will Smile So Evilly
At Every Happy Soul He Will Meet
Tho' They Pass by Him Civilly.

"Aye, Well Remember I,"
Saith The Swain
As He Contemplates the Now Dawn-Colored Sky
And Silently Takes God's Name in Vain.

He Has Lived His Natural Span
Knowing and Hearing Many a Tale
While Wandering 'Round Earth's Land
Over Many a Hill and Dale.

The Swain's Old Ears Perk Up;
He Hears the Sound of Hoofs
That along the Ground Do Gallop
Sounding Like Rain Splattering on House Top Roofs.

Soon Aurora Unfolds Her Multi-Colored Dawn,
And Apollo Follows Not Far Behind.
To This Wind Swept Place a Villager Is Drawn
To Search for One of His Own Kind.

On the Hillside They Found the Swain's Body There
With a Face Now So Content,
They Bore His Body to the Village Square
Where His Homeward Steps Were So Often Bent.

They Buried Him in the Earthy Clay.
To Sleep Peacefully in His Grave
They Placed Him Not One Yard Away
From the Slain Girl to Whom His Love He Gave.

Oh, Love Is Sweet

And Love Is Kind;

But Death Will We Always Meet;

The Mortal Fear of Each Man's Mind.

So Was It When Life Started,

So Is It Now,

And Not One Fear Hath Departed

From Man's Eternal Brow.

NOTE: This poem was written in the style of Alfred Noyes' poem "The Highwayman," and it is dedicated to Ben F. Turner.

ACKNOWLEDGMENTS

Writing a book is never easy. As it takes form—especially when extensively edited—there are myriad details that have to be checked and rechecked. As I write, the words flow, but when finished I find I need to either find and fix minor discrepancies or clarify and fine tune certain descriptions and conversations. The author is extremely grateful to several people who helped bring *The Other Side* to fruition.

First, I would like to thank my publisher, Julie Castro, who not only published my second book, *Letters From Potsdam: Colonel John S. Wise's Impressions of the 1945 Berlin Conference*, but also did an outstanding job editing it. Every writer needs a cheerleader and not only was she incredibly helpful with that book, but she also went out of her way to encourage me in the completion of *The Other Side*. Her comments, ideas, probing questions, and suggestions enabled me to make this a much better book. Lastly, her faith in me is deeply appreciated.

I would especially like to thank my editor, Michelle Williamson, for a great job at not only editing, but for turning it into a finer book. It is interesting to me to see how someone else views your writing and can, by small, but important changes, improve the book. With her skills and perceptiveness, plus her encouraging thoughts and comments about each story, she helped me make this a more interesting book for you, the reader, to savor and enjoy.

A special thank you to Stefan Hansen of Creative Instincts for his skill in creating not only the cover for this book, but also the interior design and typesetting. His idea to have a mirror with a scene pertinent to the subject of each poem and short story was absolutely outstanding and much appreciated by the author. His vision and artistry enhanced this book far beyond what I could have ever imagined. The importance of an enticing design not only brings a book alive but also sets the mood for the reader.

For over fifty years, my dear friend, Cindy Conte (1952-2021), encouraged me to write. Her faith in my ability has always been an inspiration. Her ongoing faith resulted in my first book: *Eleven Bravo: A Skytrooper's Memoir of War in Vietnam*, along with my second book mentioned above, and now this—my third book that you hold before you. It was especially nice to have a good friend cheer me on for so many years. Sadly, she will be missed. RIP.

The author thanks Donna Nardi for her phenomenal proofreading expertise. Due to her eagle eyes, she made this a much better book.

With profound appreciation, I would like to thank Braden McKinley, former Worship Pastor and Choir Master for Scottsdale Bible Church, North Ridge. The worship hymns at each Scottsdale Bible Church service are both inspiring and uplifting. During one particular Sunday service, several hymns gave me a few ideas, which I was able to incorporate into my story titled *The Cabin, The Journey, And The Vision*. Braden gladly and happily supplied me with the lyrics of those hymns, which I found most useful and helpful in completing that story.

The author would also like to thank Jamie Rasmussen, the senior pastor of Scottsdale Bible Church. His sermons, without any doubt, are the most awe-inspiring and historically informative discussions of biblical history the author has ever heard in his more than seventy years of periodic church attendance. The biblical research information that he imparts during his sermons is particularly fascinating to the author who has also been a historian for more than thirty years. The idea for several of the short stories included herein came about from information Pastor Jamie examined during his sermons, which I was able to jot down in brief notes that I later included in *The Other Side* tales.

Finally, I especially want to thank the many friends I have made through Scottsdale Bible Church who, in many subtle and different ways, encouraged me to write my books—Erick and Bev K., Yoko L., Steve S., Arnold A., Dan S., Brian K., Eddie C., Pastor James D., and Pastor Kevin Y. Without their friendship and warm-heartedness, I would not have been able to find the inspiration to finish these books and stories, some of which languished for more than twenty years in my filing cabinets.

Books also by
E. Tayloe Wise

Eleven Bravo:
A Skytrooper's Memoir of War in Vietnam

A narrative of the author's 1969-1970 combat tour in Vietnam

Letters From Potsdam:
Colonel John S. Wise's Impressions of the 1945 Berlin Conference

Letters to Colonel Wise's wife from the editor's father who attended the 1945 Potsdam Conference